GREED

By Kim Hunter

INDEX

Copyright
Authors other works
Quotes
Introduction
Index of characters
Chapter one
Chapter two
Chapter three
Chapter four
Chapter five
Chapter six
Chapter seven
Chapter eight
Chapter nine
Chapter ten
Chapter eleven
Chapter twelve
Chapter thirteen
Chapter fourteen
Chapter fifteen
Chapter sixteen
Chapter seventeen
Chapter eighteen
Chapter nineteen
Chapter twenty
Chapter twenty-one
Chapter twenty-two
Chapter twenty-three
Chapter twenty-four
Chapter twenty-five
Chapter twenty-six

QUOTES

The Transaction.

'What value does a human life hold' she asked?
'Whatever someone is willing to pay'.
'And once purchased, what will you do with that life?' she asked
'Torture it to death and in doing so, satisfy my lust'.
'Then I'm afraid the price will be high' she replied.

Unknown

INTRODUCTION

SNUFF - FACT OR FICTION?

FICTION

Supposedly 'circulated amongst a few for the purpose of entertainment', snuff movies have been an urban legend since the first mention of the term in a book back in 1971. Not predominantly for financial gain, these supposed movies did gain momentum in the mid 1980's via the Japanese horror film series 'Guinea Pig'.
In 1991, actor Charlie Sheen was so convinced that the second film in the series depicted a real murder, he contacted the FBI. Investigations were closed when it was proven that the film used only special effects.

In 1980 the Italian director Ruggero Deodato was arrested when his film Cannibal Holocaust depicted the killing of an actress. Deodato was able to prove to the court that the actress was fine and that the realism of the killing was purely down to special effects but his licence was still revoked for three years causing media attention to escalate.

FACT

On the 18th of January 2018, Peter Madsen was charged in connection with the murder and

disappearance of Kim Wall a Swedish journalist. Kim was last seen alive on Madsen's privately owned submarine. When a torso washed up on the coast of Amager, it was soon confirmed to be that of the journalist. Madsen was arrested and charged with her murder. A post-mortem revealed knife wounds to her genitals and ribcage. In court it was revealed that police found snuff videos on Madsen's computer showing the murder of women via decapitation and asphyxiation sex. The jury accepted that he had sought sexual pleasure from the death and torture of a woman. Irrefutable evidence was provided that Peter Madsen was a prolific user of violent pornography.
On April the 25th 2018 Peter Madsen was found guilty of all charges and sentenced to life imprisonment without the chance of parole. His psychiatric evaluation described him as a narcissistic psychopath.

Porn apologists have long since claimed that snuff movies do not exist but several years before the rise of the internet, a woman entered a UK porn shop and asked if they had anything really extreme. The woman was given a video depicting a South American being raped and having her hand sawn off while she was still alive. The victim was then murdered. Hardened crime reporters left the room to be physically sick after viewing the video. Experts verified that there were no camera tricks involved in the making of the footage. A local journalist reported the film to the police. No action was taken.

Index of main character

Brice McKay. Born in 1946. The son of a steel worker, Brice had a tough upbringing. A nice man who was liked by many, his world would fall apart, at least for a time, when he met Bonnie Wilson one cold February night in 1967 at the long since closed 'Old Granny Blacks' pub in Glasgow.

Bonnie Wilson. Born in 1947. A young woman out for all she could get and one who had no intentions of getting tied down. By day she worked on the production line at the Singer factory but by night she partied like it was going out of fashion. Hung over most days, Bonnie could drink many a man under the table but would meet her match in Brice McKay.

Maggie McKay. Born at the beginning of December in 1967, little Maggie was the apple of her father's eye but loathed by her mother. Her days would be spent ducking slaps from her mother and being told she was a waste of space but in the evenings she was showered with love, at least from one of her parents.

Bobbie McKay. Born 1988, Bobby was another unwanted pregnancy but for entirely different reasons to Maggie's birth. From day one it was noted that there was something wrong with him and as he grew Bobby was labelled as slow. That didn't stop him being adored by everyone he came into contact with, everyone except for Maggie. If she'd had her way she would have smothered him at any given opportunity and measures had to be taken so that they were never to be left alone.

Kenneth Voss. Aged fifty nine, Kenny had worked for the Pimms crime firm since he was seventeen, long before Brice McKay had come onto the scene. A giant of a man, he instilled fear purely due to his size but he was also incredibly hard. Becoming the honorary uncle to the McKay children he took his responsibility very serious and would have died rather than see a single hair on either of their heads come to harm.

Anna Draycott. Born in 1980. Anna was a remarkable police officer and had joined the Metropolitan force at just eighteen years of age. Quickly rising through the ranks, she soon reached the position of Detective Inspector and was now only months away from retirement after serving a little over twenty years in a job she adored.

Lou Garnet. Chief Inspector Garnet was now in his sixtieth year and there wasn't much he hadn't either been witness to or investigated in his long and successful career. Being surrounded by an excellent team meant that Tottenham Station had an exemplary record for solving cases and much of that was down to Detective Anna Draycott who Lou adored. Having been on his team for the last ten years, Lou looked upon the high flying officer as the daughter he never had and with every case she solved he became convinced that she would become his natural successor.

Asti Marku. A thirty eight year old Albanian migrant and a man with absolutely no morals. Asti would literally undertake any task, no matter how horrific if the price was right. Available for hire, he was regularly employed by Maggie McKay.

CHAPTER ONE
1971

The McKay's hailed from Clyde Street in Glasgow and would eventually move down to London in the summer of 1972. At twenty one years of age, Brice McKay, had married Bonnie Wilson early in 1967 after a drunken one night stand has resulted in an unwanted pregnancy. Neither had any desire to marry but back then it was still frowned upon to be a single mother so reluctantly Brice had done the honourable thing. From the off the couple constantly bickered and because of this Bonnie had and would continue to make sure there were no further offspring's. The 1970s were, like so many other industrial areas, a depressing period in Glasgow with many factories, shipyards, mines and other heavy industries going out of business. The high levels of urban decay and mass unemployment would see Brice finally make the decision to once and for all turn his back on Scotland and head south.

"Bonnie!"
When she heard her husband's voice Bonnie McKay poked her head out of the tiny kitchen that in reality was little more than an alcove with a curtain separating it from the front room. It was only just after eleven and there was no way he should be

home from work yet. Hearing her Daddy come in, little Maggie ran from the sitting room and wrapped her small arms tightly around her father's legs.
"Hello my wee angel, been a good girl for your mam?"
Maggie vigorously nodded her head, she had just turned four but to her the man whose leg she now clung onto was a superhero. Bonnie walked into the compact hallway and sharply pulling her daughter away, proceeded to open the bedroom door and roughly pushed the child inside.
"Stay there until I say you can come out!"
Brice furrowed his brow, for the life of him he just couldn't work out why his wife was so bloody cold and mean spirited when it came down to their daughter.
"I've been laid off again Bonnie! I'm sick and tired of this, let's pack up and leave this shite hole once and for all?"
"Leave Glasgee?!! My family, my friends, everyone I know is here, so in answer to your question, NO!!!"

Life sadly continued as it was but now due to the lack of any income, the couple fought like cat and dog with each outburst becoming more and more violent. It was bad enough when Brice was bringing a wage home but now poor little Maggie spent most of her time shut away in her room with her hands over her ears desperately trying to stop the sound of her parents fighting.

Almost a year later and the family were constantly struggling to live off of the meagre amount given to them by the state. When the atmosphere in the flat became so toxic that you could virtually cut it with a knife, Brice gave his wife an ultimatum.
"I'm leaving Bonnie, there's nothing left for me here. I bumped into Ewan Drummond at the weekend when he came back for a visit to see his brother in Barlinnie. We met down the Glen for a few jars and he said he can get me work in London if I want it. When I'm set up with a place to live I'll call you and you can come and join me if you want, the choice will be yours."
"Ewan Drummond?! He's been locked up in Barlinnie more times than his brother! You're a fool Brice McKay and you'll end up just the same."
"Maybe I will and maybe I won't but I have to give it a try and like I said, the choice is yours."
With that Brice grabbed a bag and stuffed a few items of clothing inside. Kissing Maggie tenderly on the top of her head he felt as if his heart would break when she began to cry and clung onto his leg in an attempt to stop him leaving. It was a futile act and a few seconds later she was grabbed by her mother and once again thrown into the only

bedroom in the tiny flat. Walking to the station Brice was in utter turmoil and he almost changed his mind several times but something deep inside pushed him on, he had to find a better way of living or he knew he would die in this godforsaken shithole. The furthest he'd ever been from the city was a day trip to Wenyss Bay when he was a boy and that had been a disaster, the sea was freezing and the wind whipped Brice's face so hard that his cheeks had stayed red for hours. Still he argued with himself, this could be a golden opportunity and there and then made up his mind to be positive not negative and push any doubtful thoughts to the back of the queue as far as his worries were concerned.

The journey took just under six hours and Ewan was waiting at Euston Station when Brice's train pulled in. The two old friends embraced and then in the tradition of their past, headed straight for the nearest pub. Three hours later and slightly the worse for wear the pair made their way to Ewan's flat on Whitelegg Road in Plaistow. When the door was opened Brice's heart sank. It wasn't a flat but a cramped bedsit and worse still, backed onto the railway line so the constant rumble of trains not only saw the building vibrate but made sleep almost impossible. Brice didn't openly complain as he was grateful just to have a roof over his head, even if it would hopefully only be a temporary arrangement.

The next day which just happened to be a Thursday, Ewan took Brice over to Roman Road market in Bow. Walking through the many stalls selling clothes and household items, much of which had no doubt fallen off of the back of a Lorry somewhere, he suddenly realised that the place was no different from Glasgow and that people were just scratching about trying to make a meagre living. This, along with the memory of the previous night spent in the bedsit had him suddenly wonder if he'd made a big mistake after all. At the end of the stretch of stalls was a burger van. In front of this were a couple of tables and sitting at one was a rather large balding man and Brice noticed that people were keeping their distance for some reason.
"That's the Boss, well the boss's right hand man at any rate! Now let me do the talking and don't speak to him unless he speaks to you okay?"
"But shouldn't I...."
Suddenly Ewan spun on his feet and his face was set in stone as he spoke.
"Do as I fucking tell you! These aren't nice people Brice, they pay well but they're complete cunts. They don't give a shite about anyone and that even includes the Law!"
Brice knowingly nodded his head and a few minutes later he had been introduced to Philip

Magarey, known to all as Pup. The man suspiciously eyed him up and down but didn't speak for a few moments. Pup worked for Harry Pimms and was responsible for recruiting bodies as and when needed. The Pimms firm worked out of a double railway arch over on Pinchin Street in Whitechapel but Pup preferred to stay away from the base when meeting any prospective new staff, just in case they didn't measure up or he didn't like the look of them for some reason.
"So, who do we have here then?"
"This is Brice Mr Margarey, Brice McKay."
"Not another fuckin' Jock? You skirt wearing cunts will be takin' over before long."
Back home if anyone, especially a southerner had made a remark like that there would have been World War Three but when Pup burst into laughter at his own joke, Ewan just joined in and Brice could only look on in total shock at his friend and then to his prospective employer.
"So, what can you do?"
"How do you mean?"
Pup looked at Ewan with a frown.
"Is he fuckin' thick or what?"
Brice didn't allow Ewan to reply, his rag was now well and truly up and in all honesty he had taken an instant dislike to this fat southerner who for some strange reason, was holding court in front of a burger van in East London.

"No, I am not thick and I can do anything I suppose. Back in Glasgee I worked on the docks so I ain't scared of hard work."

"Maybe you ain't but unloading fuckin' boats ain't in our remit sunshine. I meant, can you fuckin' handle yourself?"

Brice again looked away from the man and then at Ewan before looking back to Pup.

"I guess so Mr Magarey."

Pup nodded and with that Ewan knew it was time to leave and pulled his pal back into the market. When they were out of earshot, Brice turned to Ewan with a deflated look on his face.

"So he didn't want to give me a job then?"

"You soppy twat, 'course he did! Brice you have to realise and I thought I'd made myself clear already, these blokes are criminals and I don't mean like the small scale Neds back home. He'll report back to the Boss and then you'll get called in. Now a word of warning, they will want to test you and it could result in you getting a beating but if you want a job then you'll just have to take it on the chin so to speak. Another bit of advice pal, like I told you before I introduced you to Pup, when you meet the Boss for fuck's sake don't speak until you're spoken to. If you think Pup is fucking odd, you ain't seen anything yet. Mr Pimms and for the life of you never address him as Harry, he's fuckin' mental and would put a bullet in your brain without a second thought."

Brice wasn't sure if his pal was exaggerating or not but he was so desperate for money, that right at this moment, he would consider doing anything just to be able to put decent food on the table back home.

The call came at just before seven the following evening via the communal payphone on the ground floor. Someone had hollered up the stairs that there was a call, no names were mentioned and it would take Brice several weeks to find out that all of the occupants of the house worked for the Pimms firm. Brice was given the address of the arches and told to attend the next day at noon, alone! He wasn't happy and would rather have had the support of his pal but as he'd been advised, he made no other comment other than 'yes and thank you'. Pinchin Street, home of the notorious murder of an unnamed woman and mistakenly assumed to be the work of Jack the Ripper back in 1889, housed a relatively small area of converted old arches over a now defunct railway bridge. Numbers ten and eleven were on a long term lease to the Pimms firm and number ten housed a front reception area with an office for the boss at the rear. The adjoining unit had no front entrance and was only accessible via the inside of number ten. This unit couldn't have been more different to its neighbour. The original brick walls were bare and if you cared to look hard enough, the concrete floor, though regularly scrubbed with bleach, still showed signs of the numerous pints of blood that had been spilt upon it over the years. Brice nervously rapped hard on the door with an understandably shaking hand but he wasn't kept waiting for long and the door creaked open almost immediately. Brice came face to face with a mountain of a man who was almost as wide as he was tall. Ken Voss had a mean looking face and that meanness was further enhanced by a scar that ran from his right eyebrow down to his chin. He didn't ask for Brice's name, or what he was doing there and instead gave a single nod of his head, indication that the stranger should step inside. Entering, Brice scanned the area and saw several men milling about. Two were counting cash out onto a desk, one was on the phone and the call sounded more than a tad heated. The final two stood by the side of a door at the far end of the unit and as Ken Voss marched towards them Brice quickly picked up his pace. Tapping on the wood Ken waited until he heard the command of 'enter' and then opening the door, beckoned for Brice to go inside. The room was nothing flash, just a desk, a filing cabinet and a solitary swivel office chair. Harry Pimms stared blankly in Brice's direction as he slowly looked his prospective employee up and down.

"Pup says you're okay but what I want to know is

can you handle yourself?"
Brice coughed nervously, this was the second time in as many days that he'd been asked the same question.
"I like to think so."
"Good to hear it but I don't take anyone's word as gospel. Now in the unit next door is a geezer that's well and truly trying to pull the fuckin' piss. He owes me money for an outstanding loan and has failed to make any fuckin' payments. In my line of work that isn't an option and for me to let it go without punishment wouldn't bode well with my street cred. I have to instil fear, or every low life cunt in this city would try and play me for a fuckin' fool. Now I want you to go in there and beat the cunt to a pulp. If you do it, then you're in, if not, then…... Let's not go down that route for now."
Brice could only stare blankly, he couldn't believe what he'd just heard or what he was expected to do. Now he had a dilemma, he was desperate for money, desperate for a job so that Bonnie and Maggie could join him but hurt someone he didn't even know?! Ken was called in and knew without being told, exactly what to do. Brice duly followed and by now he was scared, more scared than he'd ever been in his life. Not a small man in any way, he'd always been able to take care of himself, coming from Glasgow it was a must if you wanted to survive your childhood years but he always tried

to avoid trouble if he could. Who would his opponent be? For all he knew the bloke could be built like a brick shit house and slaughter Brice before he'd even done a day's work for the Pimms firm. Walking through the entrance that linked the two areas, he turned sharply when he heard the door slam behind him and then the sound of a key being turned in the lock. The space was lit with a single bulb in the centre of the room and the surrounding walls appeared to be in darkness. Giving his eyes a few brief seconds to adjust, he noticed a closed circuit camera as it slowly scanned the space and then he spotted a solitary figure leaning against the rear wall. The man was average in height and build and Brice breathed a sigh of relief as he imagined that he must be just as scared as Brice was. Walking towards the stranger, he stopped just a few feet away.
"Who the fuck are you?!!"
Brice began to explain but was stopped after just a few words.
"Another scotch cunt! Well do your best mate 'cause only one of us will be walkin' out of here and it ain't fuckin' gonna be you! I'm fuckin' sick of foreigners comin' here to do the shit that Pimms ain't got the fuckin' balls for! You must think............"
Suddenly and out of nowhere, a rage seemed to take over Brice, all the pent-up anger regarding Bonnie,

the shithole he'd come to and now in effect having to fight for his life! Without warning he swung a punch and the fight was on. His opponent, who Brice would later learn was a robbing weasel called Stevie Graham, tried to fight back but it was absolutely no contest. Brice reigned down blow after blow and even when his victim fell to the floor Brice straddled him and continued the beating. Each connection of flesh seemed to ease his own frustration and he only stopped when exhaustion eventually forced him to. Brice was sweating profusely, his hair flopped down lankly over his eyes and his knuckles were sore and grazed. Stevie Graham was unrecognisable, teeth lay on the floor beside the body and blood was coming from the victim's nose and mouth in a kind of frothy foam. Struggling to his feet, Brice then staggered over to the door and beat on the wood as hard as he could. Again it was Ken Voss who opened up and handing Brice a towel he smiled, which was strange and somehow made him look even more menacing.
"Back in the office, the boss wants to see you again. Nice fuckin' work by the way sunshine!"
Entering, Brice suddenly noticed the screen on the wall. He'd missed it the first time round but could now clearly see the adjoining unit and the motionless body lying on the bare concrete.
"You've proved yourself well Mac, that's what you'll be known as from now on. Pup has some

cash to tide you over, sort some decent threads out and be back here Monday morning at ten sharp."
"I don't wish to speak out of turn Mr Pimms but I would rather go by my given name. I have enough trouble when blokes hear my accent without being referred to as Mack and being the brunt of their fuckin' jokes."
"Fair enough."
With that Harry Pimms lowered his head and began to glance at some paperwork on his desk. After collecting the money, which turned out to be five hundred pounds and more money than Brice had seen in a long, long time, he slowly made his way back to Ewan's bedsit. This was all surreal, how could he earn that much just for giving some wanker a pasting? It slowly dawned on him that maybe Stevie Graham was dead! That thought now opened a whole new can of worms emotionally and the weekend would be spent fighting his demons, demons that would only be laid to rest with the help of a bottle of scotch.

CHAPTER TWO
1972

Early the following year Bonnie was ready to make the leap and join her husband. She had little love for Brice but financially things were so tight that she had no real choice in the matter. Bonnie McKay was a spender and finally all of her friends and family had found out that borrowing from them meant actually giving with no hope of a repayment, at least as far as Bonnie was concerned. After clearing her rent and stocking up on fags and vodka, there was little left over for treats let alone food for the brat that she had the misfortune to be saddled with. Brice had been over the moon when his wife informed him on one of his weekly Sunday afternoon telephone calls, that by the end of that month she would be joining him. Still camped out at Ewan's bedsit, it was now finally all systems go to find a place for his little family to live and even though back then finding accommodation wasn't that difficult, a bit of additional help went a long way. Harry Pimms had connections all over the City and that included one of the housing officers at Tower Hamlets Council. The man was a compulsive gambler and used the loan services of the Pimms firm on a regular basis. As such he was never able to deny a request and as Brice had become a valuable member of Harry's team, within a few days two properties had miraculously become available. The first was a flat on the fifteenth floor of Keeling House in Bethnal Green. Built in 1957, by the 70's it was already showing signs of urban decay and social problems. On first inspection Brice rejected it outright knowing Bonnie would be back on the train home as soon as she saw the place. The second was a twenty third storey three bedroomed flat on the newly constructed Crossways Estate in Bow. The rooms were bright and airy and Brice felt as though he'd won the pools. Deciding to just buy the basics so that Bonnie could furnish the place just how she wanted, he eagerly awaited the arrival of his little family.

When the train pulled into Euston station, Bonnie McKay was already tired and craving a drink. Struggling with the cases she then roughly yanked Maggie off of the train and the child instantly cried out in pain.
"Shut the fuck up ya wee bitch or I'll give ya somethin' to really fuckin' cry about!"
Maggie promptly did as she was told, her treatment was an all too familiar occurrence and even at such a tender age, she knew what the outcome would be if she didn't do exactly as she'd been told. Brice ran along the platform clutching a bunch of roses but his wife just sneered and leaving the cases and her daughter, marched off in the direction of the exit. It was nothing new and Brice just shrugged his

shoulders, picked up Maggie and gently hugged her to him. The little girl again began to cry but this time they were tears of joy and as she nuzzled into his neck she whispered 'Love you daddy'.
"I love you too my princess. Come on let's go and find your mam and then go and have a look at the new place. Oh Maggie I know you're going to like it, it's like being up in the clouds and looking down on the whole city just like a real princess does from her castle!"
Things didn't however go to plan and as soon as Bonnie stepped out of the cab and looked up at the stark high rise flat that they'd been allocated she turned on her husband with a vengeance.
"What a fucking shite hole! You expect us to live here like fucking rabbits in a cage?! The big shot ain't so big after all are you Brice, you're a fucking loser!"
Entering the pristine building and taking the shiny, almost new lift, up to the twenty third floor, still did nothing to endear Bonnie McKay to her new home or in fact to London. She incessantly continued to complain before the key was even placed into the lock.
"You imagined the streets were paved with gold didn't you, you twat! Why the fuck I ever let you shag me I will never know."
Poking her finger viciously into his chest, she glared in Maggie's direction as she continued her

onslaught.

"You ain't that good in the sack pal and all I ever got out of it was that little fucker!"

With her vicious words, Brice promptly came back down to earth with a bump.

"You are one spiteful bitch Bonnie! This shite hole as you called it, is almost new and far better than the squalor we lived in back home. You didn't have to come and now I'm beginning to wonder why you did? Maybe a phone call to your old Mam might enlighten me."

Bonnie momentarily panicked. If he found out she had left Glasgow owing a mountain of debts to friends and family he would hit the roof! Then again, her husband didn't like confrontation so she knew he was bluffing and would never make that call.

"All I ask is that you give it a chance hen. I'm making good money and you can buy anything you want for the place. Here!"

Handing over a wad of cash instantly saw a change of heart and over the next few days there was a slight improvement in his wife's mood, so much so that even Maggie picked up on it. Little Maggie McKay was a quiet child and from as early as she could remember, it had been made blatantly obvious that her mother detested her. In her own little way she tried to please her mam whenever she could but nothing she did was ever good enough, she was never good enough and the only happy time in her day was when her father came home but Brice's work was demanding and over the ensuing months it sadly felt like he was there less and less.

Ten years later

Maggie was now fifteen and a stroppier teenager you would be hard pushed to find. She talked back to her mother and on one occasion even raised a hand to Bonnie in the form of a so-called slap. It had only ever happened the once and she'd regretted it instantly. Her mother had recently sunk deeper and deeper into alcoholism and spent most of her time lying in a comatose stupor in bed. Bonnie only ventured out to buy vodka and that was only on the odd occasion when she couldn't get anyone else to go for her. Brice showed little interest in his wife, it was after all now only a marriage on paper and he had moved out of the family home some ten months earlier. He still paid the rent and household bills but the only contact he had was when he came to collect Maggie on a Friday evening. His new house on Buxton Street in Whitechapel, a recently modernised Victorian mid terrace, was bought and paid for. Maggie loved her time there, so much so that she informed her father on one particular weekend stay that she no longer wished to live with Bonnie. It hurt Brice when his daughter referred to her mother by her Christian name but then he reasoned that Bonnie had never been much of a parent to their daughter. Agreeing to the request, strict ground rules were laid down. There would be no more bunking off and she had to knuckle down at school and take her exams. Maggie flung her arms around her father and on returning to the flat the following morning to collect her belongings, she opened the door to Bonnie's bedroom for one last time. It was just before ten and the stench of stale alcohol and what she could only guess was urine filled her nostrils as she entered. The television was blaring out some inane morning show and her mother was propped up in bed smoking a cigarette and already swigging from a vodka bottle.

"I'm moving in with dad."

Bonnie momentarily stared at her daughter and the glazed look she gave Maggie as she spoke, was one of utter disgust. Her words came out in a fine shower of spittle and were full of venom.

"You always were a fuckin' ungrateful wee bitch! I am your mother and you will not be going anywhere, do you understand me!?!!"

Aware that this would be the case, Maggie came right back with an answer that she knew would without doubt, change Bonnie's mind.

"Dad said you would say that and he told me to tell you that if you said no, there will be no more payments for rent, fags and booze!"

Bonnie suddenly looked scared, she couldn't live

without her bottles and if Brice stopped paying, there was no way on God's earth she could survive. About to open her mouth again, she wasn't able to get a word out as Maggie quickly added to her last statement.

"You are a total piss head Bonnie and personally I doubt whether you'll live much longer but you have a choice, drink yourself to death with his help, or die crawling up the walls in desperation for a drink. As for you being my mother? You conceived and gave birth to me and that is the sum total of motherhood, at least as far as you're concerned. Let's not beat about the fuckin' bush, I hate you as much as you hate me! I'm going now, so keep your trap shut and dad will send more money next week."

With that Maggie quickly turned and stormed out of the place that had never felt like home, a place full of only sad, cruel memories.

As far as the firm was concerned Brice McKay had done really well for himself over the years and he was now second in command to Harry Pimms, since Harry's health had sadly taken a turn for the worse. The two men got on really well and the rest of the employees not only respected Brice but they actually liked him, a rare thing for a boss in the London underworld. He always seemed to have time if one of them had a problem or wasn't happy about something and would listen fairly before making any decisions. Sometimes he agreed with what was being said and sometimes he didn't but his judgement was always the end of the matter, whether you agreed with it or not. Initially Brice had been concerned that he was stepping on another man's toes but Pup had taken the announcement of Brice's promotion with a pinch of salt. Being a right hard bastard was one thing but he was too old to step up and in all honesty it wasn't something he'd ever aspired to. A short time later, Ken Voss would push Pup further out and take over as Brice's right hand man but he only stayed in that position for a couple of years. Ewan Drummond hadn't worked at the firm for over five years and was currently doing an eight stretch in Barlinnie, after a trip home to see relatives had somehow resulted in Ewan stupidly taking part in an ill thought out random raid on a security van. The robbery was doomed from the off and after the guard and driver were shot but thankfully not killed, Ewan was arrested within hours. When the news had made it back to the firm Brice took it on the chin and Ken Voss was immediately dispatched to find a replacement. It wasn't a cold or unfeeling decision, just part and parcel of underworld life, no one was indispensable and Brice knew that term even included him!

A verbal contract had been agreed several months

earlier, that when Harry passed, Brice would take over the company. Sadly for Harry but a gift from the gods as far as Brice was concerned, this would happen far quicker than anyone could have possibly imagined. A massive heart attack late one Saturday night had put Harry Pimms in an early grave and overnight, promoted Brice to Guvnor. The transition for the new owner had been smooth as all the blokes preferred Brice to Harry so there wasn't much heartache over their former boss's death. Harry Pimms had always referred to his little empire as 'the Company' but on his death it swiftly became known as the McKay firm. Apart from the name change it was business as usual in the short term. Money laundering was still a large contributor to the firm's income but sex and drugs were becoming far bigger money spinners and Brice had plans to branch out into even better things over the next few years.

Around the same time Bonnie passed away. Her body was discovered when a neighbour reported a terrible stench coming from the flat opposite. When the Police forced entry, the bedroom was swarming with flies and it was estimated that she had been dead for at least a week. After tracking him down, Brice was informed but all he did was nonchalantly shrug his shoulders. However, he was concerned about breaking the news to Maggie, after all she was still his daughter's mother. Leaving it until Maggie came home from school, even Brice was surprised at the response he got.

"Sit down for a minute hen."

"I didn't do it!"

"Didn't do what sweetheart?"

"Whatever you're going to accuse me of!"

Brice smiled, he wanted to laugh but this really wasn't a time for joviality.

"I'm not going to blame you for anything love, actually I have some bad news. Your mam has passed away."

For a few minutes Maggie didn't say anything as she reminisced about all that had happened over the years, all the cruel words and beatings that she'd received from Bonnie for doing absolutely nothing wrong.

"Honestly dad, I don't give a rat's arse about that evil old bitch. Actually, I hope she fuckin' rots in hell!"

"Maggie!"

"What?!"

"You're a beautiful young lady, so please don't use language like that."

Suddenly they both burst out laughing, it was in bad taste but neither could deny that all they actually felt was relief.

Naturally Brice paid for the funeral and as the attendees would all be from Glasgow, he decided to

hold the service and wake back in their old home city. Maggie flatly refused to attend but Brice felt a sense of duty, so ten days later and accompanied by Ciaran O'Connor, his now right hand man, the two boarded a train. The funeral service went off without a hitch but it was a different story when it came to the wake. Too much whisky, which had been supplied free of charge by Brice, was consumed and within a couple of hours Bonnies family viciously turned on Brice. The debts she had left behind were temporarily forgotten about and he was blamed for taking her away from her home and even blamed for her death. It got so bad that Brice and Ciaran had to make a hasty retreat to the station with Brice swearing that he would never again set foot in this shithole of a place, a shithole he had once been proud to call home.
"What a bunch of ungrateful cunt's Ciaran!"
"No worries Boss, we're out of it now thank fuck."

Ciaran O'Connor was twenty four years old and originally hailed from Belfast. Born in Ardoyne in the north area of the city in 1958, he had been forced to grow up fast in his teens. As the Troubles escalated, each street was a potential tinder box just waiting to go up at any given time. He shied away from any factions both political and religious but it was still tough and joining a local boxing club, he quickly honed his skills as a fighter. Ciaran would never make it in the professional world of boxing as his temper was too fiery and by the age of twenty he had put Ireland behind him and moved over to London. After seeking out work with a couple of small firms, his path soon crossed that of Ken Voss and Ciaran was put forward as a potential employee. Brice had instantly warmed to the youngster, probably due to the fact that unlike the rest of the firm, they both hailed from other parts of the United Kingdom. After his initiation and with detailed instruction, he had soon become Brice's personal minder but being liked didn't just stop with his boss. Maggie had instantly fallen in love at their first meeting and although Ciaran didn't outwardly encourage the teenager, he knew that it wouldn't do any harm to keep her on side as she could twist the guvnor around her little finger.

CHAPTER THREE
1988

Just as planned, the firm had gone from strength to strength. Maggie was now working alongside her father but as yet her input was only in a clerical capacity. It wasn't what Brice wanted for his daughter but Maggie had been adamant so he'd relented on the understanding that she would attend college and take courses in accounting and business management. Maggie McKay, never really one for study, rose to the challenge and had finished her education with a distinction in both of her subjects. Still hankering after Ciaran O'Connor, the young woman's heart skipped a beat whenever he entered a room or on the odd occasion when he winked at her, something he did sporadically and which made Maggie's cheeks flush with embarrassment. Brice wasn't stupid, he noticed the new clothes and carefully applied make up but he reasoned it was just a silly girl's crush and she would grow out of it. He totally trusted Ciaran and was sure he would never take things further so in reality, there wasn't too much harm being done.

Maggie's twenty-first birthday was fast approaching and Brice had a few surprises in store for his beloved princess, the first being dinner at renowned Michelin restaurant Le Gavroche in

Mayfair. It was arranged that Ciaran would collect her from home and drive her to the restaurant, Brice had been really busy of late so he would join her as soon as he could, until then Ciaran was to stay by her side. Knowing who was collecting her, Maggie had gone all out with her dress and was ready well ahead of time. When she heard the car horn in the street she purposefully didn't venture outside. Ciaran sighed in frustration, Daddy's little princess wanted him to go to the door and he knew he didn't have a choice in the matter. Exiting the car he was about to ring the bell when he noticed that the door was on the latch. Pushing it open he called out her name.

"Maggie?! Maggie are you about?"

"I'm in the front room Ciaran, come through."

As soon as he saw her he knew what she wanted, dressed up to the nines with makeup plastered on thicker than a street Tom. Swiftly moving across the room he took her into his arms and roughly pushed her to the floor. Maggie was momentarily stunned, this wasn't what she wanted, and this wasn't how it was supposed to be. Instantly her romantic dreams of him taking her in his arms were shattered into a million pieces.

"Stop!!! What do you think you're doing Ciaran? Get off of me!!!"

By now his hand was up inside her dress and realising that she wasn't wearing any knickers had him hard in seconds.

"You want it, you know you do you dirty little slut! You've been flirting with me for years, ever since you was a kid, well you ain't a kid anymore and it's time to pay the fuckin' piper!"

With one hand Ciaran pushed hard on her chest as he struggled with the other to open his trouser fly. Maggie was hysterical and raising her head as much as she could, she looked down and saw his erect penis.

"No! No! nooooo!!!!!"

Forcing her legs apart he rammed himself inside of her and Maggie screamed out in pain. Except for her mother's beatings when she was growing up, Maggie had been shielded from any violence since her teens and now that this was happening she didn't know what to do! It didn't last more than a couple of minutes and when she heard Ciaran grunt loudly, knew that the ordeal had come to an end. Standing up he casually tucked in his shirt and then offered his hand to help Maggie to her feet. Her mascara was smeared by her tears and her previously pristine hairdo now looked like a birds nest.

"Go and clean yourself up, you look like a fuckin' panda! Don't be too long or you'll be late and the guvnor will start to worry and I'll be the one to get it in the fuckin' neck not you!"

Up in the bathroom Maggie broke down sobbing,

she was physically shaking and didn't know what to do, to tell her father would break his heart and she would rather die than do that. Five minutes later she had pulled herself together and walking down the stairs, followed her attacker to the car. The drive over to Mayfair was taken in complete silence but Ciaran was sure that he didn't have to tell the stupid bitch to keep her trap shut, she adored him it was obvious and there was no way she would ever tell Brice what had occurred. His big headed assumption was a huge mistake, as four months later Maggie had no option but to spill the beans.

On the day in question she hadn't gone into work, preferring to wait until the end of the day when she knew everyone would have gone home. Phoning ahead, Maggie had told her father that she wanted to talk to him with no one else around, not even Ciaran. Just as he always did, Brice honoured his daughter's wishes and sent his minder on an errand with instruction that after that, to call it a day. As she walked into the office Brice looked up from his desk and with just a single glance his brow became furrowed with concern. His beautiful Maggie was dressed down in jeans, trainers and a bomber jacket. Her hair was pulled back into a harsh ponytail and she wasn't wearing a scrap of makeup, making her look washed out and weary.

"Hi dad."

"You okay hen?"

Flopping down into the facing chair, Maggie's eyes instantly filled with tears.

"No not really."

"What is it my little darlin', tell your daddy and I'll sort it out for you."

"You can't sort this one out Dad, really you can't."

"Well not if you don't tell me I can't!"

Maggie swallowed hard, this was far more difficult than she thought it would be. Would he hate her? Would he think that she was now damaged goods, an old slapper just like her mother?

"You have to promise me that you'll stay calm dad and not go up like a bottle of pop because if you do then I'm out of here!"

"I won't I promise, now tell me for God's sake because you're startin' to worry me."

"Remember the night of my birthday? The night Ciaran came to collect me?"

The question was rhetorical but Brice nodded his head all the same.

"I left the door on the latch and he came into the house. He raped me dad, raped me!!!!! He said it was what I wanted but it wasn't, oh I admit I had a crush on him but it was a romantic thing, I didn't want sex and now I'm pregnant and I don't know what to do!!!"

Maggie began to sob, heartfelt, gut wrenching sobs

and at the same time she stared at her father's face desperately looking for a sign that he was disappointed with her. There was none but neither did Brice speak. The look on his face was one of pure rage and Maggie recognised the coldness in his eyes, she'd seen it so many times over the years and knew what it meant. Standing up her father walked around the table and taking her hands, slowly lifted Maggie to her feet. Tenderly taking his most precious possession into his arms, he hugged her lovingly.
"Don't you worry about a thing hen, everything will be fine. I'll make sure it is."

At noon the next day, Ciaran nonchalantly strolled into the arches without a care in the world. Apart from Brice, only Ken knew of what had actually happened. Everyone else was still aware that he had pissed the guvnor off big style in some way or another but no one showed it or knew exactly why. Ken Voss, who had idolised Maggie since she was a little girl, struggled to hold his anger inside but he managed and just smiled in the Irishman's direction. Ciaran took it that Ken was pleased to see him but it was a smile of satisfaction, satisfaction in the knowledge that he knew what the cunt was about to go through.
"Guvnor's next door. He said to tell you to join him as soon as you got here."

Shrugging his shoulders Ciaran calmly walked through the door and into the dimly lit space.
"Ken said you wanted to see me……."
Ciaran stopped his sentence dead in its tracks when he spied a padded bench, complete with restraining straps, which had been set up in the middle of the floor.
"Who's that for?"
His boss was decked out in a long plastic butcher's apron and he just slowly tilted his head at the question but offered no answer. Ciaran was suddenly grabbed from behind by Ken and Albie Mitchell and then he heard Ken whisper into his ear 'You! You cunt!' Roughly bundled onto the bench, within seconds the restraining straps had been tightened and Ciaran was unable to move. Albie was told to leave and wait in the office area until he was called.
"Please Brice, what's all this about!!!?!!"
Ken Voss ripped off a wide strip of duct tape and slapped it roughly over Ciaran's mouth before pulling a Stanley knife from his pocket. Ciaran's eyes were out on stalks and as fear raged through him a solitary tear escaped and ran down the side of his temple. He wasn't stupid, he'd seen enough of what went on here, much of which he'd been party to himself and he wasn't getting out of this place alive, of that he was certain. For a few seconds Brice slowly and menacingly circled the table just silently

glaring down coldly at the young man, a man he'd naively believed he could trust.

"You raped my girl, my beautiful, beautiful Maggie!!!!!"

When Brice nodded his head, Ciaran knew that his life on this mortal coil was about to come to an end. Ken quickly undid the Irishman's trousers and in the blink of an eye they had been pulled down and were now wedged around his knees. Brice stepped forward, this was one act of violence he definitely wanted to carry out personally. Ken handed over the Stanley knife and his boss grabbed Ciaran's penis and roughly yanked it up so that the flaccid cock was stretched out tightly. Taking his time he slowly drew the razor sharp blade around the skin and as he did so the blood began to flow freely. Ciaran's screams or at least his attempt at screaming, was audible even through the tape but Brice had no intention of putting his former minder out of his misery. Instead he took his time and it was almost a full minute before the penis was detached from Ciaran's groin. Brice knew that this act alone probably wouldn't kill the bastard and in all honesty he didn't care. At this stage, the punishment was purely for his own satisfaction. Ciaran had instantly passed out so Ken reached under the bench and pulled out a bucket of iced water and then threw half of its contents into the victim's face. Ciaran O'Connor started to gasp and

splutter and his whole body began to shake with shock but he knew the assault was far from over when Brice grabbed hold of his entire scrotum. Once again using the knife he repeated the process and yet again Ciaran passed out and had to be revived.
"I think that's about it! Finish up here will you Ken and then get rid of this cunt!"
Brice removed the apron and as he walked towards the door, Ken pulled out a Bowie hunting knife and staring directly into Ciaran's face began to grin from ear to ear.

Under duress from her father, Maggie agreed to proceed with the pregnancy. She desperately wanted a termination but Brice had pleaded with her that this was his grandchild and promised that if she gave birth he would purchase a flat and install a fulltime nanny. Maggie would not be forced to have any contact and Brice would raise the child as his own. He was praying that once the baby was born, his daughter would instantly fall in love but that wasn't to be the case and when Bobby Brice McKay came into the world screaming and kicking on November the first 1988, his twenty one year old mother had never in her life felt so much hatred for another living thing.

Now in her thirties, Maggie McKay, with the help

and guidance of Ken Voss, was all but running the firm. Years of heavy smoking had caused Brice to develop Chronic Obstructive Pulmonary Disease and his illness was so severe that he wasn't expected to live much longer. Maggie idolised her father and had taken the news badly so had thrown herself into business as a way of taking her mind off of the situation. Brice spent most of his life in bed or at best propped up in his armchair with piped oxygen circulating around his bedroom. Bobby, now seventeen, wasn't a typical teenager and during daylight hours he became Brice's fulltime caregiver with Maggie taking over in the evenings for a few hours. His sister, as far as he knew that was who she was, cared about nothing but money or at least that was how he viewed her. Their relationship was strained and Maggie could barely look at him when she visited let alone have any kind of a conversation with the boy. With Brice knowing that his time was almost up, he had to find a way for young Bobby to be taken care of because if Maggie had her way, the boy would be out on his ear as soon as Brice died.

David Granger, a senior partner at Granger, Granger and Hobbs, having represented the McKay firm with any legal issues from the day Brice had taken over from Harry Pimms, was invited to the house on a day Brice knew that his daughter would be busy and therefore not able to pop back home, which was often the case. Brice asked his grandson to make sure that after he'd been to the shops he was back in time to let David in. From thereon in, he was told to make himself scarce and with the added instruction not to mention a word of the visitor to his sister.

"Hello Mr McKay, how are you today?"

"Hi David, I'm hanging on in there but I can feel the fuckin' life of me being sucked out a bit more each day."

David Granger was about to say that he hoped Brice would feel better soon but that would be a ridiculous statement as he knew exactly why he was here. Suddenly Brice began to gasp for breath and it looked as if he was going to expire before any business was carried out but slowly his breathing regulated and he pointed to a chair which had been situated next to the bed.

"I take it you wish to put your affairs in order Mr McKay?"

Brice only nodded his head in an attempt to conserve what little energy he had left. For several seconds the room remained silent, save for the sound of oxygen being pumped by a compressor. Finally Brice at last felt able to continue.

"It's pretty simple, everything goes to Maggie, the house, the business and most of the money and shares, both legit and otherwise. Regarding my

boy, I know he ain't the full ticket but I want a trust fund set up for my Bobby and a position found within the firm, there will be no negotiation on the latter as I know my daughter well enough to know that she will oust the kid at the first opportunity."
"Is there anything else?"
"No that's it but I need this all done as soon as possible and that I can't stress strongly enough!"
"It will be ready for you to sign by tomorrow, should I pop back at say lunchtime?"
Exhausted, Brice could only nod his head and as he slowly closed his eyes it was a signal to David Granger that the meeting was over. The McKay's had paid handsomely over the years for his services and David hoped it would continue with Maggie. For a fleeting moment he toyed with the idea of forewarning her but professionalism and the added fact that she would then view his company as untrustworthy, made him dismiss the idea out of hand. Bobby saw the visitor out and after making his dad a cup of tea in the special non spill plastic beaker that Brice absolutely hated using, he made his way back into the bedroom.
"Everything okay dad?"
"All good son, now I want you to call Uncle Kenny. Tell him to come over this afternoon and again, I don't want your sister knowing."
"Okay dad will do."
Bobby was a good kid, he loved his little family

even if that love wasn't returned by a certain someone. He wasn't exactly smart and had never really achieved much at school but his nature was so kind, that everyone he came into contact with genuinely adored him. Doing as he was asked, a little over an hour later he again opened the front door with a broad grin on his face.
"Hello Bobby boy, how's it hanging?"
The teenager giggled and at the same time his face reddened with embarrassment.
"Fine thank you Uncle Kenny. Dad told me to take you straight through as soon as you arrived."
Kenneth Voss was a giant of a man standing over six feet tall. His love of beer had seen his waist line expand over the years and his heavily thinning hair showed his age. Ken continually breathed hard and he knew that if he didn't start to change his lifestyle, then just like his boss, his years on this mortal coil would be greatly reduced but at his age it would be like trying to teach an old dog new tricks. Bobby loved Kenny and even with his limited intelligence he could see that his uncle wasn't in the best of health and it worried him. They both headed in the direction of the back room that had been set up as a temporary bedroom for his father. With Ken inside and not needing to be told twice, Bobby left the two men to their business and went back to watching television in the kitchen.
"That's a great kid you have there and if I do say so

myself, you look a bit brighter today guvnor!"
"Fuck off Kenny, we both know I'm about to peg it. Tell me, how's that girl of mine doing?"
Ken laughed, Brice always referred to her as my girl, he obviously didn't want to see the hard faced thirty something woman who could make grown men piss themselves in fear, something she actually did on occasion.
"Running a tight ship as always boss, Maggie is tougher than both of us put together and that's not an overstatement."
"Good, she's a woman in a man's world and if she wasn't tough every cunt in the Smoke would run rings around her. Right, let's get down to business. We both know I'm about to snuff it and I've put all of my affairs in order regarding the firm and finances but there's something I want you to make sure of. Bobby has to come into the business and Maggie will do her best to stop it from happening. Apart from me and her, you are the only other living person who knows the exact details of what that cunt Ciaran did to her so when she kicks off I want you to remind her of that and that this is my dying wish regarding her son, tell her about you being here and what I have said to you."
"That goes without saying Mr McKay. You know I've always adored her, right from when she was a little kid but I also care deeply for your Bobby and I swear to you I'll make sure nothing bad happens to

him. What about the crew, especially Albie and Pup, you made any arrangements for them?"
"Ken my old mukka, it ain't for me to dictate to Mags who she does and doesn't employ. Obviously you'll be okay but if she chooses to have a reshuffle and get rid of some of the dead wood then that's her affair."

Four days later when Brice McKay gasped his last breath, he was surrounded by Bobby, Ken and a weeping and heartbroken Maggie. It was one of only a handful of times that Ken had ever seen her cry and it tore him up inside to witness it. The funeral was attended by over a hundred people, many of whom were known London faces but unusually they weren't there to try an attempt at a takeover but purely down to paying their respects to a well loved and respected fellow villain.

At the reading of the Will, Maggie McKay's face was set in stone. Grateful that everything had been left to her, she was also furious about the late addition of a codicil to the Will regarding Bobby. Later that day she had even contacted David Granger with a view to contesting but was instantly informed that the document had been made watertight in the event of just such a situation arising. Maggie was absolutely livid, if that little shit had to come into the firm then she would make his life unbearable, so bloody unbearable that he would leave, or at least that was the plan.

CHAPTER FOUR

Even though it had really gone against the grain as far as Maggie was concerned, she had nonetheless honoured her father's dying wish and Bobby was given a position within the firm but it was as menial as she could find and only consisted of manning the phones, keeping the place clean and tidy and making tea as and when anyone wanted one. Almost eleven long years of taking abuse and much to Maggie's annoyance, her so called brother had never once complained and as every day passed, he'd endeared himself more and more to the men that he worked alongside. They always had a kind word for young Bobby and disliked the treatment he received from his sister but none dared to voice an opinion, at least not within earshot of Maggie McKay.
"Bobby!!! Get your fuckin' arse in here now!!"
The young man looked in Ken's direction and the pure embarrassment he felt showed on his face. Shrugging his shoulders he wearily stood up and making his way to her office, closed the door behind him. He needn't have bothered as Maggie's voice was so shrill that everyone in the arches heard her every word.
"You are a fuckin' joke, a complete waste of space do you hear me? All you have to do is man the phones and you can't even fuckin' manage that!

I've been waiting for a call from Frankie Tennent for three days now, only to find out this morning that he rang on Monday and you soppy bollocks, didn't have the nous to tell me."
"I'm sorry Mags but you weren't here, I did leave you a message though."
"Where?"
"On your desk, I propped it up beside dad's picture to make sure you saw it."
Maggie scanned the desk but there was nothing visible.
"Well it ain't fuckin' here now is it? I don't know why dad even gave you the time of day! Now get out of my sight you useless twat!"
When Bobby came out of the office Ken noticed him wipe a tear from his eye. This was bang out of order and marching forward he entered without an invite. Maggie glanced up from reading the scrap of paper that she'd strangely just found under a pile of letters."
"What!"
"Good job the old man ain't alive 'cause princess or not, he would have hauled you over the fuckin' coals for talking to the kid like that. You may hate him, though God above knows why but….."
"You know why Kenny, I never wanted him but dad made me keep the little bastard."
"And was any of that Bobby's fault? He didn't ask to be born, that was your choice."

Profit wise 2005 and the year her father had passed away, was a surprisingly lucrative year for the McKay firm. The Tom's brought in a fair amount but now with the rapid rise of lap dancing clubs, frequented by the rich and famous, classy skirt was "No it wasn't, you knew how dad could be and he would never have forgiven me if I'd got rid. I didn't ask to get fuckin' raped but we don't always get what we want in life so if you have nothing else to say, get back to work!"
When she was in this mood Ken knew better than to push her any further. Her tongue could cut you like a knife and she had none of her father's endearing qualities of that he was sure. Since Brice had passed, Ken felt he was being pushed further and further away from the arches and his daily workload now consisted of taking care of the Soho properties that Maggie hated and found boring. They did bring in regular cash though so she wouldn't get rid of them as they were far too lucrative but she was happier when she didn't have to deal with them and Ken's new appointment as properties manager made sure she didn't have to.

Profit wise 2005 and the year her father had passed away, was a surprisingly lucrative year for the McKay firm. The Tom's brought in a fair amount but now with the rapid rise of lap dancing clubs, frequented by the rich and famous, classy skirt was required and Maggie McKay soon became known for providing some of the best women in London. This had continued until 2009 when some bright spark in government reclassified the clubs as 'sex encounter venues' and by early 2012 all of the clubs had to reapply for their licences. Many were refused and the decline of such premises quickly escalated. With the reclassification three years before the change in licences, Maggie had weighed up the situation and it wasn't rocket science to see what the future held and what was in the pipeline for the now, most profitable part of her business. Over the years she had built up quite a file of contacts and on numerous occasions had been asked to supply an alternative to lap dancers. She had always politely declined, choosing to keep the clubs separate from her Tom's but now with a wealth of rich clientele, Maggie had decided to branch out into private sex parties. It seemed like the more high profile the men were, the sicker their fantasies and the more they were prepared to pay. It wasn't just the cash she would earn from these so called parties but also the list of names, not to mention the recordings she would discreetly make, that would one day probably come in handy for her own personal retirement fund. It had been in conjunction with Sam Wenner, a club and events planner and after Sam had secured the exclusive weekend use of Hatton Hall, a mere hour's drive

from the capital, it was all systems go. They started off in a small way just to test the waster and see what the demand was but they needn't have bothered. From the onset every weekend was a sell out and it wasn't long before Sam went on a second scouting mission which resulted in the use of Boreham Manor in Basildon. Many of the girls previously used in the lap dancing clubs had come to Maggie in fear of losing their livelihoods. One such woman, Alina Balan would freely moan to anyone who was prepared to listen that she'd been seduced into thinking that lap dancing was safe and secure but the regular verbal and sometimes physical abuse she received from customers had damaged her. There was just one problem, she desperately needed to earn money. Maggie knew she could trust the girl with her new venture as Alina was only too aware of what would happen to her if she ever opened her trap. Getting a call out of the blue and being invited over to the arches was something of a surprise and Alina was more than a little nervous as she was shown towards the office by Chris Freeman. Chris was a trusted but sex mad employee of around five years and he was physically undressing the young woman with his eyes as she nervously walked past him.
"Strip me in your head all you like you fucking pervert because you'll never get a woman like me unless she's dead or drugged out of her head."

With her sudden outburst now over, Alina knocked on the office door and went inside to see her boss.

"So how are you Alina, how's work?"

"Dead and I can't see it changing, my pay is a pittance to what it was and I don't know how much longer I can survive. I hate the work Ms McKay, hate all of those dirty perverts mauling me and making me feel like just a piece of meat that they can touch whenever the mood takes them."

"Sadly Alina we are living in a generation where everything has become a commodity. Now, I'm in the process of setting up a new business, a business I think you would fit into perfectly. I want you to run the two places I currently have but I hope to expand upon these initial two in the not too distant future."

Explaining the details to Alina and they were very limited details at that, Maggie couldn't help but notice the look of absolute horror and disgust on Alina's face.

"Excuse me Ms McKay but have you not heard a single word that I've just said?"

"Of course I have sweetie but I ain't askin' you to take your drawers off, only manage the fuckin' Tom's that do. If you want in then you will be paid handsomely, if not, then we will say our goodbyes here and now."

"I would be lying if I said I'm not interested Ms McKay but I have to admit that I also fear for some of those poor women. Before the Go-Go club shut its doors it had become a no holds barred place, oh I know a lot of the blokes came in because in their pathetic minds they loved the women but there were a lot of others who used it only to vent their bitterness and frustration on the girls. They weren't being challenged about it either, not by the owners nor the security that was there to allegedly protect us, which was a joke and that damaged a lot of those girls."

Maggie knowingly and sympathetically nodded her head while Alina spoke but in reality she was bored, totally uninterested and just wanted this simple piece of business wrapped up as quickly as possible. These women who sold their arses for a few quid were starting to get on her nerves with all of their whining and winging about being treated like a piece of meat.

"Believe me Alina, my places are all run in the correct way. My employees are one hundred percent safe and there is enough security to form a small army. No one, and I repeat no one, will be forced to do anything they are not happy with. My clientele have more cash to spend than you can poke a stick at and I know some of the sick bastards want stuff they can't get off of their little woman back home, so it obviously isn't just the missionary position. That said, as long as any girl in question doesn't have a problem with that then they can do what they like and they get paid handsomely for their services into the bargain. So?"

"What's in it for me?"

Maggie had to stop herself from laughing. For all of the damaged goods speech that the young woman had just spouted off about, when it came down to cold hard facts, it was all about the cash, just as it always was.

"How does six hundred a week sound? Plus, the added bonus of expenses and a car of course. For that you will be required to work from Friday evening until Monday morning. The parties are held from eight each night until the early hours so there will be some time to rest up although I will expect you to cover both properties at some time or another over the weekend. You will have a small office that houses the most up to date Closed-circuit television. The monitors will cover the social areas and hallways but most importantly of all, the bedrooms. Your role will be to observe and act upon anything being carried out that you deem to be unsafe. You won't be required to get involved physically, there will be security for that but you have a kind way about you Alina, you know the business so to speak and are better prepared for what is acceptable than any man would be."

For several seconds Alina Balan didn't utter a word. She acted as if she was mulling over the offer as she obviously didn't want to seem too eager. Inside she

was jumping for joy, six hundred a week for doing almost nothing and a car chucked in for good measure was like winning the lottery.
"I'm in and thank you very much for choosing me Ms McKay."

Hatton Hall did well but Boreham Manor in Essex was the real money spinner. Gangsters, celebrities, politicians and Premier League footballers all mingled together at the weekly invitation only events and although Maggie never personally attended, she took great delight in reviewing the recordings every Monday afternoon. It was her little weekly treat to herself and something she enjoyed immensely. A lot of the footage was the boring, Tom and client stuff that you would expect to see and for the most part these were fast forwarded and stored for future reference. The images Maggie was really interested in were the sick fantasies such as the High Court Judge who liked to have one of the whores defecate into his mouth or the premier league footballer who got off on being fisted by a woman and who would take great delight in examining every Tom working that night before choosing the one with the biggest hands. The lengths these men would go to was at times unimaginable and could in the future turn out to be very lucrative for Maggie.

While Hatton had been ready to go from the off, Maggie was the most proud of Boreham Manor because it had taken a lot more work. A boarding school until six months before she took over, the rooms were barren and the upstairs still housed the metal framed beds in the dormitories. The whole place had an overpowering smell of Jeyes Fluid which the caretaker must have obviously been a tad too fond of using. The Manor was soon decorated from top to bottom and the hardwood floors were covered with expensive shag pile carpet. Beds replaced school desks and high end furnishings, some of which it could be said were a little on the tacky side but suited the new use perfectly, were put into place. At the end of it all Maggie came for a final inspection and as soon as she gave it the thumbs up, the first weekend went into planning.

Ken Voss and the others at the arches weren't privy to what was going on not a million miles away. They still ran the loan sharking, street girls and any robberies that were in the pipeline but Maggie knew that the less people involved the safer her clients' secrets would be. Even the security guards were driven to the venues in a van with blacked out windows. All mobile phones were switched off and confiscated before departure and were not given back until the van returned to London on Monday so that no one could track where they had been taken. Latex gloves were handed out to everyone, guests included and strict instructions were given that they were to be worn at all times. It wasn't rocket science to work out why and no one complained as they simply didn't want any evidence coming to light that they had ever been in attendance. The setup worked well, worked well for many months in fact and brought in so much cash that the money became the be all and end all as far as Maggie was concerned. A small investment company had to be set up as well as a warehouse offering cut price high end electrical goods, all a front to launder the money. Maggie lost fifteen percent of her takings but she reasoned it was worth it to appear clean and besides, she was coining in so much that it really didn't matter. A house in Chelsea was purchased along with a Bentley and designer goods of the highest calibre which included both Cartier and Bulgari jewellery. Ken Voss knew better than to question Brice's daughter but he wasn't stupid, something was going down that her father wouldn't have approved of but there was little Ken could do to stop it.

By the end of 2016 the parties were running like a well-oiled machine but they came to an abrupt halt at the end of the following year when the bodies of a well-known television presenter and his chosen

Tom for that evening were found face down in the Jacuzzi. Maggie was contacted at two in the morning and straight away she drove over to Basildon. All guests had congregated in the main sitting room and even though several had tired, none of them had been allowed to leave.
"Good morning everyone. Now what happened here tonight was nothing more than a tragedy but I am also aware that due to you high profiles, you do not wish to be associated in any of this for fear of damaging your careers. I advise you all to collect your belongings and do a double check that you have left nothing behind. When everyone has left the site the police will be notified. I cannot stress enough that you should never breathe a word of these events to another living soul, if you do, then I cannot guarantee that you won't be incriminated in some way. Do I make myself perfectly clear?"
Everyone in the room vigorously nodded their heads before scattering at an alarming rate. The security crew were returned to London in the same manner in which they had arrived and pretty soon, save for the two deceased, it was just Maggie and Sam Wenner left at the Manor.
"Right, now we have to do closure on this fuckin' mess Sam. The owner, does he know you, know your name?"
"No Maggie, I was very careful on that score. His only contact with me is via a burner phone which

has already been disposed of. An envelope of cash was left for him to collect here every Monday afternoon but apart from that there was no other contact and no questions asked."

"Good. Right, so the only thing left to do is to collect all of tonight's recording."

"What about the equipment?"

"There isn't time and besides, I can well afford to leave it. Just make sure you wipe the machines as you go round. When you get back to London, find a payphone, disguise your voice and report the deaths to the Old Bill. Don't contact me for a couple of months until the dust settles and then hopefully we can start over again. In the meantime I can run Hatton on my own but I'll reduce the frequency of the events. For now, I'm sorry to say it's a case of see you around Sam!"

With that Maggie left and got into her car and as she did so she sighed heavily. Shit happens but now she was going to be out of pocket by a huge amount, an amount she had quickly gotten used to and liked.

CHAPTER FIVE

With a population of almost six hundred thousand, Bacau is one of, if not the, poorest city in Romania and still has the highest poverty rate among all of the country's regions. Supposedly, the Securitale, Nicolae Ceausescu's secret police, were disbanded after the overthrow of the dictator in 1989 but in reality their various intelligence tasks were just reassigned to numerous other institutions under the guise of several different names such as the SRI, the SRE and the SPP to list but a few. The Securitate were one of the most brutal secret police forces in the world and were responsible for the arrests, torture and deaths of thousands of Romanian nationals and absolutely nowhere was safe, not even in hospitals or schools. The Securitate previously deployed one agent or informer for every 43 Romanians, making it almost impossible to form any activist groups, no matter how small in numbers.

Alina Balan was born exactly three months to the day that Ceausescu was executed. The eldest daughter of Elena Balan, the fear of torture and poverty from her mother's earlier life still hadn't faded by the time Alina started school. Dread still gripped the population and conversations were always carried out in hushed tones, even regarding the most menial of topics. Elena had been heavily pregnant with Alina when her husband had disappeared and Elena would continually relay to Alina and her two elder brothers, the story of when the Securitale had called late one evening and forcibly taken her husband away. Florin had kicked out and screamed that he had done no wrong but his pleas went unheard. His wife had spent months searching for him, asking anyone with influence to help her but her begging fell upon deaf and frightened ears until she finally accepted that he would never return home again. The children had been too young and hardly remembered their father, so the tears shed by Elena every time she recalled that fateful night, received little to no compassion from her babies.

By the time Alina was six she was already helping her mother with the vast amounts of washing that Elena was forced to take in just to put food on the table. When business was slow there would be sewing and baking bread for people if they could provide the ingredients. That said Alina's childhood was a happy one with plenty of love, making up for all of the missing essentials.

School was hit and miss during Alina's formative years and although compulsory, the law regarding learning was seldom imposed, with illiteracy being higher than the previous generation. Elena was concerned about her daughters prospects, the boys could probably get labouring work when they were old enough but she wanted better for her girl. Walking five miles to take freshly baked bread to the local doctor, Elena beseeched the physician to help her. Doctor Cazau was an elderly man who was also incredibly kind and a deal was struck. Two evenings a week he would teach Alina literacy and as a well-educated man, he also taught the young girl a good command of the English language and all for the princely sum of a loaf of freshly baked bread.

Home was a ramshackle house, in reality little more than a shack on the edge of an industrial zone. Elena had grown up there with her parents when it was all still farmland and her husband had moved in as soon as they were married. Now some forty years later the homes were due to be demolished and the residents would be expected to find alternative accommodation. Alina celebrated her nineteenth birthday the day before the bulldozers were due to raze the area to the ground and the birthday gift from her mother was an envelope containing a passport and a few dollars. Back then it equated to roughly fifty pounds or three hundred Leu, not a vast amount but in Romania it was a King's ransom. The money had been changed on the black market, a highly dangerous act but Elena knew that her country's currency wouldn't be much use outside of Romania so she had taken the risk. Alina had argued that the family couldn't afford it but her mother was insistent as she explained that she had saved every spare Leu she could over the years and the gift was to get her daughter away from Bacau and out of Romania if possible.

"But when will I see you again Mama?"

"I don't know my darling, I suppose there is a possibility we may never see each other again but if that's God's plan, then so be it, because I will die a happy woman just knowing that you are no longer living in this hellhole. Write to me every week and tell me what you are doing and how successful you are, send the letters to Uncle Marius until I know where me and your brothers will finally be able to call home."

Many tears were shed between the two women and finally after packing a small suitcase, Alina set off for the coastal town of Split in Croatia. The thousand and six mile trip would take several train and bus journeys and almost twenty long and tiring hours to complete.

Due to the fact that she was able to speak English well, and was able to converse with the tourists, Alina gained work almost immediately in one of the beach side cafes. By taking a budget room in one of the hostels, she would hopefully be able to send any spare money home to her mother. Alina had hoped that the work would last for the summer season but everything would change only a month into her new life when she was innocently introduced to a lone diner by the name of Adam Thompson. Adam was on holiday and the pair seemingly fell head over heels in love, well at least on Alina's part. Two weeks after Adam's return to the UK, Alina received a one way plane ticket and it took only seconds for her to make a decision. Stay here and hope to continue working until the winter, or go to England, the land of milk and honey and be with her love?

When flight LHR416 landed at Heathrow airport, Alina was full of trepidation. Would she still feel the same? Would she even like him now that they were on his home territory? Would England turn out to be all she had hoped for? She needn't have worried as her heart missed a beat as soon as she saw him standing at the arrivals gate. He was as handsome as ever and holding the most gigantic bunch of red roses. On the drive into the city, Adam explained that he had carried out some research and for her to remain in the country, it would be best if they married. Naively she believed him and two weeks later on the day they tied the knot at Hounslow registry office, Alina's nightmare

would began.
She wasn't allowed to work, making it impossible to send money home and leaving the flat was a definite no, no, save for doing the weekly shopping. She wasn't allowed to write to her mother, phone or to use anyone else's phone to call her family. Overnight her life had become a prison, one she had no means of escape from. When Adam started to show his true colours and would beat her at least once a week, a beating that was carried out for absolutely no reason other than to break her spirit, Alina knew that she had to get out. Luck was on her side when she saw an advert in the Local newspaper for advice on women's shelter, now she just had to figure out a way of contacting them.

After finally locating her passport that Adam had hidden, she began to put a plan into action. She had no money and it would mean putting all of her trust in these people but what choice did she have? With the shopping budget accounted for down to the last penny, she reasoned that if they could help her, then she wouldn't have to return and face his wrath for spending a few pence on a phone call. The following Friday she stepped out of the front door for what she hoped was the last time and after entering the main foyer of the supermarket, headed straight for the payphone. Placing two twenty pence pieces into the slot she nervously tapped in

the number and almost instantly she heard the soft gentle tone of a woman's voice.
"Hello my dear, I take it that you are in trouble?"
"Yes and I need help, please, please help me!!!"
Out of nowhere Alina started to cry but stopped when the woman softly began to speak.
"I know you probably have limited funds, so I want you to give me the number you're calling from, hang up and I will ring you straight back."
Alina did as she was told and at the same time nervously glanced all around the supermarkets entrance trying to see if anyone was watching the strange woman who was crying as she used the payphone. Seconds later the phone rang and Alina snatched up the receiver and listened intently. Less than thirty minutes later a taxi had been dispatched and Alina found herself being driven to a secret destination. Later she learned that she was now in Hounslow at the St Mary's charity Refuge for women of domestic abuse. The place was filled to capacity with other women and their children but as busy as the rooms and hallways were there was also a feeling of peace and safety. Alina Balan spent time with the in-house therapist and just six weeks later had been settled into council accommodation on Sussex Gardens in Paddington. Part time work in a café was found by the refuge, with the remainder of her rent and bills being temporarily met by the charity. The job didn't last more than a

few weeks, Alina hated the work, the customers and even her employer. Something had changed in her, the kind innocent young woman that had arrived on English soil less than a year earlier was now gone and in her place was a woman with attitude, a woman that had suffered abuse both physical and mental. Now Alina was out for her and her alone and wanted to earn as much money as she possibly could so that she could send plenty home to her family and also save enough to provide a good life back in Romania for herself one day. This country, this supposedly land of milk and honey had given her nothing and now she was going to take what she felt she deserved.

The discreet advertisement in the Evening Standard for lap dancers somehow appealed, she was pretty, had a good figure and swivelling around a pole really couldn't be that difficult, could it? On her initial meeting with Maggie McKay, Alina was instantly offered a position and she was good, so good that in little more than a year her tips alone allowed her to move into a far nicer, not to mention larger, flat. Her slim dark Romanian body was something different at that time and the Soho punters lapped it up. That said, it was still hard work, especially at the weekends when the venues were at their busiest and more girls were on duty, especially those that had weekday employment and only wanted to earn a bit of extra cash so would offer discount rated dances. Alina met all kinds of women, some who were trying to get into glamour modelling and others who just needed to pay the rent. There was also a big problem with unwanted pregnancies, drink and drugs amongst a lot of the women but fortunately Alina was bright enough to steer clear when offered anything. Initially in the first few days she had naively believed it was just dancing but very few of the girls stuck to the three feet rule and after their dance would disappear into one of the private rooms with whoever had stuffed enough twenty pound notes into their crotch. The women always seemed to emerge with a smile on their faces, so at the first real opportunity Alina gave it a go. She never actually thought of it as prostitution, it was just a mutual respect between two consenting adults and ten minutes later she emerged one hundred and fifty pounds better off. It was hard work but Alina was good, so good in fact that even after paying the club a dance fee for every single dance, she couldn't work without doing so, then paying Maggie McKay a fee, the job was still very lucrative. So lucrative that money was soon being regularly sent home and her mother and brothers were no longer living hand to mouth.

The decline of the lap dancing clubs began slowly with the reclassification of the venues in 2009 and by 2012 Alina's earnings had dropped by over fifty percent while the closure of more and more clubs rose rapidly. Now hardly able to meet her rent, when the unexpected call came through from Maggie McKay, Alina had jumped for joy. When she first heard what the position entailed she was sceptical to say the least but running the sex parties turned out to be her saving grace financially. True the pay wasn't as good as the club work had been in the early days but it was regular and she only had to work on a weekend, so if on the off chance any dance work came up midweek, she would still be free to take it. Everything fell into place and within a month her bills were up to date and money was once again being sent back to Romania. Alina was again riding high but at the beginning of 2016 when the deaths at Boreham Manor occurred, her world once more fell apart and she quickly spiralled into debt.

Silently, Alina blamed Maggie though she knew better than to ever voice that opinion but it didn't stop her calling into the arches at least twice a week in search of work. Ken Voss was told to send her away with the excuse that Maggie was not there or was in a business meeting but occasionally she slipped through the net and would knock on her former employer's door without warning. Maggie became more and more annoyed with the foreigner and normally she would have been dealt with and possibly made to disappear but Maggie also knew that Alina was good at her job and could probably come in handy again one day. A few charitable bank notes would be passed across the desk to tide her over but it was never enough and the woman was now seen as a continual nuisance and a problem that would inevitably need dealing with in the not too distant future.

CHAPTER SIX

Maggie had kept a discreetly low profile over the next couple of months, dealing in only the usual business that the firm was known for and even though things were ticking along nicely, she missed the buzz of a new project and most of all she was missing the vast amounts of money that the private parties had generated. Poor Bobby was now receiving the wrath of her pent up frustration on a daily basis but still he didn't complain. He'd recently rented out the apartment that had been left to him in his father's Will and moved into the old family home. Maggie hadn't tried to stop him, some deep rooted loyalty to her father's memory had emotionally blocked her every time she'd considered selling the house. At least with Bobby staying there it wouldn't suffer from any damp or decay.

Out of the blue late one Friday afternoon Bobby took a call for her. The man didn't give his name, so placing him on hold Bobby innocently popped his head around the door to his sister's office.
"Got a bloke on the blower Mags, wants to speak to you but won't give me his name."
"Well put him through you moron!"
Maggie knew instantly who it was and smiled as she picked up the receiver.

"Long time no hear babe, how are you?"
"Good thanks darlin'. I'm missing our little venture and that's why I've called."
"Pray, tell me more, you've got me wet already."
Sam Wenner took a moment before he continued as he wasn't exactly sure how she would receive his offer. He then decided that talking over the phone wasn't safe as you never knew who was listening in, especially in the McKay's line of work. He asked her if she'd like to meet him later that night for a few drinks and maybe a bite to eat. Sam was handsome, you wouldn't say he was rugged or a pretty boy either, it was more about the way he carried himself. He wasn't cocky but he was confident and his piercing blue eyes seemed to follow your every move. Well at least that's how Maggie felt. He was the first man to get under her skin in God only knew how long, probably since her silly infatuation with that bastard Ciaran O'Connor. Sam was different though, he was kind and so sexy that he would never have had to resort to rape but still, Maggie wasn't naive and she knew he didn't look at her in that way and she would never embarrass herself by making a stupid play for him and then getting rejected. It would only ever be a friendship and she accepted that but it didn't stop her X-rated fantasies when alone in her bed.

La Bleuet Restaurant on South Molton Street in

Mayfair was welcoming and whilst Sam knew that Maggie preferred the finer things in life, more importantly it was a quiet, select venue. The restaurant was high-end and had been on the street close on twenty years. With an overly lavish interior of blue velvet seating and the finest crystal chandeliers, its food was well rated and the prices unsurprisingly matched the interior. Maggie and Sam had been there a few times before and although they weren't exactly regulars, Maggie's face was remembered by the maître d' and she was greeted warmly. Shown to a table at the rear which had been specifically requested by Mr Wenner, she opted for a tonic water so that her head was clear for business plus she didn't know how long she would have to wait, luckily it was only a couple of minutes before her companion for the evening arrived. Bending over Sam kissed her on the cheek but it was a purely friendly gesture. The hard-faced blonde really wasn't his type and besides, Maggie could turn on a person in an instant and he was always careful not to let his guard down when he was around her.

"Hello sweetheart, looking radiant as ever."

Maggie rolled her eyes and laughed, he really was a schmoozer and a liar to boot. Now more than just a few pounds overweight and with her short peroxide bob, she knew how she looked, knew how men viewed her but all the same, it was nice to receive a

compliment.
"So, what do you have for me?"
"Fuckin' hell Mags, you're keen! Can I at least get a bloody drink first?"
"You know me babe, always chomping at the bit when it comes to making a few quid."
"When you hear what I've got to say you'll realise that it's considerably more than just a few quid!"
After placing his order and then nervously glancing around to make sure no one had been seated close enough for them to listen in, he began.
"This is for your ears alone and that's only if you're interested. Personally I'm staying well away from it but we have an agreement to put all available deals on the table so that's what I'm about to do. What I'm going to tell you is nasty, really fuckin' nasty and you'll probably discard it straight away but like I said, I feel duty bound to…………"
"For fucks sake Sam! Just spit it out will you?!"
"Okay, remember the Judge?"
"I do indeed, the dirty old bastard. That cunt ruined more of my girls than anyone I know, scared the shit out of them, literally I kid you not but then he paid handsomely for the privilege."
Sam inhaled deeply before he continued.
"I have been approached on his behalf by a guy named Dennis Havers. He resembles a City type and is the kind of bloke who looks down on everyone but is still willing to make some fast coin

for doing that old tosser's sick bidding. Anyway, they want, along with a private club of a few other members, to err, make a snuff movie! Apparently it's been on the Judge's bucket list for quite some time and as he ain't gettin' any younger, he wants to make his fantasy into a reality as soon as possible." As he talked, Sammy studied her face for any sign of distaste but just as he'd expected, there was none. "Obviously they can't procure a victim themselves so via this Dennis geezer and then me, I've been asked to contact you?"
"Who gave them my name?"
"I suppose after the sex parties they just imagined it would be somethin' you'd be interested in but does it really matter?"
"How much?"
"Fifty grand."
"Male or female?"
"Female."
Maggie was silent as she mentally went through her list of contacts and tried to think of someone who could be used. It wouldn't be difficult to snatch some sad body off of the streets, there were plenty of homeless that after a good scrub could end up being presentable but it would be much easier if she used one of her girls, at least to begin with because she had an inkling that there was a good chance this wouldn't be a one off. Suddenly she had a lightbulb moment. Alina Balan had been a thorn in her side

since the parties had come to an end. The woman was constantly hassling her for handouts, not to mention the fact that she was privy to far too much information and there was always a risk of her going to the Old Bill, or at least threatening to and no one threatened Maggie McKay.

"I have someone in mind but I want seventy five grand. If they kick off tell them that's the deal and there will be no negotiations. After all, I'm the one taking all of the risks. Right, can we order now?"

She never ceased to amaze him and while in business together everything had been fine, he definitely wouldn't want to cross her. Maggie's old man had earned a reputation for being a hard bastard but it paled into insignificance when put up against that of his daughter.

"You do know that once you cross that line there's no going back?"

Maggie laughed, if it was as lucrative as he was saying why on earth would she ever want to go back?

Two days later at the arches, Maggie again received a call, which after previously learning his lesson, Bobby put through without querying the person's name.

"Hello you!"

"Morning sweetheart, it's on by the way. Those sick cunts didn't even try to argue the price down. The location details and date will be with you tomorrow

and the cash will be with you on the day of delivery. Seems like the sadistic bastards, are more than a tad eager to get the ball rolling!"
With that the line went dead and Maggie leaned back in her chair with a wide grin on her face. She felt no remorse for what she was about to do, Maggie McKay never felt sorry for anyone, least of all a former Tom and that was exactly what Alina was. Maggie remembered back to the girl's first visit to her office when Alina had said she was a dancer and nothing more and then security had informed Maggie that her newest recruit had willingly laid two punters within her first week of work but she was never challenged by her boss, so all in all she was a good choice to test the water and Maggie was now under no illusion, this new deal would definitely progress to many more in the future, of that she was certain.

The following day and just as she'd been told, Maggie received a time and venue. It would take place on Friday in a semi-derelict barn close to Waltham Abbey on the edge of Epping Forest. The cash would be dropped off at five that evening and the cargo was expected for delivery at eight on the dot. It all appeared to be simple enough so Maggie telephoned Alina and asked her to come by the office at seven on the ruse that there was a lucrative job in the offing. Then she called someone that she privately referred to as the cruellest and hardest bastard she had ever known.

Asti Marku was Albanian, thirty eight years old and had originally hailed from the foothills of a small town called Kruja. His family were farmers and after a long standing land feud with a neighbouring family, Asti's mother, father, two brothers and a sister were murdered. Asti had witnessed the shootings but luckily for him he had managed to escape and at the tender age of twenty had landed totally alone on British soil. So damaged by his loss and the horrific sight he was forced to witness, he no longer cared about anything, himself included. Life was cheap as far as he was concerned and he was happy to carry out any task asked of him, for a price of course. Asti arrived within an hour of Maggie's call and when he walked into the arches everyone else there moved out of his way. Ken led the visitor through to the office and then making a hasty retreat himself, shook his head in utter despair. Whatever the Hell was going down wouldn't be good, as Brice had only ever called on the services of the Albanian when there was some serious shit happening. As he entered Maggie looked up and even though nothing in her demeanour showed it, Asti Marku instantly put the shits up even her.
"Hello Asti, long time no see! I have a job for you

and it's a good earner."
He didn't speak, Asti never did, well not unless it was absolutely necessary and instead he would just nod his approval. Maggie didn't explain exactly what would be happening, there was no need to reveal any more than was absolutely necessary. All she did was tell him what his role would entail. Passing over a scrap of paper which had the address of venue, she then continued with what he would be expected to do.
"I need you to do a recce of the place and install a couple of hidden cameras and a recording device. I then want you to collect a woman here on Friday evening, take her to the location in question and hand her over. Understandably she will probably be reluctant but that isn't anything you can't handle. I will then need you to return either later that night or the following morning and that's when things will get a bit messy."
Asti casually shrugged his shoulders as if to say 'so what'?
"You have to dispose of her in such a way that identification will be near impossible."
Asti nodded his head and then strangely and totally out of character, asked how much he would be paid.
"Ten grand."
Again the man nodded and then turning around he left the building. Maggie let out a low sigh of relief, everything had been put into place and now she

could finally relax, at least for the time being. She could feel the adrenalin surging through her veins and she liked it, in fact she had actually really missed it over the last few months but now thankfully it was all systems go again.

On Friday, Alina was punctual. She had dressed up in a smart suit as she was trying to appear professional and business-like after hearing Maggie say that there could be lucrative work in the offing. Knocking on the roller door she was kept waiting for a couple of minutes as Maggie had sent everyone home and had to come through from the office herself to let the poor girl inside.
"Good evening Alina, nice to see you've made the effort. Please come through."
With the area now void of the usual leering men, Alina found the space a little eerie but it was also nice not to be ogled by the perverts Maggie employed.
"Now I'm really busy so unfortunately I won't have time to take you to view the prospective building. However, I have asked one of my men to escort you on my behalf. He's a decent bloke and won't try it on so you can relax. Have a good look at the place and report back to me if you feel it's suitable to restart up the parties?"
"Is that it?"
"Is what it?"

"You just want me to check out a property for you?"
"Well, with the view of running it for me. Why, is that a problem?"
"No, no of course not, I'm just a little surprised that's all. I'm sorry Ms McKay I'm rambling on I know but I'm just so happy to be working again that's all. Thank you so much."

By the time Asti arrived and the two set off from the arches, Alina was grinning from ear to ear. The assignment she'd been given made her feel important and even though this Asti guy didn't open his mouth for the entire journey, she felt safe in his company. She talked nonstop about her new role within the firm and Asti realised that he wouldn't have to take her inside, she was so excited that she would probably run in without giving him a second thought. Her feelings of safety instantly changed when they pulled up outside a dilapidated building that might just have been a house or a barn at some time. It was hard to tell as a large section of the roof was missing and the windows were boarded up. The location was remote to say the least and there were no other building's in sight, however she did feel a little more confidant when she spied three high end cars parked outside. The place was void of any outside lighting so Asti directed the car headlights towards a concrete path that ran along the right hand side of the building.

"Go inside! I have an errand to run so I will collect you in, let's say an hour."

As soon as she was out of the car Asti removed a long range remote control and pressed record to engage the hidden recording equipment that he had set up and checked earlier. Doing as she was told, Alina began to make her way around the back of the building but momentarily stopped when she heard his car pull away. Smoothing down her hair she chastised herself for being so silly, this was her chance to make a good impression, though she doubted very much that she would be recommending this place to Ms McKay. Pushing on the creaky rear door she hesitantly stepped inside and for a moment was stunned at what she saw. There was a dirty old double bed in the centre and it was covered in heavy duty polythene. What she guessed were film cameras had been placed on three sides and a large light on a tripod was situated at the back and already switched on. Hearing the door slam behind her she swiftly turned and came face to face with four naked men. The Judge she recognised from the previous parties but the other three were strangers.

"Good evening Sir."

Alina was somewhat confused when none of the men acknowledged her greeting but with Dennis Havers next sentence she suddenly became frightened.

"Looks like McKay has come up trumps your Honour!"

Judge Michael Lemmings was in his mid-sixties, badly balding and with a large paunch, there was absolutely nothing attractive about him at all. As he slowly stepped forward and smiled in the dim light, his teeth appeared to be illuminated in some strange way. Looking closer, Alina saw that he was wearing a kind of metal brace, like the steel teeth of the character Jaws in the Bond movie. Grabbing her hand he forcibly dragged Alina over to the bed and shoved her roughly down but he didn't speak a word. Instead Dennis Havers stepped forward as Alina struggled to prop her upper body up on her elbows.

"Stop! Stop, leave me alone!"

"I do not know your name my dear, nor do I wish to. I will now explain what is going to happen and you will obey the Judges' commands, if you want to remain relatively pain free. Do you understand me?"

Alina began to scream in terror but her captors only laughed in her face.

"Scream all you like my dear, no one will hear you. Now this will become very ugly if you do not comply. So, what's it to be?"

Suddenly the realisation hit her, Maggie McKay had set her up in the most spectacular way and she was now about to be raped. She could try and make a desperate run for it but in all honesty, she knew that would be pointless and besides, there was simply nowhere to run to as she was miles from anywhere. Slowly she nodded her head in submission and silently prayed that her ordeal would swiftly be over.

A few moments later and now donning a black leather gimp mask, a naked Judge Lemmings stepped forward. He was fully erect and as he smiled menacingly through the open zipped mouthpiece Alina once again saw the metal teeth guard. The sight of his wrinkled body made her feel like gagging. Tears streamed down her cheeks and unable to control her bodily function, as he stepped towards her she retched and then vomited onto the plastic.

"Open your legs my dear."

Obediently obeying the command in the vain hope that he would go easy on her was a wasted tactic as the rape was both rough and painful. She tried hard to remain as still as possible and at the same time she watched the others as they filmed the scene and just couldn't understand how they could be a party to this, not only a party but obviously enjoying it as a couple of them also had visible erections! When the Judge eventually grunted Alina knew that he had climaxed but as he got off of the bed, another took his place and each one seemed to escalate in force. All in all Alina was raped four

times but the worst was by the one who chose to invade her anally. The pain was excruciating and she actually felt her anus as it was ripped open. Just when she thought her ordeal was finally over the Judge made his way back to the bed and thinking that he was up for seconds, she was startled when he suddenly moved in the direction of her face. It was clear that they had lied to her regarding letting her go but thankfully Alina couldn't possibly have known what would happen next. The Judge thrust his left hand up inside of her and at the same time used his right to grab a handful of hair and forcibly yank Alina's head back. Wide eyed she stared up at him and seconds later he bit down and viciously ripped out her throat. Alina's life was snuffed out on film and as the Judge raised his head, his victim's blood ran down onto his chest.
"How was that?"
Hugo Burnside, a long term friend and the cameraman for this event raised his head and smiled.
"Oh bravo Sir, bravo! You looked magnificent."

When Asti arrived in the early hours to remove the body, the sight that greeted him confirmed the reason he was being paid so well. It was a bloodbath and he knew that whatever had gone on here would have been gruesome. Aside from the woman's body on the bed, all of the other equipment had been removed and Asti quickly climbed up onto the overhead rafters to make sure Maggie's hidden recording paraphernalia was intact. Everything was still where it had been placed and as instructed, he left the camera and only ejected the disc from a small well concealed recorder. With Maggie McKay's prized treasure safe and secure in the upper pocket of his jacket, he set about his disposal. This would all take time but hopefully by daybreak there would be nothing left in the place to reveal what had gone on just a few hours earlier. Carefully removing the victim's teeth just in case there were any recorded dental records, he placed them into his jacket pocket as a sick kind of trophy and then after slicing off the finger tips, began dismembering the corpse.

It was just starting to get light by the time Asti finished, so leaving the derelict building, he had a good look about outside. There was a small wooded area to the north of the barn and spying an abandoned well he lifted the heavy metal lid. Momentarily he stepped back as the stench of stagnant water invaded his nostrils. Deciding it would be a good place to get rid of the limbs he retrieved them and dropped them one at a time into the hole. It seemed like an age before he heard the first arm hit the water, so he was quietly confident that there was very little chance of them ever being found. Pleased with his work he packed the remainder of Alina into the van and set off for London. On Newham Way and close to Canning Town he spied a refuse lorry parked up at the side of JJ's greasy spoon. The bin men had obviously popped in for a bit of breakfast, so quickly pulling up behind he stopped and tossed the wrapped head into the back. It was now almost completely daylight and he was still stuck with the torso. Deciding to temporarily store it in his chest freezer for a while, he returned home to get some well-earned shut eye.

CHAPTER SEVEN

Three months later a second call came through from Sam Wenner. Bobby had bounded into Maggie's office to inform her that the same strange man was on the telephone again. Maggie frowned and sneered her distaste as she barked at him to put the call through. When Bobby sat back down at his desk, he wasn't his usual dejected self after receiving yet another undeserved dressing down from his bully of a sister. Ken noticed a change in the young man and if the truth be told, he'd actually begun to notice a subtle change in Bobby over the last couple of weeks. He was happy, happy beyond belief in fact but it was more than that, Bobby was almost childlike and was acting far younger, more immature than his twenty eight years. He was slow, everyone was aware of that but this was a different kind of behaviour.

"You're in a good mood sunshine, anything you feel like sharing with your old Uncle Kenny?"

Bobby's face turned bright red with embarrassment but at the same time he was bursting to share his news.

"Only if you don't tell her?"

He pointed over his shoulder in the direction of Maggie's office as he spoke.

"Why would I?"

Bobby slowly tilted his head sideways giving a

knowing look. Uncle Kenny looked out for him but he was also loyal to Maggie and Bobby didn't want her to spoil things like she usually did. Maggie had a way of pissing on the matches whenever she heard good news that didn't involve her or at least that's what his dad used to tell him. For a moment Bobby was lost in thought about Brice and how much he still missed his old dad.
"I won't, I promise."
"I've got a girlfriend."
Bobby giggled in that same childlike manner again and Ken smiled, the man, because at twenty eighth that's exactly what he was, was a little bit simple. Kenny hated to use the term and it was used loosely as the kid was able to look after himself and do work here at the arches but there was definitely something missing in his brain. Brice had always covered for the boy, made excuses for him and the one and only time Ken had raised the subject, Brice had become angry and had flatly refused to get Bobby checked out with a specialist. Suddenly Ken was worried, Bobby didn't go out or mingle and he had no friends to speak of save for the blokes here at the arches, so where exactly had he met a girl?
"Tell me more, what's her name?"
"Diane or Di but I call her my princess."
Again Bobby began to giggle.
"So where did you meet her Bob?"
"In the shop at the end of my road, she works there

part time on account of her little girl Lisa."
A kid?! This was going from bad to worse. Ken suddenly had a decision to make and quickly, tell Maggie and watch the shit hit the fan or wait and see if this so called relationship petered out. Not sure if he was making the right choice, he opted for the latter.
"Well I'm really pleased for you Bobby but take it slow mate and remember to always wear a condom."
Bobby's face instantly turned red again and he hung his head but still wore a slight grin.
"Uncle Kenny!"

That night Maggie met up again with Sam Wenner at the same restaurant in Mayfair. They were shown to the same quiet table as before but this time it hadn't been requested. Sam had tipped the maître d well on their last visit and now they were being looked after royally.
"Hi darlin', I take it they want second helpings?"
"You're correct Maggie, seems the dirty sick bastards have been desperate to contact you but that Dennis Havers geezer advised them to wait to see if there was any fallout from the last time."
"I knew it! I knew after the first one that this would become a regular fuckin' event. So when and where? The price has gone up by the way!"
"Hold your horses, I ain't told you everything yet.

Seems one of the members of their perverted little group is a surgeon. I never knew how much money was involved in organ trafficking but fuck me Mag's, its huge! This surgeon, some Harley Street Paki and we all know about those robbin' bastards, anyway, he has come up with a great idea, well as sick as it is I think it sounds great. After they have had their revolting bit of fun, they want to strip the body of organs and then transport them to a private hospital over on Beaumont Square."

"Seems simple enough to me."

"Not so fast darlin', this is a whole new ballgame. Your guy can't just wrap them up in plastic and that's it! They have to be treated with respect. The tissues, such as bone, skin, heart valves and corneas can last up to twenty for hours but it's not the same for the vital organs as they quickly become unusable for transplantation."

"Listen to Doctor Wenner!"

"Maggie, I'm being fuckin' serious here! Through Havers, the surgeon has given me all this info and what he would need doing, especially for what they are prepared to pay!"

"And just how much is that exactly?"

Sammy took in a deep breath, even he was still flabbergasted at the amounts that had been mentioned.

"Five hundred K for a heart, add another two hundred if the lungs are included. Two fifty for the

kidneys and then three hundred K for a liver. All that is without the eyes, skin etc. All in all, were talkin' well over a million and a half per body."
"So is that what they're offering?"
"Don't be daft, that's the street value. You'll be getting' five hundred K."
Maggie was silent for several seconds as she took in the enormity of what was on offer. Now she felt like kicking herself, all that money gone to waste with Alina's body. Well there was no point in crying over spilt milk, it was onwards and upwards and she was already mentally working out how much she could rake in over the remaining year.
"So what happens now?"
"We have to find a new venue and it has to be sterile. The Judge can have his fun but then Mr Dewala will need to step in as soon as the old man is finished."
"Who the hell is Mr Dewala?"
"The surgeon you silly cow! Anyway, he will remove what's suitable and then it will be down to your man to do a thorough clear up and remove whatever's left. They really are keen to get going, so how quick can you set somethin' up?"
"I'm not sure, this needs thinking about. Anyway, all of this has given me a hell of an appetite so shall we order?"

Later that night when she was finally back in her

office, Maggie scoured the internet for disused hospitals and clinics. There were many but they were either totally derelict, earmarked for housing or where residential houses were so close that it would be far too risky. After half an hour she sat back in her chair and racked her brains as she desperately tried to think of somewhere. There was nothing for it, she would have to use the adjoining archway and it felt as if she was shitting on her own manor, something you just didn't do in their line of work. It wasn't ideal and she would have to lay out a considerable sum to make it sterile which went totally against the grain but the wealth of cash coming her way would make it worthwhile, she was sure of that.

Putting all of the aggravation to one side, the Judge's sick little side-line would always be carried out at night, so providing she made sure that her men had all left the building and she called in the spare keys that were held by Ken Voss, no one would have access without her knowing. Being mean with money, something that she'd inherited from her parents Scottish genes and a well-trodden cliché, she decided that it would be too costly to convert the entire archway but surely she could have some kind of a structure built within it, it would also give a large amount of soundproofing and extra security from the prying eyes of her blokes. Telephoning Eryk Kowalska, a Polish builder from over Haringey way, she arranged for him to visit the arches the following night at nine.

Eryk Kowalska had arrived in London some five years earlier from Poland. A builder by trade, he took tremendous pride in whatever work he carried out. His aim was to earn enough money to be able to return home and build his dream home and a small bar on the beach at Kolobrzegon. Eryk had completed building works and the like for many London firms since he first set foot on English soil but this would be a first for Maggie McKay. Eryk had been warned that the woman was as hard as nails and never to cross her and he in turn, had come highly recommended to Maggie. His work was spot on and the team of men he employed, all Polish, knew to keep their mouths shut. As he approached the arches and waited to be let inside, he felt no unease, no trepidation at all regarding what would greet him, in fact, Eryk felt no emotion of any kind. These people were hardened criminals but he knew that as long as he did what was asked of him, he would be paid well and remain relatively safe. As she opened up, Maggie smiled in his direction but he wasn't stupid, these people always gave the impression that they were friendly but would turn on a person in a nanosecond if you said anything they didn't like, therefore, it was always

best to keep the conversation to a minimum.
"Good evening Mr Kowalska."
"Ms McKay."
Maggie led him through to the adjoining unit and began to explain exactly what she wanted but not why.
"The structure needs to be approximately twenty feet by twenty feet. Do you understand feet and inches?"
Eryk just stared at the woman in silence, unable to believe her rudeness. She was talking to him like he was an idiot but it didn't matter, he would load the bill to cover her impoliteness.
"Let's just say six metres so there's no confusion and it needs to have a smaller area added at the rear and accessed through an adjoin door, say three by three. That's metres by the way. The walls have to be totally sterile and in the far room I need a large sink installed."
When she said the word sterile, Maggie studied his face for some kind of response but there was none so she handed over a rough sketch she'd drawn on a spiral pad.
"So, how long and how much will it be?"
Eryk began to write down his own notes on an A4 pad and after a couple of minutes turned to face her.
"If I make sterile with tiles, then fifteen thousand. High gloss walls would be twelve. Time? Two weeks but if we are only working in the evenings

then three."

Maggie mulled over the estimate, she had been warned not to try and barter on the price as the man was fair and might take offense but she really didn't want to have to wait so long.

"I'll go for the second option as I think this will only be a temporary solution to my problem. There's absolutely no way your men can be here in the daytime but isn't there any way you could get the work done sooner?"

Again she studied him but Eryk's face was a blank canvas so she continued.

"When can you start?"

"Tomorrow, around six. We can work for five hours each night only, my men are working in daytime as well and will need to rest. Time maybe shorter if we come in on weekend but will only be on Saturdays as to make noise on Sunday will draw attention to place."

Hands were shaken and the deal was struck and after showing her newly acquired contractor out of the building, Maggie returned to her office to call Sammy with a date.

Ken Voss was less than pleased when his keys were taken away from him and it almost felt as if he'd been demoted. When the lock was changed on the internal door that separated the two spaces and no one was allowed access, it caused tongues within

the firm to start wagging. Not knowing, is always far worse than knowing and the Chinese whispers began to circulate among the men almost immediately, so much so that in the end Ken realised he had to confront his boss. Tapping on the door, he waited to hear the word 'enter'.
"What can I do for you Kenny?"
"I know you'll probably fly off the handle but all the same the question needs to be asked. The men are all speculating because they've been kept in the dark and we both know that's never a good thing. So, what exactly is going on next door?"
Maggie had been expecting this and as such had already concocted her story.
"You know when we were supplying the lap dancers?"
The question was rhetorical and Ken knew not to answer.
"I also had a little side line in sex parties."
"You mean orgies?!"
"Call it what you like but all the same it was lucrative, very lucrative. I have decided to resurrect them but in a much smaller way and next door seemed to fit the brief. I don't want the men involved in anyway, they are to carry on as normal and if any of them open their fuckin' traps outside of this building, I will know where it's come from. Do I make myself clear?"
"Your old man would have hated this Maggie."

"Maybe but he ain't here is he and I have to make fuckin' money or we go under."
Ken slowly nodded his head, it wasn't ideal but at least he had some answers and could now put the whispers to bed once and for all. Retreating to the front area he gathered the six men who were on duty that day and explained what he'd been told. He also repeated Maggie's threat regarding loose lips outside of the firm. There were a few disgruntled murmurs after he'd explained what was happening but in no time at all it was back to business as usual. True to his word, Eryk Kowalska finished on time and the second event in Maggie's new business was scheduled to happen two days later on Friday night. Asti Marku was given instructions to retrieve and refit the cameras from the barn and add another in the room where the organs would be extracted. He was then told to find a girl but she had to be clean and not a Tom. He could source from wherever he liked but Maggie advised him it would probably be best to go out of the city. She then handed him a syringe and after explaining that it was a strong sedative, he went on his way without even asking a question.

Doing as advised, Asti set out on Thursday afternoon and an hour and a half later arrived in Cambridge. His reasoning was the fact that the city was full of innocent students so grabbing someone would be far easier here. Parking up he settled down in his seat to get a bit of shut eye as he had to wait until it was chucking out time from the many bars and pubs.

Khristina Chernyshevsky, the daughter of a successful Russian businessman, was coming to the end of her first year of studying the classics at Corpus Christi. She didn't normally socialise on a weeknight but it was her course tutor's birthday so five students along with their tutor had all met up for a few drinks and a bite to eat. By eleven thirty the group were well and truly oiled and enjoying a raucous night but not Khristina, all she wanted was to return to her home, study for a short while and then crawl into bed. Her father had rented a private flat above the medical practice on Trumpington Street and being only a stone's throw away from the University it was ideal. Leaving The Pint Shop, it was a short walk home so Khristina was happy to go alone even though she'd been told on numerous occasions by her father never to be unescorted at night. Unusually the street was quiet and Asti had watched the party enter the venue. He parked in the correct direction, a few hundred yards away and waited for a woman, any woman, to leave. Poor Khristina didn't know what hit her and within seconds had been bundled into the back of a van and was now feeling so very drowsy. As she lived alone, it would be a further five days before she was reported missing and by then far too late.

It was the early hours of Friday morning when the van pulled up outside the arches. Dragging his prey inside, Asti had already secured her ankles, wrists and then gagged her. Maggie had given her men the day off so there would be no interruptions and by seven that night, everything was in place. The Judge had the most stomach churning, depraved fun to date only this time he chose a razor sharp Bowie knife. When everyone in attendance had satisfied their desires it was finally time for the kill. Glancing in the cameraman's direction, the Judge began to saw through Khristina's neck. Her screams were bloodcurdling but when the jugular was severed and blood spurted out spraying the ceiling and walls, there was a deathly silence. Mr Dewala then took over and was overjoyed at the standard of organs he had been able to harvest. Less than twenty four hours after the abduction of Khristina Chernyshevsky, her body had been raped, butchered, her organs removed and what was left was now about to be disposed of.

Asti Marku returned to clean up the remaining evidence but first he ejected the recorded disk. Removing her teeth for safe keeping and cutting off her finger tips, he then used an electric saw to dismember the limbs of the victim and after wrapping them and her torso in polythene, he placed the mutilated body parts into the back of his van. With the aid of a high pressure hose he cleaned down the room and then drove the sixty five miles back towards Cambridge. Asti reasoned that should she ever surface, the manhunt would be carried out in the area where she'd resided. It would take away any heat from London and therefore the police would concentrate their efforts on looking for a local culprit. Weighting down the torso with bricks, Asti pushed the young girl's remains into Bourn Brook, a small waterway seven and a half miles out of the city. Now with a spade in hand and a large holdall slung over his shoulder, he continued on until he came across several scattered dykes that had become heavily silted. Testing the mass with his spade, Asti found the ground thick but still very wet. He quickly dug away as much of the murky sludge as he could before it resettled and then placed the limbs into their watery grave. With the back of the spade he pulled the black wet sediment over the top and watched closely for the few seconds that it took for the slurry to move over, leaving no evidence whatsoever that it had ever been disturbed. Happy that all was as it should be, he quickly set off for London to collect his well-earned pay.

CHAPTER EIGHT

Born into a relatively prosperous family, Dimitri Chernyshevsky's childhood was charmed. His father's entire career had been spent in the military and he'd reached the respectable rank of Colonel With that came a favourable salary and throughout his career Colonel Chernyshevsky had saved every Ruble he could. Two years before he retired he was able to purchase a large amount of shares in a paper and pulp factory on the outskirts of Moscow. It wasn't a prestigious business and nor did it, or would it ever earn him anything like the wealth of the future oligarchs but it was healthy nonetheless and growing month by month. Slowly over the ensuing years he increased his holding until he eventually owned the factory outright.

As an only child, Dimitri finished his education and at the age of twenty three and just as expected, joined the family business. A kind hearted young man, he had plans for the future, not only did he have aspirations of taking 'Dimi Paper' onto the Moscow Exchange and becoming one of the top one hundred companies but he also had dreams of a better world and to do that the company had to reduce the impact it had on the echo-system of the country. By 2020 he finally achieved his latter goal but long before that, his world would be ripped apart.

Within two years of father and son working side by side, the Colonel passed away suddenly and shortly after Dimitri married his childhood sweetheart Annika. Life was good and when he was given the news that he was to become a father Dimitri thought he finally had it all but that ideal was short lived after Annika tragically died from childbirth complications less than a year later. He could have easily given it all up and wallowed in his own grief but little Khristina needed a father and Dimitri swore to make it his life's work to raise and care for his only child.

The years quickly passed and Dimitri's daughter grew into the most beautiful young woman. He absolutely doted on her and they did everything and went everywhere, together. The day that Khristina announced she wanted to finish her education in England almost broke his heart but he couldn't stand in her way. Had she have lived, Annika would never have allowed him to stop her and besides, Dimitri knew that to try and prevent her from leaving Russia would be to deny the world of someone very special. Khristina was exceptionally bright and after securing a place at Cambridge University, Dimitri soon came around to accepting that from now on, for the majority of time at least, he would unfortunately be alone. His baby had flown the nest and he had to, as much as it pained him, allow her to spread her wings. On the day she departed he had taken her to the airport and before he left her in a flood of tears, Dimitri had laid down a few ground rules. She must never be out alone at night, she must phone him every other day just so that he knew she was fine and she was to return home to Russia on every holiday when the universities closed. Khristina would have agreed to anything just to be allowed to attend Cambridge but she also adored her father and nothing he ever had asked of her was difficult or unfair.

Almost a year later and everything had turned out fine. Both father and daughter were looking forward to spending the impending holidays together. In their thrice weekly telephone calls they would talk about all that they would do and the places they were going to visit. There were just over four weeks to go and Dimitri was so excited, he talked nonstop like an excitable child to anyone, his staff included, who would listen. Two days after her murder and when there had been no phone call he began to worry. By the time she had missed a second call he was going out of his mind and made a frantic telephone call to the university. He spoke to the Welfare Fellow whose job it was to take care of students with non-academic problems and also the university chaplain. Both said they would look into the matter but that they were extremely busy with the end of term approaching so it could take some time. He decided to give it three days and if by then no one had been in contact, he would fly to England himself.

With his case packed, Dimitri was just about to leave for the airport when the university chaplain rang. Snatching up the receiver as he didn't want to miss his flight, Dimitri was taken aback when he realised just who was on the other end. Brian Castle went on to explain that the onus of Khristina going missing had been fully passed over to him as the Welfare Fellow just didn't have the time. This angered Dimitri but he tried to stay calm as he listened intently to what was being said. The chaplain further explained that he had gone to Khristina's flat several times the previous day but there had been no reply. He had also contacted the few people that she mixed with but there really weren't very many as she only socialised occasionally but no one had seen her since a night out for her tutor's birthday almost a week earlier. He had then contacted the medical practice on the ground floor below the flat but the receptionist confirmed that there had been no sight or sound from the first floor apartment for several days.
"Mr Chernyshevsky, I am really quite concerned

regarding your daughters welfare. If you wish I can contact the local police on your behalf to report her missing or you could do it yourself?"

Dimitri thought for a moment. If he flew to England, Khristina might be on her way back and then he would miss her. If he had to go to Cambridge, it would probably be for the best if he waited a while longer.

"I was about to come over Mr Castle but it's probably more sensible if I postpone my trip for a few days, just in case she turns up here. Could you report this to the police on my behalf and pass over my telephone number? Maybe they will take you more seriously?"

Naturally Brian agreed to the request and after promising that he would do everything he could, the conversation came to an end. An hour later and Brian Castle made his way to Parkside police station to file a missing person's report. During his time at the university he had carried out the same task on a number of occasion and the students in question had always turned up a couple of days later, a week at the most but there was something different about this situation. He couldn't put his finger on what but he'd managed to find out that Khristina Chernyshevsky had almost no friends, she was a loner and because of that fact, Brian couldn't see any reason for her going off without telling anyone, especially her father. Instantly recognised by Linda

Watson, a woman while not in the force, was the first point of contact for the general public. He smiled but Linda could instantly tell that something was troubling the gentle man, a man who always had time for those in need.

"Good afternoon Chaplain, how can I help?

Brian explained about the missing girl and that he was growing more and more concerned by the hour. He further explained about Khristina's father and that as the family were based in Russia, he was taking over until such a time as it was deemed that Dimitri should come to England. Linda took the chaplain at his word and straightaway escalated the case up to the CID department. A small investigation began but due to her age and the fact that there was nothing suspicious to be found, Khristina's case was listed as just another missing person. Many of the students who would have been questioned had already left for the summer and resources were definitely not available for officers to travel to various parts of the country on the probability of a wild goose chase. However, one person the police were able to question was the tutor who happened to live locally.

Tasha Grenfell was in her late forties and taught a couple of the classics, namely art history, at Corpus Christi. Dressing in billowing blouses, long flowing skirts and Jesus sandals, she would have been called a throwback from the sixties if she'd been old enough to have been a hippy. Tasha informed the detectives that she liked Khristina immensely and had been somewhat concerned when the girl missed several lectures. That said, it wasn't uncommon so she had made the decision to wait until the beginning of term. If there was still no news on Khristina or she was still absent, only then had she planned to report her worries. Tasha then gave a list of the others who attended her birthday celebrations but had to admit she was too drunk herself to remember Khristina leaving. The list was filed but sadly no further action was to be taken at this time.

A few days later Brian Castle phoned Russia and relayed all that had happened and also that he had to regretfully inform Dimitri that his daughter whereabouts was unfortunately not high on the police's list of priorities. Brian calmly advised Dimitri to hold tight a little longer, as the end of term was just a week away and with any luck the silly girl would arrive home with her tail between her legs. He wasn't convincing Dimitri and deep down he wasn't even able to convince himself that what he was saying would turn out to be correct. Apologising further, he asked Dimitri to call him if his daughter surfaced, or if he had any further concerns. Ending the call, Brian still had the phone to his ear as he anxiously rubbed his chin with the back of his hand. This wasn't going to end well, he didn't know why but he had a gut feeling that all was not good.

On the previously agreed date for her return, Dimitri made his way to the airport to wait at the arrivals, just in case his beloved Khristina walked through the doors. Every time the electronic doors opened he strained to see if his heartbreak and worrying would stop but by the time the last passenger had emerged Dimitri stood with tears streaming down his face. Making his way over to the reservations desk, he booked a flight for later that day, returned home to collect his luggage and with a heavy heart, then made his way back to Sheremetyevo International Airport. The three and a half hour flight seemed to go on forever and he was already exhausted by the time the plane landed at Stansted. Deciding to stay at the flat just in case she returned home, Dimitri boarded a train to Cambridge and finally placed his key in the lock at a little after eleven that night. Desperately tired, he decided to call it a night and start afresh the following day.

Beginning at the downstairs medical centre, he nervously introduced himself and although friendly enough, the staff could tell him no more than they had told the chaplain. Dimitri didn't know any of Khristina's friends and besides, they would all have returned home for the holidays by now. After walking the streets and universities for several hours he finally realised that it was like searching for a needle in a haystack. There was nothing left but to go to the police and he wasn't about to be fobbed off, not even when Linda Watson politely informed him from behind the protective screen that all the details had been logged but as they had no reason to suspect foul play, then there was very little more they could do. Dimitri was adamant that he wanted to speak to a senior officer, so after reluctantly taking a seat and waiting patiently for over an hour, he was finally approached by Detective Steve Moore.

"Mr Chernyshevsky? Would you like to follow me?"

Steve led Dimitri through to one of the interview rooms that would allow more privacy.

"Please take a seat Sir. Now my colleague has explained the situation to you so I really don't know what more I can add. I understand that you are very concerned but in my experience they usually show up sooner or later. I have found that when it involves a missing young woman then there's usually a boy in tow somewhere along the line. That's probably not what you wanted to hear but we were both young once, so you know what I'm

referring to."
Dimitri leaned forward, placed his palms down flat on the table and stared into the officer's face. Steve Moore instantly saw the pools of tears in Dimitri's eyes and his heart went out to the man. The father of two young daughters himself, Steve knew only too well that if he was in the same situation he would be going out of his mind with worry. He decided to let Dimitri explain things, even though nothing would change, it might just help the man in some way.
"Please tell me about your daughter Mr Chernyshevsky, in your own time."
Dimitri started at the beginning and explained about the death of his wife, raising Khristina alone and how close the two of them were. He told about their planned holiday together, how studious his daughter was and the fact that she didn't really have many friends.
"Please detective I'm begging you! My daughter would not go off with anyone and I know in my heart that something bad has happened to her!"
Steve made some notes, he really hated to see this caring, desperate father in such distress and as much as it pained him to admit it, apart from having a few posters made asking for anyone to come forward, there was little more he could do.
"I suggest you return home Mr Chernyshevsky as this could all take time with no guarantee of

reaching a conclusion. I will, of course do all that I can and feel free to call me anytime for an update." Dimitri slowly nodded his head, he knew what the officer was telling him was the sensible thing to do but returning to Moscow would feel as if he was just turning his back on his daughter but he had no other option, there was a factory to run and to just sit in the flat waiting for news would serve no purpose at all. Boarding his flight he stared out of the window and suddenly shivered. He had a feeling of foreboding and wondered if he would ever return to the UK, other than to identify the body of his beautiful Khristina.

Meanwhile, Steve Moore placed the manila file containing the notes he'd taken in his meeting with Dimitri, into a mesh tray on his desk. By the end of the day the tray was once again overflowing and even though he thought about the file from time to time, whenever Dimitri called the station for an update, nothing more would be done regarding the missing girl for several months. By then it was far too late but in all honesty it had been far too late from the moment Asti Marku had set off from London.

CHAPTER NINE

Since his father's death, Robert Brice McKay, or plain old Bobby to all that knew him, was desperately lonely. He had sold his flat and moved back into the family home on Buxton Street but Maggie had moved out within days of her father dying. It had probably been for the best as he had long guessed that his sister hated him, actually he was sure of that fact, though he didn't have the first clue why. Caring for his sick father had taken up a lot of his time but now that it was over, he realised that he didn't have anyone and he longed to have someone who would love him or at the very least liked him. Uncle Kenny was kind but he got paid to be nice so that really didn't count. Meeting Diane, had as far as he knew, happened by chance but in reality, nothing could have been further from the truth.

At thirty three, Diane Buckle was a good five years older than her newest boyfriend. After getting pregnant three times in her teens and with all of the babies being adopted at birth, she had then ventured into the world of prostitution. Working the streets for the next ten or so years had taken its toll and Diane was now hardened and haggard looking. A slip up at the age of thirty had resulted in one final pregnancy but this time Diane chose to keep her child. Was it for love, or the fact that she was given a flat by the local authority due to her predicament? Only Diane knew the answer to that one. Luckily gaining part time employment in the little convenience shop owned by Madur Singh on the corner of Buxton Street turned out to be very lucrative. Diane kept small foil wraps of cannabis tucked away under the counter, which she discreetly sold without the shop keeper's knowledge. All of her food was supplied free of charge, once again without her boss's knowledge. Treating the place like her own she rarely sought permission to do anything and if the truth be told, Mr Singh was a little scared of his employee and wished he'd never taken her on. All in all life could have been far worse but Diane Buckle wanted more, far more.

Bobby McKay was a regular in the shop when he collected milk, bread and the daily paper which he then took to the arches for his sister. He always smiled in Diane's direction, so much so that she thought he was odd. Six months later while having a conversation with Mavis Tyne who worked alongside Diane on one of the two cash registers, she had mentioned the strange customer and said that he gave her the willies and that he was definitely a brick short of a load.
"You do know who he is Di?"

"Some bleedin' retard, who probably goes back home for a wank after he's been in here and dribbled at the sight of us, well me at least!"
Mavis laughed and then shook her head.
"You wouldn't want his sister to hear you say that, probably order a fuckin' hit on you."
Mavis had made the comment in a joking manner but deep down she knew that it could, to all intent and purpose, be a distinct possibility.
"For gawd's sake, what are you goin' on about?!"
"You heard of the McKay's?"
"What? Of course I have you silly cow, don't think there's many around these parts that haven't. Why?"
"Because, Maggie McKay is only his big sister, that's why! Pity the poor little sod is a bit slow 'cause he must be worth a packet. I heard when old man McKay popped his clogs he set the boy up for the rest of his life."
This was music to Diane's ears and from then on she set out to trap poor Bobby. It started with just a smile and a simple kind word and within a week she had asked him out for a burger. Bobby was so excited and spent hours preparing for his first ever date. After trawling the internet to find out exactly how he should behave, he then spent an age choosing what to wear, showering and getting ready. When he finally walked up to her outside McDonald's on Commercial Road he was smiling

from ear to ear. The sudden overpowering smell of Brut made Diane take a step back.
"You smell nice Bobby but you didn't need to use the whole can babe! Shall we go in?"
Rapidly moving his head like one of the nodding dogs people once had on the parcel shelves of their cars, he followed her inside. Remembering his research, Bobby tried to be a gentleman and pulled out her chair only it didn't go to plan. The chair got stuck and he had to yank so hard that it finally shot out and one of the legs hit Diana squarely on the shin. Yelling out in pain she momentarily wondered what the hell she was doing here but then thoughts of money, lots of money, calmed her down and she smiled at him sweetly. When their burgers arrived he started to chat, he asked her about her life, about her daughter and any hobbies she had. Within minutes his inane droning was grating on Diane's nerves but she just smiled and answered his questions, reasoning she could at least put up with the muppet for a few months until she was able to get some cash out of him. The date came to an end and after walking her home Bobby McKay returned to Buxton Road feeling like he'd won the lottery. His feet felt as if they were gliding on air as he mentally recalled every last detail of the evening. Several more dates followed and within two weeks Diane had reeled him in with a blow job and the promise of her undying love. It was now

time to step up the ante and when he called at her small flat one Sunday afternoon, he found his princess in tears.

"Di, Di whatever's the matter sweetheart?"

"Oh Bobby I don't know what to do! My mum, she lives up in Scotland by the way, well she died and I'm her only relative."

"I'm so sorry babe, I know how that feels."

"We weren't close Bob but they're askin' me to cough up for the funeral and I don't have that kind of money! Actually I ain't got two bleedin' pennies to rub together! Whatever am I goin' to do?"

"How much is it babe?"

"Five grand! I feel so bad that I can't even afford to bury my own mum."

Taking her into his arms, Bobby gently stroked her back as he tried to soothe her.

"Don't you worry your pretty head about anything, you will have the money by tomorrow. When is the funeral? How are we gettin' there?"

Now Diane began to panic, she hadn't thought this through properly. Obviously there was no funeral and she had to quickly think on her feet.

"I need you to stay here and look after Tasha, she's far too young to go to such a sad event and besides, I have no one else to take care of her. Will you do that for me Bob, please!!!!"

Whatever his princess wanted, he would grant her and nodding his head he tenderly kissed her on the cheek. Diane repaid him with sex, though Bobby didn't see it as that, he loved her or at least his immature idea of what love should be.

Turning up at work the next day, Bobby carried bags from several high end stores and it didn't go unnoticed by Kenny.

"What you got there Bob?"

"Just some stuff for my Di, her mum passed away and she needed a dress and shoes to wear at the funeral. Said she'd seen some stuff in Selfridges so I popped to Oxford Street as soon as they opened. Lucky for me 'cause I wouldn't have a clue what to get otherwise."

True, Diane was a regular in the store but only ever when she was on a shoplifting spree. Now she had Bobby that wasn't necessary anymore and besides, she couldn't risk getting caught and possibly being banged up.

"I bet that little lot set you back a pretty fuckin' penny?"

"I don't care Uncle Kenny, she's worth it and more besides!"

Over the course of the next ten months, Diane Buckle would manage to con Bobby McKay out of almost twenty thousand pounds.

Around a month after Bobby had fallen in love, Sam Wenner had received his third telephone call from Dennis Havers. He listened intently until Havers said this time they wanted a man as Mr Dewala required skin from a penis, as a rich patient had been badly burnt and grafts were necessary. The victim didn't want to be scarred any further than he'd already been so a donor was sought. The idea sickened Sam, so as tactfully as he could he brought the conversation to an abrupt halt. Meeting Maggie at their usual haunt in Mayfair, he relayed the message and she could see he wasn't happy about something.

"What's up Sammy?"

"Don't you think this is all getting a bit out of hand?"

"You're unbelievable, you didn't give a rat's arse about the women but as soon as a fuckin' bloke is wanted and they go on to mention cocks, well you want to run away like a fuckin' little girl!"

"That's got nothing to do with it Maggie but for Christ's sake, how far are these sick fuckers prepared to go? I mean, what's to stop them askin' for a kid next?"

"And?"

Sam stared at Maggie as if he was somehow seeing her for the first time. He'd always known she was a hard-nosed bitch, probably the hardest bitch in London but this was different. She had an icy coldness about her, as if she didn't care about anyone, something he'd never seen before. They were taking too many risks, too often and sooner or

later the shit would hit the fan and the Old Bill would come down on them like a ton of bricks.
He'd always liked her, and would probably even go as far as to say he was actually fond of her but there wasn't anything or anyone that he would risk his liberty for. Spending the rest of his life locked up at Her Majesty's Pleasure wasn't on his bucket list and he wanted out, as soon as possible.
"What say you deal with Havers directly from now on?"
Maggie shrugged her shoulders but as soon as she answered, he could tell she was well pissed off with him.
"Sure, whatever!"
Eating their meal in silence, Sammy quickly picked up the bill and they promptly called it a night.
Back at the arches, Maggie phoned Asti Marku and he arrived just over an hour later. Being invited into the office and even stranger being offered a seat, told Asti that something about the impending job was going to be different.
"We have another order but they want a male this time."
Maggie studied his face but there was no change in the usual blank expression.
"I realise that this could be more problematic, so I'm giving you a week to locate our cargo. Befriend him, maybe have a few drinks and get him to trust you. You know the score, so I don't really know

why I even said that but just be on your guard Asti, a young healthy male is goin' to put up much more of a fight than the girl did!"
Maggie removed a small brown bottle of chloroform from her desk drawer and pushed it towards him "I got you this a while ago but after I did some research, I found out that it wasn't as simple as it's shown to be on the big screen. Contrary to belief, it takes at least five minutes to knock a body out with this stuff but all the same, it might come in useful." Once again reopening her desk, she removed a manila envelope and placed it beside the bottle. "Now obviously there will be some extra costs, so there's a grand in there for expenses. You will also need a better mode of transport so there's a white Combi van parked outside, the keys are tucked under the sun visor. It's a ringer of the same make so unless you get pulled over by the Old Bill, there shouldn't be a problem if anyone tries to check up. Call and let me know when you're on your way back. I will try and meet you here but on the off chance that I can't make it, here's a set of keys but make sure you lock up after you've dumped the cargo off. Once everything is secure you can torch the motor and we'll be good to go."

Maggie then returned to her mews house on Rowland Way. She liked living in Chelsea, though in all honesty she spent little time there but still, the house was exquisite and it was her safe haven away from all the badness and crime that seemed to fill her every waking moment. Kicking off her shoes she opened a bottle of Moet & Chandon pink, anyone who knew her, knew that it always had to be pink and then climbing the stairs she flicked on the television. Propping herself up against the sumptuous headboard Maggie momentarily felt lonely but she instantly dismissed the emotion. She had the world at her fingertips, she was unstoppable, the money was pouring in so she had nothing to worry about and besides, men were a waste of time and energy, in her book they were good for only one thing and Maggie had yet to meet her match in the bedroom and it wasn't for the lack of trying. There had been plenty over the years who were, even if they didn't fancy her, happy to fuck a London underworld boss! Taking a sip from the glass, she placed it onto the bedside cabinet and was soon sound asleep and dreaming of the infinite amount of money that would be coming her way in the not too distant future.

Setting off first thing the next morning, Asti drove around a hundred miles and ended up in Lincolnshire, the market town of Boston to be exact. Not that it made any difference, but what Asti wasn't aware of, was the fact that just a month earlier Boston had been named the most murderous town in England. After parking up, he strolled around for a while to get the feel of the place. He'd chosen this area as he knew the Eastern European population was high and for some reason, crimes against these people never seemed to be investigated as fully as crimes committed against natives of this country. That said, he was hoping to be in and out without anyone knowing and long before anyone had been reported missing.

The Folly pub, situated on the market place was quiet for a lunchtime and taking a seat at the bar Asti struck up a conversation with the barman. He explained that he was looking for work and wondered if the man had heard of anything going. "There's plenty of land work if you don't mind breaking your back, personally I'd leave that to the Lithuanians and Poles. There's usually a day's work to be had out there on the market, if you don't mind heavy lifting and it's only on Wednesdays and Saturdays but they move about, so if you're any good I suppose you might get extra days."
With that a customer walked up to the bar and the barman moved along to serve him bringing the conversation to an end. Asti was pleased with his work so far and now it was time to secure some accommodation. Deciding that it was best to find somewhere a decent way from Boston, he drove thirty miles back in the direction of Peterborough.

The Dog in the Doublet was located six miles out of the city and offered basic accommodation, which suited Asti well. His room was situated at the rear of the pub with its own private entrance, so he could come and go without being seen and the booking was on a night to night basis only. After being given a key and knowing that he had a long day ahead, he turned in for the night.

By five the next morning Asti was standing on the market place as the stall holders began to set up for the day's trading. It only took a couple of inquiries before he was taken on by a bloke with a heavy southern accent who everyone strangely referred to as 'Smiffy' but whose name was in fact Jack Keeler. It was a fruit and veg stall so the boxes were heavy and as lunchtime approached, Asti could really feel that he'd already done a half a day's work. His muscles ached badly and there were still three or four hours left to go. On the upside he'd palled up with a bloke in his late twenties named Peteris Jonsons. After chatting and sharing a few jokes and with the added fact that Peteris had told him he was living alone at the moment, due to his girlfriend Sofija having returned to Latvia a day earlier to visit her family, Asti reasoned that this unfortunate man would be a perfect victim. After work the pair went into the Folly for a few drinks and happily chatted away like two old friends. Two hours later and

Peteris said his farewell and added that he hoped their paths would cross again someday.

Saturday morning duly came around and once again Asti gained a day's employment from Smiffy. When his new found friend spied him over a stack of banana boxes he smiled from ear to ear. The day passed quickly and finally when everything had been packed away, Peteris again invited Asti for a few drinks, only this time it was back at his flat. Stopping off at a Londis store close to Peteris' home and as Asti didn't want to risk being captured on the shop's CCTV, he handed over a twenty pound note and asked his friend to get him a bottle of vodka. Five minutes later and Peteris emerged with a carrier bag containing several bottles so it looked like he was planning a heavy night. He loved England, loved the people and the opportunities and knew that opting to move here two years earlier with his girlfriend Sofija, was the best decision he had ever made. Now it looked as if he had a new friend and drinking partner so all in all, as far as he was concerned life couldn't get any better.

As soon as they walked through the door the drinking began in earnest but Peteris wasn't privy to the fact that at every opportunity, Asti was sneakily tipping his measures down the side of the sofa. By ten o'clock Peteris couldn't string a

coherent sentence together let alone walk very far. Asti hauled his victim up, slung one of the man's arms around his own shoulder and then slowly dragged him outside. Slurring, Peteris tried really hard to speak.
"Where we gggoing?"
"To get more Vodka."
"Vodka!! Goooood, vodka is goooood!"
Outside, the cold night air seemed to slightly rouse Peteris but Asti had come prepared and as he opened the rear doors and placed his victim down onto a mattress he'd had the foresight to install before leaving London, he grabbed the bottle of chloroform and liberally doused a tea towel. Loosely holding it over Peteris' nose and mouth for a few minutes, he waited until there was no further resistance and as he closed the rear doors, Asti could hear his victim begin to snore. The effects could begin to wear off anything from thirty minutes to two hours but considering the amount of vodka that had been consumed, Asti reasoned it would probably be closer to the latter. With only a mesh guard separating the driving compartment from the rear, he knew he would be notified when the acute shivering and vomiting started, which would enable him to pull over and administer more of the chemical. With one last task to perform, the van was driven back to the Dog in a Doublet where he checked out and collected his belongings.

The return journey was noneventful and Asti called Maggie when he turned onto Newham Way, which allowing for traffic, would give her a good half an hour to get to the arches and prepare. Everything went like clockwork and by one thirty Peteris Jonsons had been installed in the newly erected room where he was tied and gagged. No words left Asti Marku's mouth and he only nodded in Maggie's direction as he left the building. It had been a long day and he still had to torch the van so he headed over to the basin at Limehouse. Pulling up where there was a break in the wall for boats and cargo to be hauled up, Asti didn't bother engaging the handbrake and instead emptied a can of petrol all over the mattress and the front cab. Trailing a rag from front to back, he lit the end and stood back. His action wasn't to destroy the vehicle, even he knew that a diesel was difficult to ignite. No, what Asti wanted was to destroy any possibility of forensic evidence and within a few seconds the interior was well and truly ablaze. He was taking a risk as there were several canal boats moored up but it was dark and until the van actually hit the water there wouldn't be any noise. Hopefully he would be long gone by the time that happened. Waiting until everything inside was a blackened mess, he then leaned heavily on the rear doors and pushed for all he was worth. Slowly the Combi began to roll forward and as the front wheels disappeared over the edge, Asti quickly walked off and headed into the shadows. All he had left to do was to dispose of the body when those sadists were finished doing whatever the hell they did and he already had a location in mind. Asti weirdly now had a bizarre ritual of going back to the place of abduction, so a trip to Boston was once again on the cards but he didn't really mind, sometimes it did a person's soul good to get out of the city and see a bit of the countryside.

It was a good eight hours later before Peteris began to wake. His head was pounding and he was desperate for a drink of water. His vision was blurry and he had to try hard to focus, when he did his surroundings were alien and feeling the bindings on his hands and ankles he naturally began to panic. Turning his head he saw a water bottle and straw just close enough to allow him to drink but he would realise a few hours later that the rehydration wasn't for his benefit but purely so that he was in a decent state for the Judge and his little gang of weirdos. With the water swiftly consumed, Peteris again fell asleep only to be woken by the sound of the door opening at seven that night. He had no concept of time and didn't have a clue how long he had been held or why but as the Judge entered, tape was instantly slapped over his mouth by Dennis Havers so that he wasn't able to ask questions.

"Suitable Your Honour?"

Michael Lemmings slowly walked around the bed and then stopping, stared directly into the eyes of a petrified Peteris.

"He'll do I suppose but then I'm not interested in his face, only his arse. Flip him over then you moron!"

With the assistance of the doctor, the two men turned Peteris over with ease. He was then dragged down the mattress until his knees hit the floor. Dennis proceeded to unbuckle his belt and pull Peteris' trousers down around his knees. By this time it wasn't rocket science to work out what was about to happen and the Latvian began to fight, fight harder than he'd ever done before but it was to no avail as Dennis and the doctor just grabbed a shoulder each and forced his upper half down onto the mattress.

This was the Judge's first time fucking a man and he was intrigued to know if he would gain as much pleasure as he did with women. Opening a large jar of Vaseline he liberally applied it to Peteris' anus, not to save his victim pain but merely to avoid any discomfort to his own penis. As he was forcibly entered, Peteris began to scream out in agony and even though the sound was horrendous, it was muffled and lowered in volume due to the tape. Almost reaching climax, the Judge withdrew and

allowed Havers to have a go, before removing a cheese wire from his pocket and with a little effort, it slid through the skin on Peteris' neck. Not happy with merely killing his victim, Michael Lemmings continued until the head, save for the wire getting entangled on the spinal cord, was almost completely decapitated. Glancing in the direction of Hugo Burnside, who was once again the designated cameraman, the Judge looked for approval.
"You never cease to amaze me Judge, a perfect execution! How was it for you?"
"Don't think I wouldn't bother again old man, no substitute for the tight arse of a woman."
The Judge nodded in the general direction of his sycophants before pulling on his coat and marching from the room. It was now time for Doctor Dewala to take over and harvest as many valuable parts as he could.

In the early hours of the next morning Asti Markku returned to the arches, let himself into the secure room and began the dismemberment of Peteris Jonson's body. Packing the torso separately from the limbs and head, he set off on his journey back towards Boston. Along the way he stopped at five different locations to dispose of the legs, arms and head. The first was a skip containing landfill rubbish, the second was a Polish lorry which was parked up for the night. Quietly he rammed both of

Peteris' arms up under the chassis, with any luck the vehicle would be on foreign soil long before the body parts were located. His third dumping ground was on farmland that had recently installed massive drainage pipes where he threw in the remaining leg. Driving further along, he stopped and lifted a manhole cover in the road and dropped the head down. It would be well decomposed if ever found and that was after the rats had feasted so once again he had no real concerns. When he reached his final destination, Asti weighted down the remains of the body and watched as they sunk into Boston's Grand Sluice Lock.

Meanwhile, Frank and Frieda Meadows arrived at the lock shortly after Asti had departed. The middle aged couple were full of excitement and enthusiasm. It was their first long journey since purchasing the narrow boat and the trip they had planned was by far, a no mean feat. Few narrow boats had attempted entering the open sea, let alone a novice couple who up until six months ago had never stepped foot on a boat of any kind. The 'Lady Patty' was to be driven into the Wash and eventually enter the River Nene where the couple would lazily motor through to Wisbech. Frieda had an old friend in the town named Bill and she really wanted to show off the Lady P to him. It turned out that the passage was a resounding success and the couple couldn't have been happier as they began to moor up at Wisbech Yacht Harbour. About to disembark, all hell suddenly broke lose when the occupant of the neighbouring vessel, Stuart Delany, spied something attached to the stern of the Lady P. It was only just visible but it was sizeable, so he quickly informed Frank and Frieda that they had snagged something. Frank used a long boat hook and after a little poking and prodding, the torso of Peteris' body suddenly floated to the surface. Still wrapped in clear plastic, it was frighteningly evident what was inside and as Frieda began to scream hysterically and while Frank tried to console her, Stuart called the police. It would be many months before it became evident that the stowaway had been with them ever since leaving Boston.

CHAPTER TEN
Two days earlier

As she stepped from the plane and even though Sofija Kalnins was already missing Peteris, she was also very excited. It was the first time she had returned home since moving to the UK a little over two years earlier. The majority of her luggage contained gifts for her grandmother, parents and two brothers. Sofija's family all lived together in a two bedroomed cramped apartment in Daugavpils. Her parents, Edgars and Lilija, having one bedroom, her brothers the other, with her grandmother sleeping on the old worn out, lumpy couch. Until a few months ago Sofija's father had worked at the prison but a vicious and unprovoked attack by an inmate had left him not only physically damaged but also psychologically, which had prematurely ended his career. Unlike many other countries in Europe, there was no care or provision for families such as the Kalnins, you didn't work, then you didn't eat, it was as simple as that and the family were now struggling just to exist. News of Sofija's impending visit had been welcomed in more ways than one and Edgars was desperately hoping that his daughter would return with cash, actually he was praying for it as he didn't know how much longer his family would be able to survive. It was fine having two strapping sons but neither of them were of working age yet and they still ate as much as adults. Knowing his wife often went hungry so that the rest of her family could eat and even though she would rather die than admit she went without, broke Edgars' heart and made him feel like a failure but there was nothing he could do to change things. The attack had naturally left him feeling scared to leave the apartment, let alone seek work and in any case, his leg which had been badly broken in the attack and had received minimal medical attention, was now set rigidly forcing him to walk with a very pronounced limp and rely heavily on the use of a stick.

It had been love at first sight for Sofija and her boyfriend Peteris Jonsons and pretty soon after becoming a couple they had swiftly begun to make plans. Eventually leaving Latvia together and due to the abundance of agricultural work, they like so many others, had settled in Boston in Lincolnshire. They both worked hard, in sometimes atrocious conditions but had still managed to make a comfortable home together, even taking second jobs in the evenings so that they could send a little money back to their struggling families. For the last three months Sofija had worked every weekend and had managed to put together almost seven hundred pounds. Not a fortune by any means but she knew the difference it would make and the happiness it would bring when she handed the cash over to her father.

The five hour coach journey from Riga to Daugavpils was exhausting but Sofija would be here for two weeks so there was plenty of time to catch up on sleep. By Latvian standards the bus was comfortable but she was too excited to nap as there was the possibility of more good news to share. Her pregnancy was yet to be confirmed, so she hadn't yet confided the hopefully impending news to Peteris but she'd had the forethought to purchase a test kit before leaving the UK. Deciding to try and wait for a couple of days, she couldn't stop imagining what it would be like to be a mother and her broad smile was evident to all for the entire journey.

There had been a lot of waiting around to make flight and coach connections, so after leaving her home in Boston almost sixteen hours earlier, Sofija finally reached the apartment a little before nine that night but there was absolutely no chance of sleep. Her family were too excited to see her and Sofija's mother had, even though they were living well below the poverty line, managed to produce a magnificent spread. It was common practise to rely on the generosity and charity of friends and neighbours when times were tough. The dark rye bread had been freshly baked and the table groaned with the weight of so much smoked fish, beetroot soup, fried mushrooms, potato pancakes and a joint of Speck so huge, that Sofija knew her mother must have called in at least a year's worth of favours to get it. When she discreetly handed her father an envelope and he looked inside to see the cash, the celebrations began in earnest. By one am she couldn't keep her eyes open any longer and making her excuses, entered the cramped bedroom. Instantly the smell of sweat and stale alcohol invaded her nostrils. Adolescent boys didn't care too much about unsavoury odours and she smiled at the thought that her mother was probably banned from ever entering the room let alone cleaning it. The two beds were unmade and she spied the corner of a porn magazine that had been concealed but not very well, underneath one of them. The curtains were thin and ancient and did nothing to reduce the frost that now covered the window panes on the inside. As she pulled on her pyjamas and socks Sofija decided that it would be best to sleep in her dressing gown. Thankfully, two days earlier as she was deciding what to take along for her trip she'd had a flashback to her formative years and had wisely chosen to pack her fleecy winter one, something she was now really grateful of. Climbing into the small single camp bed that had been set up in her honour, she shivered as she felt the cold that seemed to radiate from the grey concrete walls. Over the years her father had attempted to paint them but there was so much damp that the paint only ever seemed to last for a few days before beginning to peel. Luckily she was so exhausted that sleep came swiftly and she didn't even hear her noisy brothers when they eventually called it a night some two hours later.

Not surfacing until just after ten the next day, Sofija smiled at the familiar sound of her two brothers snoring softly. As quietly as she could, she slipped the test into the pocket of her dressing gown and made her way to the cold barren bathroom. There were no soft fluffy towels like she had back in her own home, just a bleak chipped bath tub and a stained toilet and sink. The sound of dripping water was constant from the faulty toilet cistern and the taps still dripped constantly, just as they had when she'd lived here. Newspapers were piled high in the corner but they were not there as reading material. Suddenly Sofija felt incredibly sad, people shouldn't have to live like this, least of all her own flesh and blood. It hadn't bothered her when she was still with her family, she hadn't known any different back then but now that she had experienced a better way of life, her parent's situation seemed far sadder and much more bleaker than she remembered. Unable to wait due to her excitement, she removed the pregnancy predictor from her pocket. Well this was it, this was when she would finally know for sure. Sofija peed onto it and then lowering the lid, sat back down to wait the required three minutes. Time seemed to pass slowly and it felt more like an hour before her wristwatch at last told her it was time to look. The two blue lines were strong and even though Sofija knew what that meant, she still forced herself to re-read the leaflet. Smiling from ear to ear she wanted to shout it from the rooftops but that wouldn't be fair to Peteris, so not until she had called her boyfriend would she share the news with her family. It was difficult, but Sofija knew she would only have to wait a short while as the time difference meant he would soon be on his lunchbreak. Quickly washing and cleaning her teeth she returned to the bedroom and got dressed behind a makeshift screen that consisted of a sheet hung over a washing line. Again taking a seat on the camp bed she scrolled down her list of contacts to find his number and with a nervous but happy heart she waited for him to answer. The phone just rang and rang which was strange, Peteris knew how she worried and would always answer her calls no matter what he was doing or how inconvenient it might be. This was so unlike him and hanging up, she redialled. Now the phone went straight to voicemail and Sofija had an uneasy feeling in her gut. She decided that if she hadn't been able to contact him by the end of the day then she would break the news to him in a text message as she was desperate to share the pregnancy with her family. In an attempt to feel better she convinced herself that perhaps he'd left his phone at home or lost it, it could be anything so she would try again later and do her best not to worry. After all, this was the best day of her life and she didn't want anything spoiling it. That evening she reluctantly sent a text and finally she could share the news with her family. Just as she'd expected there was crying and laughing all at the same time, especially from her father as he held her in an overly long bear hug, desperately trying to hide his unmanly tears of joy.

Over the next ten days the family enjoyed several outings, mostly for free of course. Lilija had taken immense pride in creating a schedule of trips in readiness for her daughter's return. There was St Boris and Gleb Cathedral, a picnic in Dubrovin Park and the one trip they'd had to pay for, a visit to Latgale Zoological Garden. As it was a budget admission, Edgars didn't mind dipping into the money his daughter had given him and he even lashed out on the purchase of a small toy monkey for the baby. Being out in the fresh air for the first time since the attack had been a big challenge for him but now surrounded by all those he loved, Edgars felt so much better and was glad that he had forced himself to finally leave the apartment.

For the entire two weeks spent in Daugavpils, Sofija still hadn't been able to contact Peteris. She had called several times each day and even sent texts asking him to please contact her urgently. Now only hours away from leaving, she couldn't wait for the time to pass. It was a very emotional farewell as her parents didn't know when or even if she would return, at least for the foreseeable future. Lilija clung to her daughter and as her husband pried her away, she gently bent over, tenderly stroked her daughter's stomach and through sobs muttered 'pieskati manu mazbērnu, pieskati manu mazbērnu'. Now it was Sofija's turn to cry and wrapping her arms around her mother again she whispered in Lilija's ear 'Of course I will take care of your grandchild māte'.

Sofija willed every hour of her flight to be over but the return journey was even worse as there was a three hour delay at Riga airport and the coach from Gatwick back to Boston was forty five minutes late. At last she finally placed her key into the lock but she found the flat empty and in darkness. Opening the fridge door, the stench of rotten milk and meat hit her nostrils so hard that she instantly slammed the door shut and began to gag. What on earth was going on? There was no note, no signs of any trouble so what on earth had happened? She just didn't have a clue but she was worried beyond belief. There was nothing she could do for now so climbing into bed she decided that after a good night's sleep she would go down to the market first thing in the morning and speak to Smiffy.

By seven the next day Sofija had made her way to the town square but as she approached the stall she didn't get the warm welcome she was expecting.
"Where the fuck is your old man? That cunt has let me down big style darlin' and I ain't a fuckin' happy bunny I can tell you!"
"Smiffy I have only just returned from my country and I haven't been able to contact Peteris for over two weeks now. The flat is empty and I just don't know what to do."
Sofija began to cry and even a hardened trader like Jack Keller wasn't able to stop his heart going out to the sweet young woman. Pulling Sofija towards him he embraced her tenderly.
"Come here you soppy mare and stop with the tears. He's probably off pissed somewhere. I know how you lot like your juice and I expect Peteris is on the mother of all benders."
Sofija slowly shook her head.
"He wouldn't do that Smiffy, there's something very wrong I just know it."
"I think you're overreacting sweetheart but just to

put your mind at rest, why don't you call in at the cop shop? Tell them what's occurred and see what they say."

Sofija slowly nodded her head and as she walked away Smiffy called out to her.

"When that useless fuckin' sack of shit does finally show his face, tell him to get his arse down here pronto, or he won't have a fuckin' job to come back to!"

Smiling through tear stained eyes, Sofija reluctantly made her way to the police station and revealed her story to Jim Granger, the desk sergeant, who was thankfully relieving Myra Thompson. Myra was a civilian and hated Eastern Europeans with a vengeance on account of them allegedly taking all of the local jobs. Her own son had been out of work since leaving school and even though Damien was a complete and utter lazy waster, Myra just couldn't see it, so she had to find someone else to blame. Sergeant Granger took all of the details, asked if an up to date photograph could be provided and then went on to inform Sofija that she would have to wait the compulsory twenty four hours. She argued that she hadn't been able to contact Peteris for over fourteen days but as she couldn't pinpoint the exact date or time that Peteris went missing, Jim Granger explained that they would have to take it from now. He also informed her that there wasn't a lot that could be done as there was no sign of foul play and

137

Peteris was an adult, so free to do as he liked and if that meant disappearing for a few days, weeks or even permanently, then he was entitled to do so. He further mentioned that as the couple were not married, she had very few rights and would have to just sit and wait it out. Sofija Kalnins did just that, in fact she waited for many months before the devastating news would finally arrive for her and their baby son, the news that Peteris would never come home again.

CHAPTER ELEVEN

Ken Voss wearily stepped from the cab and made his way inside of 55 Old Compton Street. He routinely and with as much enthusiasm as a child has when handed a copy of War and Peace, half-heartedly walked around the shop's two floors, checked in with the manager and then left again. The main area wasn't too bad but he hated going down to the large basement where the hard-core magazines and DVD's were displayed. There was a strong smell of, well he could only describe it as sex. Close circuit cameras covered the area but he didn't suppose the young lad working the counter would risk interrupting if two gays were getting stuck into each other or if a Tom hadn't been able to find a room so was entertaining a customer in one of the corners. It went on frequently but the shop assistant wasn't paid enough to risk the wrath of a Tom, even Ken himself would have been reluctant to try and come between a brass and her hard earned cash. Lately he had begun to feel like a spare part as far as the firm was concerned, checking these premises was a total waste of his time but he knew better than try to argue with Maggie.

The shop had been one of Brice McKay's first purchases when he'd started to make some real money three years after arriving in the capital. He hadn't been underhand and had gained permission from Harry Pimms before signing on the dotted line. Brice swore his allegiance to his boss and promised that this was just a side line and that he would always remain as Harry's right hand man. Staff were installed and the place ran like clockwork as they were all in too much fear to skim off of the top. Two more shops followed in quick succession and all three buildings housed a vast selection of the most up to date porn magazines and sex aids of the time. It was only a few years after the infamous corruption findings of the Obscene Publications Squad which had resulted in lengthy prison sentences for several of the Mets detectives but contrary to the general public's belief, it hadn't stopped bent coppers from continuing to take brown envelopes once a month to top up their pay. Back then it was still a time of high corruption and the red light district continued to be referred to as 'the jungle'. Unsavoury characters, especially on weekends, would invade the small area of Soho in search of some sexual relief and that search came in many forms from street Tom's, to rent boys and down to the most obscene reading material you could imagine. After the scandal, the new bodies in the Met had made themselves impervious to being caught and the heads of the crime firms were even more protective of their allies than ever before. Brice had cultivated his own detective and Joe

Monroe, for a healthy bung each month, would inform Brice of any impending raids. The setup worked well and over the years the McKay businesses received only a handful of raids to make it look fair but all were well notified of in advance. Joe Monroe had retired just a few months before Brice's death but before he left the force had passed over his secondary source of earning to Derek Stevens, a detective at the same station and even more bent than Joe, if that was possible.

Demand for porn had been at an all-time high and Brice had done very well but by the time Maggie took over five years into the millennium, Soho was a mere shadow of its former self. No longer were the depraved its main source of footfall, now it was predominantly tourists who more often than not, would only enter an establishment in the attempt at gaining a glimpse of the past, or young men on an away-day stag do who would finger the merchandise, laugh and banter with each other before leaving without purchasing a thing. Ken had advised Maggie on numerous occasions to offload the buildings, property in the area was commanding huge sums and she would have made a fortune but something stopped her, maybe it was some kind of misguided loyalty and respect to her late father but whatever the reason, she wouldn't budge on the matter and now some months they were running at a loss.

Tucked away on the Shaftesbury Avenue side of Rupert Street was the old Starlight basement porn Cinema. It had shown films of a dubious nature for years but because of its semi hidden location had been relatively left alone. It ran movies twice a day, a matinee at two and a slightly more hard-core evening showing at nine. Since Ken had taken over he had made sure that nothing on the screen could ever bring the law down onto the firm but that said, it still brought in a regular following, especially when gay films were being played. The older dirty mac brigade could always be found on the front row, wanking over some young toned males as they rutted each other senseless on the screen and the back rows were unofficially reserved for the rent boys, who were happy to pay the price of a ticket in order to satisfy their clients without interruption. The paint on the crimson walls and ceiling was peeling badly, the fabric on the chairs was ripped and stained with God only knew what and all in all, the place wanted demolishing but it wasn't his call. To be honest and he wouldn't admit it but the whole ethos of the venue turned Ken's stomach and the smell of sex always seemed to invade his nostrils, which he found totally abhorrent.

After the success with Alina, Khristina and Peteris and now with the Judge requesting another victim,

Maggie had suddenly come up with a fantastic business idea, well it was to her and whatever she wanted it somehow always happened. The secret recordings collected by Asti would be aired at the Starlight. Each edition would be shown only once and to a select, heavily vetted clientele who would each pay ten grand for the privilege. Picking up her mobile and while still full of enthusiasm, Maggie took a moment to recall Sam's number. Her contact list was blank, it didn't bode well, should you ever get your collar felt by the Old Bill to hand them a phone containing a list of villain's telephone numbers. Sam was sitting at the bar of the Morgan Arms over in Bow when his mobile played the familiar tune that related to her number.
"Hello darlin' how's it goin'?"
"I need to see you as soon as possible."
"Usual place and time?"
Maggie didn't reply and when the line went dead, Sam Wenner knew he had a dinner date later that evening. Arriving at La Bleuet Restaurant in Mayfair at just before eight, he was surprised to see her already seated at their table.
"You're fuckin' keen ain't you?"
Maggie laughed, he was funny, very attractive and should she have been in the market for a lover and more importantly had he been interested in her, then Sam would have been ideal. Sometimes it saddened Maggie that she was alone but she never

allowed the thought to get her down for too long.
"You know how I get when I've had a new idea, especially when it involves cash."
Taking his seat, they ordered drinks and then got down to business. Maggie revealed her plan and Sam listened without interruption.
"This will be like taking candy from a baby, so, what do you think?"
"In principle it sounds good but I have a couple of questions."
"Now there's a surprise!"
Maggie laughed as she spoke but Sam always had a couple of questions and it felt to her as if he was continually trying to piss on the matches, which in turn always got her back up.
"You say select clientele, that they will be vetted? How are you going to do that?"
"Don't fuck about Sammy, I know you can find as many rich fuckin' perverts as you want who are in the market for this type of shit! I will require a photocopy of their passports along with an envelope of cash."
Sammy chuckled as he took a sip of his drink but as he placed his glass back onto the table, his face was suddenly serious.
"Do you really think anyone would be willing to expose themselves to that degree?"
"Of course I do. Listen, those sick bastards will do anything for a chance like this and it will show they

are committed. It safeguards my back should everything go tits up and you know as well as I do that they won't be able to resist being part of some sordid fuckin' secret society! They have so much money that they can only get their kicks from doing something outside of the law and that's exactly what I will be giving them the chance to do."

"You need to make sure no one in the films can be recognised."

"Yeah I know and I had already thought of that. Micky Burton over in Soho worked in the porn industry for years as a finisher. He's changed images right from the old frame by frame reels through to the modern disc system so it's not a problem. He knows how to blur or remove people and we've already agreed a price. Well, it's up to you but the rewards could be vast and I'm offering you fifteen percent?"

"Twenty!"

Bingo, she had him on board and had always been willing to offer twenty but as her dear old dad had taught her, in negotiations you could always go up but you could never go down once negotiations had started.

"Right, I need a couple of weeks to smarten the place up and get a few bodies on board and as soon as we have a full house we're set. Keep me up to date on who you've managed to get signed up babe so I can keep a track of numbers."

"Will do, now can we order? I'm fuckin' starvin'."

Derek Stevens worked in vice and had been a model detective until the death of his young wife by a drunk driver several years earlier. The culprit had been caught red handed but a technicality had seen the killer get off scot free and Derek's attitude towards the force and the law had instantly changed overnight. Now he didn't care about his career and would take a drink from almost anyone willing to engage his services. Maggie had been introduced to the detective by her father. Brice normally kept his contacts close to his chest but knowing he wouldn't be about much longer, forced him to reveal every shady body in the business, anything to ease her path after he wasn't around to help out. Maggie made the call when she was back at the arches and an hour later Derek Stevens strolled in as if he owned the place.
"Ms McKay, what can I do for you?"
"Evening Detective, please take a seat."
"Don't mind if I do, any scotch on the go?"
Maggie hated the man, he always tried to lord it over her, treat her like a little woman and she would gladly have put a 9mm in his brain had she not have needed him so badly and the bastard was well aware of that fact. Retrieving a bottle and two crystal glasses from the double depth draw in her desk, she poured them both a glass and continued

to explain her plan, apart from stating the obvious that was. Derek wasn't really interested in what was being shown in that shithole of a cinema anyway. He had a good idea but as long as his pocket was substantially lined he didn't give a rat's arse about the content of the films.
"Can't see any problems with your request Maggie, just let me know when you're about to start up." With that Detective Stevens swigged the last of his drink, stood up and walked out of the office.

The services of Eryk Kowalska were once again requested and a week later, with no questions asked, the old fleapit had been totally transformed. Freshly painted and with the carpets cleaned, there were no longer any distasteful odours. An upholsterer had also been brought in to repair what seats he could and recover those that he couldn't and when Maggie called in to check on the progress, she was pleasantly surprised. Eryk had built a small bar area to one side and Maggie planned to sell alcohol at exorbitantly inflated prices, she had never missed a trick to make money and she definitely wasn't about to start now. Finally a week later it was all systems go and as the finer details and arrangements regarding clientele had been left to Sam Wenner, she just had to sit back and wait to coin in it. Initially it had really gone against the grain for Sam and it had taken him several days of battling with his conscience before he was ready to proceed. There was simply too much cash involved to just walk away and as he wouldn't actually be involved in the making of the movies or knowing the victims in the flesh he was able to justify to himself that staying on board really wasn't so bad. Maggie was earning well, so she shouldn't be averse to giving a healthy handshake to him for arranging a few viewings.

On the opening night, Maggie had sensibly installed a couple of her trusted doormen but as soon as all the guests had arrived, the men were sent home and the entrance doors were locked from the inside. The only staff on duty was a barman, who was an ex-convicted paedophile and old Bertie Lancaster who was there to work the machinery. Now in his seventies, Bertie had spent his entire adult life in Soho and had experimented with every sexual practice known to man. There wasn't anything that was out of bounds to Bertie and his mantra had always been 'as long as you don't scare the horses then anything goes'. The first screening hadn't gone as smoothly as Maggie had hoped. Oh there wasn't any complaints about what was offered but the occupancy of the Starlight was only at just over seventy five percent. It was still very lucrative but she was greedy and wanted the place full to bursting. Maggie needn't have worried as word amongst the closed hard-core society of sexual deviants quickly spread and when two months later a new title was announced, the event sold out within twenty four hours. There was a minor setback when the Judge got wind and Maggie received a rather irate phone call from Dennis Havers. Maggie asked for a meeting which luckily was held that same day. She explained to Michael Lemmings that his identity would never be known to anyone other than those in his own circle so he had nothing to fear and after pondering the idea for all of a few seconds he nodded his agreement. On the second screening the Judge was actually in attendance and he took great pleasure in knowing he was up on the big screen and not a single viewer knew it was him.

The initial closure of the Starlight hadn't gone down well with the dirty mac brigade and the rent boy community but in all honesty the place was never full and wasn't even covering its costs, so when approached, Ken Voss wasn't able to assure them that it would ever reopen to the public. Relaying the problem to his boss he had suggested opening the place as usual and only closing when she was having one of her special evenings, though he wasn't sure exactly what those evenings entailed but she wouldn't hear of it. The refit had cost an arm and a leg and there was no way on earth she would allow those filthy bastards to soil it. When he quizzed Maggie further regarding what was actually happening with the place he drew a blank but he was still convinced there was something very shady, something far and beyond their usual villainous practices going on. Whatever it was, for once Ken was happy to be kept in the dark. His weekly visits to Soho still continued and he checked out the shops but the Starlight was taken away from him and for once he couldn't have been more pleased.

CHAPTER TWELVE
March 2018

Just as she did every morning, Anna Draycott religiously walked up the concrete rear steps of Tottenham Police station and entered a world that she loved. It was going to be hard leaving and every day since she'd made her decision, she had tried to convince herself that all would be fine and she must simply look upon retirement as a new adventure. Every day she had tried to convince herself that it was the right thing to do but as soon as she stepped inside the station, all of her fears and worries would resurface. Just as she took off her coat and hung it on a hook on the wall, Drew Payton tapped on the office door and not waiting to be invited inside, walked straight over to Anna's desk and parked himself on the corner of the highly polished wood. Anna glared in the direction of the arrogant young detective and her expression spoke volumes. The desk belonged to Anna personally, it had been a gift from her husband and she adored it.
"The Chief wants to see you, ASAP!"
"Get your arse off of my desk now Drew!! In the future you will address me as Ma'am and only that, do I make myself clear?!"
Detective Payton hung his head and as he nodded Anna could see that his cheeks had turned scarlet with embarrassment.

"Don't let me have to tell you again."
Drew again nodded his head and then made a swift exit with the more than embarrassed expression still plastered all over his face. The Met, even though the powers above had tried their best to eradicate unacceptable opinions regarding certain minority officers, had failed dismally, especially when it came down to the female members of staff. The place was full of old timers with chauvinistic attitudes towards women and the young inexperienced officers were still being heavily influenced and not in a good way. Well this particular officer had better start pulling his socks up pretty damn quickly or she would make sure he saw her bad side, the side that had seen her obtain a record for solving cases that was second to none and which had also propelled her to the rank of Detective Inspector.

Knocking on the Chief's door she mustered up the best smile she could manage as she entered. It was fake and Chief Inspector Lou Garnet could read her like a book, he also knew the reason, she was being forced to quit the force by Jake.
"Right, let's get down to business. The body of a Caucasian child washed up in the Thames early this morning, well the torso at least. It was retrieved by a man named Andy Case whilst he was out fishing for eels apparently. The silly fucker was reluctant to

report it at first as he hadn't got a licence but thankfully his conscious got the better of him and it was called in at just before seven. Marine Support were initially on scene but then handed it over to Limehouse, who as you know are absolutely inundated at the moment, so they have kindly passed it on to us."

The sarcasm in his voice didn't go unnoticed but Anna didn't comment.

"Michael Hanks stated that the victim was killed approximately two days ago but you know Mike, he wouldn't comment further until he'd carried out a full autopsy, which he did at nine this morning and the results have just been emailed through."

"So, it is murder then?"

For a second the Chief looked at her quizzically as if she'd lost the plot.

"I mean, it's not the result of a boat propeller or something?"

"I'm coming to that. Seems the child, a girl, was around eight years of age and all of her primary organs, heart, liver, lungs and kidneys had been removed so no, in answer to your question this was no accident. As for the rest of her, who knows what the poor little might was forced to endure."

"What?! Oh my God!"

"Gets better, if that's the correct term? Mike said that they had been professionally taken out and in his expert opinion, was willing to state that he firmly believed it was for the illegal transplant trade."

Anna's right palm instantly covered her mouth. In all her time on the force and especially the last ten years in CID, she'd seen horrors too vile to even think about, but this? This was about as bad as it got and her heart broke for that poor little girl, a sad innocent child who Anna would have adored, had she ever have been blessed.

"The sick bastards! So what's the plan of action Sir?"

"I want you to lead the team."

"But I only have ten months left until I retire Sir, what if we haven't concluded by then? I mean, I will do my damnedest to solve this but we're both under no illusions that these types of cases can take many months, if not years!"

"Then, you will have gathered enough to make your successor's transition to the case far easier. Why you want to retire at the age of thirty eight is beyond me, what on earth will you do with your time?"

"Travel a bit I suppose but in all honesty I haven't really figured that out yet. This institution has all but owned me since I was eighteen and after twenty years on the force I think I deserve a rest and Jake has so many plans for us, even if they are his and not mine and……….."

Lou Garnet, a portly man due to the overindulgent

excess of alcohol and bad food choices during his long career, was only three years shy of retirement and he couldn't wait. Dealing with violent cases seemed to suck the life out of most officers no matter how strong you were and Lou Garnet had definitely seen his fill over the years. The newest case to land on his desk was no exception and the beginning of another sick murder and he just didn't have time for idle chatter, at least not today, so out of character he cut his Inspector off mid-sentence.
"Anna, I need you to set up an incident room asap. You have four officers at your disposal plus Drew Payton. I know he's still a bit wet behind the ears but he'll come in useful I'm sure and it goes without saying, as many plods as the station can spare when and if."

Nodding her head Anna walked out into the central shared office area and headed in the direction of Incident Room 2.

Her team consisted of Detective Constable Beth Saunders who was five years into her time with the Met and DC Carl Shaw and DC Dave Wilson, both experienced officers with over twenty years combined under their belts. Her Sergeant was Steve Johnson, who Anna really got on well with, not to mention the fact that in the past the pair had worked on several successful cases together. Then there was of course Drew, not a lot to say about him but Anna just hoped he would be more of a help than a hindrance. As she entered she was pleased to see that the room had already been set up with wipe boards containing images of the body and a detailed location map. Her team were quietly seated around a large central table and the mood was most definitely sombre, it always was when a child was involved. Anna was small in stature, and stood little more than five feet tall. Thin, with a dark brown bob, at times she resembled a child but anyone confusing her appearance as someone they could run rings around had been sorely ill informed. Anna was fair but she didn't suffer fools gladly and had a record for solving cases no matter how long it took. If you cut the mustard then you were a welcome addition to the team, if not, then she would have you off of the case without a second thought.

"Morning all! Well you've obviously been briefed already so let's get down to business. Steve, me and you will pay Mike Hanks a visit and then go down to the location at Limehouse. Beth, you and Dave get a few plods together and start a door to door. It's mostly high end apartments and warehouse conversions so I very much doubt you'll come up with anything but we still need to go through the motions. Drew, I want you to shadow Carl, the pair of you need to go over past files and see if there's anything similar that's been reported regarding missing kids. If there is then look into the parents and other relatives etcetera. Dave, when you get back go through the usual suspects. See if we have anyone on the books who's been charged, recently released or have had their collars felt in connection with anything remotely similar. Come on then you lot, what are you waiting for?"

The forensics and pathology lab was situated in the lower ground floor of St John & St Elizabeth hospital in St John's wood. Quite frankly, Anna wasn't looking forward to the visit and it had little to do with the case. As far as she was concerned, Michael Hanks was an awful human being who treated women and in particular police women, as lower class citizens. They had clashed several times over the years but as he was held in such high esteem by the Met, she had been warned not to offend him in any way.

The laboratory had no natural light and as she and Steve Johnson emerged from the lift, Anna immediately found the surroundings oppressive and somewhat claustrophobic. Situated right next to the hospital mortuary area, as far as Anna was concerned, not much thought had gone into the planning. To reach the lab you had to walk along a corridor with windows that looked directly into the autopsy rooms. The pathologists must have been so used to their working conditions that they hadn't thought to lower the internal blinds and as Anna and Steve passed they had a full view of a post mortem in progress.

"You okay Guv?"

Anna smiled and nodded her head. Steve must have thought that the sight bothered her as she wasn't sure if he was aware of her feelings towards the pathologist and even if he was, now wasn't really the time to discuss it at any great length.

"I've been to plenty of autopsies Steve, some of them up close but you'd think they would drop the venetians, just in case it upset anyone who wasn't familiar with the procedure."

"I don't mind admitting that it still turns my stomach. How anyone could choose to do that for a living I'll never know."

Ringing the bell, the officers waited to be let inside and to say Anna was shocked when the door was opened by a pretty young blonde was something of an understatement. After displaying their warrant cards, Anna and Steve were shown through to the mortuary and directed towards a small office at the far end. The door was ajar and as he saw them approach, Michael with a curt wave of his hand, beckoned for them to enter. He was on the phone and Anna felt like a right lemon as she just stood there waiting for him to finally end the call and give her his attention.

"Inspector Draycott, we meet again!"
"Good morning Sir, obviously you know why we are here? Chief Garnet has briefed me on the autopsy report and obviously there is very little for you to add so……."
"There you go as usual Anna, jumping the gun without all of the facts! Actually I have carried out some further tests and I do indeed have more to offer."
The meeting was beginning to feel awkward and for a moment Anna didn't speak but at the same time she noticed that Michael Hanks appeared to be taking great delight in her discomfort and it was something that really pissed her off.
"That has always been your problem Inspector, jumping in with both feet before you've bothered to inquire further. As I was about to say before I was so rudely interrupted, the stomach contents, which weren't listed in my initial report as I had to carry out further tests, were some form of liquid beetroot and a half-digested cabbage roll. In my experience it is a diet typical of eastern Europeans and in particular Romanians, though obviously I cannot categorically confirm the latter. It has now also come to light that the corpse had suffered sexual abuse shortly after her death. Traces of semen were extracted from the vaginal cavity which we are presently in the process of running through the DNA database. As for prints? Well, as we all know

that's not possible and probably the reason they removed the limbs and head, though why we would have any records on a child so young is beyond me anyway. I hope that I am wrong but I think there could be more to follow. It's a highly lucrative trade and if the extraction was successful, there's a high demand and whoever is responsible will be eager to carry out more of the same if they haven't done so already!"

Anna didn't know which offended her the most, the revelation of sex abuse or the fact that Hanks had just referred to the poor little mite as a corpse. Whichever it was, this case had now escalated further and a whole new can of worms had been opened up. Reluctantly having to thank the man as he handed over the folder cut deep but remembering her earlier warning, Anna was gracious.

"Wait there and I'll get Trudy to show you both out."

Michael pressed a buzzer and within seconds the pretty young blonde reappeared and walked them both out towards an area marked 'exit'. As she entered the lift Anna turned and still feeling peeved, looked directly into the young woman's face. She couldn't resist asking one final question that had been on her mind since she'd arrived.

"How on earth do you work for a complete fuckin' moron like Hanks?"

The young woman only stared at her in uncomfortable silence until just before the doors closed. Suddenly Anna noticed Trudy as she gave the slightest hint of a smile.

"Because, he's my father."

When the doors had finally shut, Anna sighed deeply and Sergeant Johnson couldn't contain the short giggle that escaped his lips. When she glared at him sideways he knew she was angry but still he couldn't remove the smirk from his face.

"Nice one Guv, you well and truly fucked up there!"

Anna sighed, closed her eyes and then slowly shook her head from side to side.

"Hopefully she'll keep her trap shut but if not? Well fuck him the arrogant bastard, if he puts in a complaint that's up to him because right at this moment in time I've got far more to worry about than some pathetic little man's ego! Drive me over to Limehouse while I phone in the twat's findings."

Steve Johnson smiled, he loved working with the Inspector and on any case she headed, it was never a dull moment. There were always fireworks of some sort between Anna and the Met's hierarchy and that was what made her special, she wouldn't be bullied when it came down to what was right.

Limehouse had been redeveloped in the 1990s and was now home to top earners and celebrities alike.

Anna was only too aware that the occupants wouldn't like being hassled by the police for whatever reason. There would obviously be complaints, so in less than two hours she had pissed off a top forensic scientist and possibly several respected residents of Limehouse, causing even more aggro than she needed.

The body, or at least what was left of it had been discovered in a small inlet between Victoria and Papermill Wharfs and as the tide was now high, no scene of crimes tent could be erected. When Anna and Steve arrived it felt as if it was just another day, as if nothing had occurred and to Anna it seemed almost as if the child's life hadn't counted for anything. Beth Saunders approached them at the water's edge and she already looked stressed up to the eyeballs. Now Anna would have to waste even more precious time placating one of her officers, instead of getting down to the matter in hand.
"Guv, Sarge, not a lot to report as yet, well actually nothing."
"You okay Beth?"
"No not really. I've never come across such rude and arrogant people! Slammed the door in our faces mostly, well at least those we could even be arsed to answer the door."
"Nature of the beast I'm afraid but you've been in the job long enough to know that's the case with

most murders."

"I know guv but we're talking about a child here, a little life that was never given the chance to grow because some sick bastard decided to end it."

Anna placed an arm around Beth's shoulder and gently guided her out of Steve's earshot. She was aware that the young officer had been desperately trying to fall pregnant for the past two years, so this case was going to be additionally hard.

"You're young Beth and a child's death is never easy to deal with, especially if you have strong maternal feelings but you must harden up. I have a feeling this might only have just begun and I need you focused."

Detective Saunder's swallowed hard, sniffed loudly and then slowly nodded her head.

"This is all just as I imagined Beth, the rich don't like being disturbed, no matter what has happened or who has got hurt, sadly they care for no one but themselves. So, how many bods have you got helping?"

"Only four and at this rate it will take us a month of bloody Sundays just to get round all of the properties."

"Leave it with me, I'll give the Chief a call and get you some more help."

True to her word, Anna phoned Chief Inspector Garnet and by noon eleven further constables had been briefed and had arrived at the scene. Anna and Steve made their way back to the station and as soon as they walked into the incident room Carl Shaw swiftly made his way over.

"I think we've got a lead Guv. Seems two similar cases have flagged up and that was only going back over the last couple of years. The only difference to our body was the fact that they were both adults, the first, a female torso, surfaced in Cambridge almost seventeen months ago and the second was male, which was more recent at six months. I think the male could be of a higher interest initially, oh and he was found in Wisbech."

"Where the fuck is Wisbech?"

"It's a small market town in the Fens. It lies northeast of Cambridgeshire and also borders Norfolk. I think…"

"I was joking and I don't need a fucking geography lesson either Carl! Get to the point will you?"

"Sorry Guv. Well the area is typical fenland and therefore has a high demand for agricultural workers, mostly migrants from Eastern Europe."

"And?!"

"Well you said in your call that the pathologist thought that the stomach contents might be from a Romanian diet?"

For a few seconds Anna chewed down gently on her bottom lip as she thought.

"I want all files from Cambridge and this Wisbech place sent over ASAP and make sure that the dozy twats include the pathology files. I know what some of those backwater stations can be like and it's not unheard of for major evidence and files to go missing. If you want me I'll be in with the Chief. Oh, and let me know as soon as it all arrives and I mean like today!"

"Yes Ma'am."

"Steve, go over anything Dave has hopefully uncovered."

With that Inspector Anna Draycott pushed on the heavy double doors and disappeared from sight. The Chief's office door was wide open as she approached and Anna walked straight in. Lou glanced up and smiled, her brow was furrowed and past experience had taught him that when his Inspector wore that look, she had managed a breakthrough of some sort.

"And?"

"I've got a bad feeling about this Sir. We could be looking at the possibility of two other cases, maybe a serial killer but my money would be on organised crime and if that's the case?"

"We're in for a shit load of aggravation!"

For a fleeting moment Anna closed her eyes and could only nod her reply. Deep down she was praying that the cases weren't in any way linked but in reality there were too many coincidences for them not to be. No copper ever wanted to leave the force half way through an investigation and she and

Jake had been so looking forward to her retirement but she had a horrible gut feeling that her pending leave date might have to be delayed which she knew would cause problems in her marriage.

CHAPTER THIRTEEN

Eight year old Kahla Hussein had been living in the United Kingdom for a little under a year. Her family were from Syria and she had made the long treacherous journey to England with her parents Mohammad and Iman and baby brother Hassan. Making their way on foot from a small village near 'Al-Sukhnah' in the centre of Syria to the border with Turkey at Idlib had taken almost a month. At times the terrain was rough, it was dangerous and only just the beginning of their journey. Still treacherous, it would have been a lot simpler to travel by sea but Iman was petrified of water to the point of hysteria whenever that option had been raised in the planning of the family's escape. At Idlib they were smuggled in the back of a farm truck all the way across Turkey until they reached Istanbul. The nine hundred mile drive took almost a week as the driver was only prepared to take the family under the cover of darkness. Mohammad had saved every Lira he could and sold every possession that they owned in order to pay for the trip and even then it would be tight as to whether they would be able to fund the entire journey. By the time they reached the Bulgarian border over half of their money had been spent. Onwards they travelled, through Romania, The Ukraine, Poland and Germany, in all the family had crossed, in horrendous conditions, eight different countries to reach the sea and now Iman had no choice in their mode of transport. When the ocean came into view she began to wail in fear and nothing her husband did could calm her. Finally she was forcibly manhandled and that was only after being slapped across the face and told to shut up. Her assailant was one of the men leading them onto the ship and Mohammad didn't dare protest for fear of being left behind.

Classed as illegal immigrants and along with many others, they then crossed the English Channel in the back of a shipping container which was supposed to be carrying potatoes. The crossing was fraught with danger, they were hungry, thirsty and the air seemed to be getting thinner by the minute. The P&O Ferry from Zeebrugge took just under fifteen hours to reach Hull and for every second of that time the people crammed inside the container were panicking that they would be caught. The highest risk, though unknown to the people being smuggled, was actually making it through customs. On average it was a fifty, fifty chance and the smugglers called this last leg 'Russian roulette' but had never disclosed this when taking almost every penny that the people on board possessed.

The port at Hull was busy, so busy in fact that there

just simply wasn't the man power or enough hours in the day to check each and every freight lorry. If the driver was compliant and didn't look too shady, they would be waved on after their papers had been checked and luckily for the Hussein family, on this occasion they dodged the bullet. At Scunthorpe the lorry came to a stop in a roadside layby. The rear doors were opened and those who had only paid for passage were told to get out, from here on in they were on their own. Thankfully Mohamed had paid for the onward journey and after being allowed to stretch their legs and after taking fresh bottled water inside, their journey to London began. Less than four hours later Mohammad breathed a huge sigh of relief when the rear doors had been opened for the last time and he was met with the most beautiful blue sky.

It had taken a while for them all to acclimatise to the cold English weather but just to live in peace with no bombs or snipers shooting at you day and night was worth more than anything to the family. Unlike her parents who spoke little to no English, Kahla had picked up many words and phrases mixing with other children since she'd been in the UK and even at such a tender age, she had become the family interpreter. Her mother and father had little choice but to rely solely on the smugglers to find them accommodation and that accommodation came in the form of a two bedroom flat in Walker House. The old council building was on Ossulton Street in Somers Town but sadly the family were not the only occupants of the property. The largest bedroom where Kahla and her family slept held two double beds and the second was also inhabited by a family of three from Senegal. The smaller bedroom had a double bed which went almost from wall to wall and its occupants were three other Syrian refugees. The front room and previously the only communal space in the flat had been turned into another bedroom which now housed eight Somalian men, also all illegals but the nightmare didn't end there. Unlike the majority of flats housed in the block, number seventeen had never been modernised which meant that although there was a separate toilet and basin, the bath was still situated in the kitchen and covered with a large piece of plywood. One bathtub for eighteen people seems absurd but they couldn't be anything but grateful, even if they were all crammed in like sardines. The one saving grace was the fact that the Somalian men all worked a night shift so at least during the day when they were asleep, there were fewer bodies to manoeuvre around.

Kahla's parents both found work in a tiny sweatshop at the rear of number seven Fonthill Road over in Finsbury Park. The business was owned by the Assam brothers and fronted by a small retail unit selling seconds. The brothers didn't care where their employees came from, paid well below the required minimum wage and expected the men and women to work like slaves. They were all illegals so there was no choice in the matter as the workers knew it was that or starve or worse still, get deported. Mohammed and Iman would leave Walker House each morning at six and not return until after seven so childcare was left to Gertie Granger who lived next door. Gertie minded most of the children in the area, well those of the illegals and she charged extortionate fees but no one could argue. Known as GG to the kids, Gertie was grossly overweight and constantly had a cigarette hanging from her lips. Permanently dressed in an old fashioned wrap over apron like her mother had worn during the war, she continually had a wet cough, the sound of which churned even the strongest of stomachs. Her flat was filthy but even so, she rarely allowed the children inside if she could help it. Save for torrential rain, they were all forced to play downstairs in the concrete courtyard. Meals were supplied by another resident, thirty year old mother of two and Romanian immigrant Agnese Ozols, who supplemented her universal credit by cooking the meagre food rations and being paid a token fee by Gertie for doing so. Kahla hated the beetroot soup and the potato pancakes that the

Romanian woman cooked, it tasted bland and was so different from the delicious dolmas, kebabs and sweet baklava of her homeland but food was scarce here in England, so Kahla ate what she was given without daring to complain.

Over at the arches, a message had reached Maggie that the Judge now wanted a child, well actually it had been Mr Dewala who had raised the question regarding if this would be possible. He'd had a request by a rich family who's little girl needed a kidney transplant and the Judge had decided that he might as well have some fun with the small victim first, until he was told in no uncertain terms that she wasn't to be touched before the organ removals had taken place. Maggie had instructed Asti to find someone suitable and after purchasing a couple of cheap dolls and a soft toy teddy, he had thrown them onto the passenger seat and then sped away in his newly replaced van. Driving around the King's Cross area for what felt like hours he started to worry that he wouldn't be able to deliver so with still no success, he parked up to take a break and enjoy a smoke. As he wound down his window he heard the sound of children playing noisily in the vicinity. Getting out of the van and stubbing out his cigarette underfoot, Asti walked towards the courtyard that wasn't secured and which had open accesses on all four corners that led

to sheds and garages situated at the far end. A mix of children were running around playing tag and as far as Asti could see, there was no adult supervision. He returned to the van and brought it closer for a speedy escape. It wasn't that he had any fear regarding his details being noted by the Old Bill as he always drove with fake registration plates but he didn't want to risk getting seen or stopped and quizzed by any of the locals. Pulling up close, he got out and opened the side door in readiness. Slowly peering around the corner he spied Kahla standing alone, she wasn't interacting and just stared at the other children as they all went about their play, blissfully unaware that they were being watched. Reaching his arm around the corner of the brickwork, Asti placed the bright pink teddy bear down onto the concrete and moved a short distance away so that he could observe unnoticed. It didn't take long for Kahla to spot the cute toy, she had none of her own so this cheap little bundle of fluff drew her attention far more than it would have with any other child. Slowly she moved away from the others towards the intriguing bear and as she bent down to pick it up, Asti quietly came over. Seeing his feet, Kahla instantly dropped the toy and stood up.
"Hello little girl, it's okay there's no need to be scared. I see you've found my friend. He's very lonely, would you like to look after him for me?"

Kahla happily nodded her head and Asti retrieved the bear from the ground and handed it to the small child. It was so soft and as Kahla stroked the silky fur she looked up at Asti and smiled.
"I have many more lonely bears in my van, would you like to see them?"
Momentarily Kahla looked back in the direction of the other children. She knew she should stay with them because if GG found out she had wandered off she would get very angry but just a few moments couldn't hurt could it? And besides, Kahla planned to be back before anyone noticed she was missing. Asti pointed to the side door of the Vauxhall Combi but as Kahla's eyes momentarily looked inside she frowned in confusion and then she became scared. There was nothing inside but a dirty old mattress and even at her tender age, she recalled the stories told to her by her parents about having anything to do with strange men. There was no time for her to react further as with a swift heavy hand, Asti grabbed her by the scruff of the neck and threw her inside. Everything felt like it was happening in slow motion as the door slammed and the van set off. Now in almost total darkness, Kahla was thrown from side to side as Asti drove the vehicle at speed in a desperate attempt to give himself some distance from the flats. Kahla suddenly felt the warm wet sensation as her bladder released itself in fear and she began to cry out for her mother.

Asti couldn't have timed the abduction any better because when he arrived at the arches, only moments earlier everyone had fortunately left for the day. Opening up, he dragged a terrified Kahla kicking and screaming from the van. Aware that there shouldn't be anyone in the vicinity who could hear, he was nonetheless still nervous until they were inside the safety of the inner soundproof room. As the girl was so small there was no need to tie her up and once the refrigerator panel door was locked there was no way she could escape. Asti had no morals but knew only too well that this latest abduction would be viewed in a far worse light should he get caught. He tried to make himself feel better about his actions by recalling Maggie's parting words 'It's a small mercy but at least her life will have ended before any abuse begins, Mr Dewala has insisted that he doesn't want any undue stress placed upon the body prior to organ removal'. Over recent months the Judge's sexual appetite had become more and more sickening and depraved, so he wasn't at all perturbed that he would be forced to explore the mutilated body of a dead girl. Necrophilia had always been of interest to him so now would be as good a chance as any and one more abhorrent fantasy to tick off of his bucket list.

By the time Mohammad and Iman returned to

Ossulton Street, the courtyard was strangely filled with lots of people, many of whom Mohammad recognised as being in the same predicament as his own family. Gertie Granger was nervously pacing up and down and when she spied the Hussein's approaching, she quickly turned the other way. It wasn't that she was worried about the Old Bill, as there was no chance the child's disappearance would be reported, not if most of the illegal community wanted to remain in the UK. No, for the first time in her life Gertie actually felt guilty and that guilt only deepened when Iman found out that her baby girl was missing. When the enormity of what that could actually mean suddenly hit her, she began to wail uncontrollably and scream hysterically. Her husband tried his best to console her but nothing could stop her feeling as if her heart had been ripped from her body. She screamed at him like never before, that he shouldn't have brought them to this terrible place and that if Kahla didn't come back to them she would never forgive him for as long as she lived.

It had been arranged that Adesh Dewala would arrive at the arches a good three hours before anyone else. Entering the secure unit he found the little girl nervously huddled on the floor in the corner of the room. Momentarily he felt bad for what he was about to do but then he thought of the vast amount of money he was going to receive and all guilt instantly disappeared. From her dress Adesh could see that the child was from a poor background and would never amount to anything, whereas the recipient came from wealthy parents, would be well educated and in turn would be able to offer something back to the human race. Walking very slowly towards Kahla he bent down and in a soft tone, began to speak.

"Hello little girl, there's no need to be frightened. I expect you are wondering why you are here? Let me explain. In this country you need to have vaccinations and once I have given you an injection you will be taken back to your parents. Will you let me do that?"

Kahla didn't like needles, she remembered back to when she was in Syria and had been vaccinated for polio. She had cried and cried and was only soothed by her mother's kind words but her mother wasn't here, so she had to be brave. Nodding her head, she stood up and followed the doctor through to the dismemberment area. Seeing the steel table and glass bottles containing all manner of things, it did at least resemble a doctor's room so she began to relax a little. Dewala pulled up her sleeve and gently injected her with Pentobarbital, a drug widely used by vets to put animals down. Within a moment poor Kahla's heart stopped and her small body dropped to the floor. Adesh immediately lifted her onto the old autopsy table, removed her clothes and then began to scrub up in readiness for the harvest. By the time the Judge arrived her body had been crudely stitched back up and was now lying on the polythene covered bed ready for him to do as he wished. Apart from the good doctor, who this time couldn't stomach abusing a child's lifeless remains, everyone else in the room took their turn.

By the time Asti returned to the arches in the early hours of the following morning, he had come to a definite decision, he was leaving England and this time it would be for good. Over the last couple of days it had begun to weigh heavily on his mind that things had started to get way, way out of hand and as much as he hadn't dwelled at all on the fate of the adults he had abducted and what had been done to them, a child was a different matter altogether and a turning point as far as he was concerned. Of course it hadn't stopped him collecting the large wedge of cash from Maggie McKay for his services but it still hadn't sat very well with his conscience. Asti was worldly wise, wise enough to know that it wouldn't be too much longer before everything came crashing down around the ears of the sickest, greediest bunch of low life's that he had ever had the misfortune to do business with.

This time, removing the evidence was difficult and

as he began to dismember Kahla's remains he was forced to place a cloth over her face as she seemed to be staring at him, her dark eyes somehow pleading with him to help her. Before he removed the head he opened the little girl's mouth and on seeing no sign of any dental work, knew that there would be no records on file so left her mouth intact. Removing her tiny teeth would have been a step too far, even for Asti. Placing the small torso into the water at Victoria wharf, Asti didn't even bother to weight it as he knew this would probably be the last job he would do for the McKay's and something deep inside of him wanted the child to be found. Her little limbs were so small and he was now feeling immense guilt, something he'd never experienced before. Individually wrapping them in black plastic bags, he drove around the East End of London and disposed of them randomly in the bins at the rear of various restaurants. With his work now complete, he made up his mind to stay for the remainder of his lease, which was now only a few months away and then he would skip this sick, shithole of a country without telling anyone. In the meantime, if Maggie McKay wanted more dirty work carried out he was adamant that he would only entertain it if the victims were adults. No matter how much she offered, from now on innocent kids were definitely off limits.

CHAPTER FOURTEEN

Even though Anna had demanded them, the reports on the Cambridge and Wisbech cases didn't arrive until early the following day but unfortunately they shed no further light on anything and Anna had a sneaking suspicion that either information had been left out, or the investigations hadn't been carried out properly. After clearing it with the Chief, Anna and Sergeant Johnson set off for the Fens at just before eleven that morning. They had an appointment with a Chief Inspector Larry Hanwell at the city station on Parkside and it had been decided in advance that rather than return to London, they would stay over in Cambridge and then move onto Wisbech early the next day. Beth had booked them into a pub for the night and had also made an appointment at the second station for ten am sharp. Steve drove while Anna made notes into her Dictaphone and he knew better than to make any attempt at idle chitchat when she was engrossed in her work.

Their timing was spot on and when they entered the Cambridge station via the custody suite at the rear, Chief Hanwell was ready and waiting for them.

"Inspector Draycott and…..?"

Anna held out her hand and then introduced her sergeant. The Chief seemed amiable enough but past experience had taught her well that first impressions could be very misleading. For a start, no force likes to have their cases looked into and even though this was just an information seeking mission, if there had been a lack of due care or if the officers had been negligent in their investigation, then without hesitation it would be reported back to the DPS.

"If you'd like to follow me to my office we can have a more detailed discussion in private."

Anna and Steve both nodded and a few minutes later they were seated in Chief Inspector Larry Hanwell's inner sanctum. The Chief outlined the case and what occurred during and after the investigation. Some ten minutes later he concluded that although it was still very much a live case, it had now been placed onto the back burner until any further evidence came to light, which he was doubtful of. Anna had already read the pathology report but what she was interested in was the fact that there was very little other paperwork.

"So Chief Hanwell, were any females reported missing around the same time?"

"None in that age group, oh we had plenty of old people, or children, mostly teens, who reappeared when they thought they had caused their parents enough worry. You know the usual suspects, kids that have fallen out with mum and dad for some inane reason and decide to set off for the bright lights of the big city but no adults of the age in question were reported I can assure you."

"Door to door near the find?"

"Yes, but it drew a blank so was called to a halt after twenty four hours."

"Who by?"

"Well me of course, why? Inspector, if you are inferring that I didn't carry out my duties properly or......"

"And the stomach contents, what did you make of those?"

"Excuse me?"

"Our autopsy report suggests an Eastern European diet and similar contents were found in the stomach of your victim. What about semen?"

The Chief just stared blankly and to Anna, if the situation hadn't have been so serious, it would have been comical. Anna knew what the answers were going to be but she felt strongly compelled to question the Chief further.

"The cases only differ in the fact that our body was a female child and yours and the one which surfaced in Wisbech, are adults. Studying all of the reports revealed that traces of semen were identified in all three cases, so there was now no doubt, that the murders were sexually motivated in some way. Obviously it was run through your database? So we are looking for people with no previous and no DNA on file."

Larry just continued to stare at her open mouthed.

Someone had fucked up big style and now he was being made to look like a complete idiot by an officer of a lesser rank, not to mention the fact that he would undoubtedly be hauled over the coals because of it. When this meeting was over, heads would roll that was for sure! Anna and Steve left the station no further forward but still wondering how a city force could have been so lapse.

The Waterman on Chesterton Road was midrange and Anna was pleasantly surprised at how nice the rooms were. Detective Saunders had booked the accommodation and Beth knew her Inspector so well, that instead of a hotel she had chosen a pub. Anna smiled to herself, that young woman would go a long way, she was bright, eager and always noted the small things, like knowing her superior was more than fond of the odd drink. Arranging to meet up with Steve in an hour's time, Anna lay on the bed and phoned Jake. Their hectic careers dictated that they couldn't always spend every night together but it was an unwritten rule between them that they spoke at least once every day, even if Anna had pulled a night shift at the station or Jake was away on business in some foreign country.
"Hi darling."
"Hello sweetheart, how's it going?"
"So, so. I really expected Wisbech to be bad and that delight still awaits me tomorrow but not

Cambridge. If it wasn't a city then I'd best describe their force as coming from some backwater yokel town. Oh the joys of being in the Met."
"Is it cold there?"
"Not too bad but I'd rather be curled up in bed with you my sexy man!"
"Don't tempt me or I might just drive over to Cambridge, right now!"
They both laughed and after telling each other that they loved one another, Anna ended the call and headed downstairs to meet her Sergeant for dinner and a few drinks. Unfortunately the planned few drinks turned into far more and when the alarm went off the following morning, Anna woke with the mother of all headaches. Holding her brow as she turned on the shower she chastised herself, would she ever learn not to mix the grape and the grain? The previous evening had started off well enough with a few pints of delicious craft beer but over dinner Anna had stupidly ordered a bottle of red wine which had quickly escalated into two. Now she was paying the price and suddenly the thought of the fried breakfast included in the room rate made her stomach heave. Luckily she was close enough to the toilet not to make a mess but this wasn't boding well for the rest of the day. Downing a couple of pints of water, by the time she joined Steve at the breakfast table she was feeling slightly better.

"Morning Ma'am."
"Steve. How you feeling?"
"Like shit but that's par for the cause where you're concerned."
Taking a seat, she smiled.
"I didn't exactly tie you to a chair and force it down your throat, now did I?"
"Might as well have Ma'am, everyone knows I could never have out drank you but I would never have been able to live it down if anyone back at the station got wind that I didn't at least try to match you drink for drink."
Anna laughed, of course he was correct and it was something she was planning on addressing once she retired. Jake hated her drinking so much and she was ashamed to admit that she'd often told him a white lie when he sometimes asked if she'd been to the pub with her team. Oddly, both of the officers declined the full English and opted instead for simple coffee and toast.

The drive to Wisbech took just over an hour and Steve continually commented on how flat it all was. His voice seemed to drone on but Anna realised that her agitation was more down to her hangover than her Sergeant's boring conversation. Initially driving by the station, Anna was somewhat surprised at the sheer size of the building, considering this was a small town. That most certainly didn't bode well and could only mean there were probably high incidents of crime. Finally parking up a few hundred yards away, the two officers strolled back to the station and entered through the main doors. It was just before ten but there was already a queue of three people before them. Anna didn't play up to her rank and instead just stood patiently and observed what was happening.

The first customer was an elderly lady of around seventy who was hard of hearing and there to report a missing cat. The desk sergeant was friendly and patient, even if he did have to explain three times and with his voice escalating each time, that they no long held lost and found animals and that she would have to contact the dog warden. The second was far more interesting, a man with an Eastern European accent who gave his name as Juris Ivanova and who was there to report a mugging from the previous evening. Again the Sergeant was polite and after phoning upstairs to a detective, politely asked the man to take a seat. The third and final was a woman named Josie Codona. The young woman stated that she was attending to report as per her bail conditions and suddenly everything changed.
"Address?"
"Ringers Lane, Travellers site."
Anna instantly noticed how the officer's tone had

drastically altered and whereas the young woman was courteous and only doing as she had too, the Sergeant was dismissive and looked at the girl as if she was dirt on his shoe. Josie didn't rise to the bait, her family had lived in the community for long enough to know this was typical treatment by Gorgios towards a traveller. Any attempt at fighting back, more often than not ended in arrest for the traveller, even if the altercation had been nothing more than verbal.

"Wait over there!"

Josie Codona obediently did as she was told without any complaint but it really had rubbed Anna up the wrong way. Walking up to the counter she momentarily stared in silence at the officer standing behind the glass screen.

"Yes Madam? How can I help?"

"Do you always talk to members of the travelling community like that?"

Suddenly Josie's ears pricked up and there was the slight hint of a smile on her lips.

"I beg your pardon?"

"You heard me well enough. So?"

The desk sergeant leaned forward so that he was able to lower his voice.

"Not that it's any of your business Madam but they are the scum of the earth. Rob their own granny for a penny and the people of Wisbech are sick and tired of their thieving ways. Now can I take your name please?"

"So you are tarring all travellers with the same brush. You blatantly discriminate against a certain sector of the public and think it's okay to behave that way?"

"I really don't have time for this, as you can see there are now several people waiting behind you. Now either give me your name or leave, the choice is yours love!"

"I'm not your love, it's Detective Inspector Anna Draycott and you are Constable?"

"Sar, Sar, Sergeant Forbes Ma'am."

"Sergeant? Well, let me tell you something Sergeant, if you were in the Met I can assure you that you would have been stripped of your rank and be back pounding the beat for speaking to a member of the general public in that way! Now, I'm here to see Chief Mulberry."

"Yes Ma'am, certainly Ma'am. Please, through those doors if you would be so kind."

As he pressed a buzzer that released the door, Anna turned and as she and Steve headed through, she winked in Josie Codona's direction. Josie gave a slight giggle and then lowered her gaze when she saw the sergeant glaring at her.

The inner hub appeared far newer than the station at Cambridge and had obviously had a recent program of modernisation. Listening intently,

Anna heard the familiar yokel drawl that had always amused her. She also noticed that there wasn't one ethnic officer in sight, at least not on this particular shift and that concerned her. About to voice her opinion to Steve, she was stopped when a thirty something, rather good looking man, raced down the stairs in her direction, taking the steps two at a time as he did so.

"Morning Inspector! Danny Mulberry pleased to meet you."

Chief Inspector Mulberry held out his hand and shook Anna's vigorously when she offered it. Again they were led into an office and Anna was pleased to see that at least more of an effort had been made with the case of the dead body in their locality. She asked the same questions as she had in Cambridge and while there was still nothing regarding the stomach contents or semen traces, a thorough search and door to door had been carried out.

"Sir, I believe that a large number of the local population are migrant workers from Eastern Europe?"

"That's correct, mostly Lithuanians, Latvians and Poles and a few Bulgarians and Romanians. In the last couple of years we've also seen a vast increase with the influx of Russians. The jury's still out on whether that's a good or a bad thing. Anyway, the poor buggers work for a pittance because our lazy bastards won't get out of bed let alone do a hard day's work."

"So were any males from here or the surrounding areas reported missing?"

Chief Mulberry sighed heavily before continuing. "When the body surfaced, I scoured our data base personally and sadly in that time frame there were none. The body was hooked up close to the propeller of a boat owned by a middle aged couple from Boston. Mr and Mrs Meadows had just completed a journey from their hometown to Wisbech. We don't know when the body became caught up, it could have actually been with them for the entire journey meaning that the victim wasn't even from this area. Obviously there wasn't much left to identify but thankfully at least there was a torso, which wouldn't have been the case had it been any closer to the propeller."

Danny Mulberry was beginning to waffle and Anna needed to get back to what was important.

"Is there any way I could possibly speak to the local community here, just in case?"

"They're a strange lot, keep themselves to themselves mostly but I can try. We have a Latvian officer here, Andris something or other, I can't remember what his surname is but even if I could I wouldn't be able to pronounce it, maybe he could have a word for you."

Though not as bad as the incident in the reception

area, Anna could still sense more prejudice but decided not to act on it. He was her senior and it wasn't for her to reprimand him. She also didn't voice her experience regarding what had happened on her arrival with the front desk sergeant, there was no point. It was sad but one disgruntled inspector from another force really wasn't going to change anything.

It was left that Chief Mulberry would contact Anna when he had some news and sure enough two days later he called. It was arranged that a meeting would be held in the Methodist church hall and Constable Andris Kalnberzinsh would attend and do his best at translating should it be needed. As it turned out there was no need for a translator as the majority of the thirty or so people that had bothered to turn up spoke varying degrees of English and those that didn't were told by their fellow countrymen what was being said.

Late afternoon on the following day, Anna and Steve again set off from London for the journey to Wisbech. The traffic was heavy and by the time they exited the M11 and were on two lane roads, it was a nightmare of lorries, not to mention the odd tractor. Making it by the skin of their teeth, the pool car pulled into the carpark at five minutes to six. They were greeted by an overly anxious Danny

Mulberry who had been frantically pacing up and down in fear that after making all of these arrangements, the London officers were going to be a no-show.

"Thank the Lord! I had visions of having to walk in there and cancel. We best get a move on before they change their minds."

Inside, Anna, Steve and the Chief Inspector sat behind a table on a raised makeshift stage so that they were visible to everyone. In all honesty, after scanning the room Anna was pleasantly surprised at the turnout. Chief Mulberry began by thanking them all and then slowly and with as much care as possible, he revealed the reason for the meeting. A couple of the women shed a tear when the child was mentioned but it wasn't until Danny explained that they had good reason to suspect that all of the victims came from an Eastern European background that a plethora of gasps were heard before the room then fell deathly silent. Suddenly a man stood up, his face was full of rage and his voice clearly rose as he spoke.

"Why our people? Why not your people and how do you even know they are our people?"

Everyone who had attended nodded vigorously and most began to murmur under their breath but obviously Anna couldn't make out what was being said. Briskly standing up, she knew she had to take back control of the situation and fast!

"Ladies and gentlemen, I am Detective Inspector Draycott from the Metropolitan Police Department. I am sorry to be the bearer of such grave news and I can only hazard a guess at how you are all feeling after hearing about these atrocities. In answer to your question Sir, we simply do not know why. I am here tonight to make you aware what has happened and could possibly happen again. Why do we suspect that the victims were Eastern European? Because of the stomach contents found during the autopsies."

There were several audible gasps from the small audience and even though Anna knew the sentence would shock some, she just couldn't see any other way of explaining.

"I am so sorry to cause you all further upset but simply, those are the facts. Now I strongly urge that if any one of you hears anything within your community that could have any connection to these cases, to come forward straight away and it doesn't matter how small or insignificant that information is. Chief Inspector Mulberry will be available to speak to you at all times. As the officers got up to leave, the room remained silent and the man who had spoken up a few minutes earlier gently nodded his head as Anna passed by. Walking to their car the Chief continued to hold onto the open door after Anna had climbed inside.

"What you said in there, about it happening again?

I could tell by your expression that you think that's a real possibility."

"Indeed I do Sir, personally I think we could have a serial killer on our hands and if that's the case, God help us all. I'll wait to hear from you Chief and when I do, I'm praying for good news and you not telling me that you have yet another body on your hands. Goodnight."

As the car pulled out of the carpark Danny Mulberry was still in shock regarding tonight's discussion and the Inspector's news from two days earlier. This was turning out to be the biggest case he had ever been involved in, even if he and his team were not first chair it was still a big thing for the Chief Inspector. If he had a choice would he have wanted to be in charge? Definitely not and thankfully that job had already been taken by Detective Inspector Anna Draycott and she was welcome to it as far as he was concerned.

CHAPTER FIFTEEN
Two weeks later

It could never be said that the investigation was gaining momentum because nothing could have be further from the truth. There were no witness statements and really nowhere further to go, at least for the time being. Anna was having sleepless nights worrying that this would be her last case before retirement and instead of going out in a blaze of glory, she would leave the station with her head hung low, feeling nothing but a failure. Deciding to go over all of the notes that they had to date, she shut herself away in her office and told everyone on her team that under no circumstances whatsoever was she to be disturbed. Two hours later and with paperwork strewn all over her desk she was still at a dead end and to top it off, there was now an annoying knock at the door even after she'd given strict instructions to be left alone.
"Enter!"
Drew Payton poked his head around the corner, just enough so that she was able to see who it was. After his previous dressing down from her he didn't want to be in the line of fire should she vent her displeasure and kick off again.
"What! I thought I told you I was not to be disturbed?"
"I know Ma'am but the Chief wants to see you in

his office like yesterday!"

Anna sighed loudly enough, for the rookie detective to hear and then closing the folder that she'd been studying, stood up and walked out of the room. This was all dragging on for far too long and she was only too aware that soon enough heads would begin to roll, for all she knew she could be about to be replaced, maybe that's what the Chief wanted? Cagily knocking on his door, for once she waited to be invited inside.

"Come!"

Taking a deep breath, Anna cleared her throat, stood up straight and after nervously turning the handle, stepped inside to meet her fate.

"You wanted to see me Sir?"

Lou Garnet momentarily stared at her without speaking and to Anna he looked as if he'd lost a fiver and found a penny. Always such a strong leader, he now resembled a lost soul at the end of his tether.

"If it's about the case, then we really are doing all that we can Sir. My team have…………."

"It's not about the case Anna. Please, sit down for a moment."

Suddenly her guard was dropped and for some strange reason she felt incredibly vulnerable. It wasn't a feeling she was used to, nor liked very much but doing as she'd been asked, Anna took a seat on the opposite side to her superior. Chief

Garnet didn't stay seated and standing up from his leather swivel chair, he walked around his desk and slowly lent against its corner. They were now less than two feet apart and Anna could feel the dryness of fear as it slowly began to invade her mouth.
"I am so sorry sweetheart but I have some terrible news to break to you."
Anna stared wide eyed in her boss's direction. Her brow was creased in confusion as she desperately tried to think of what on earth he was going to say. For starters, he had never referred to her as sweetheart, oh there had been times outside of work when he'd dropped the formalities of rank but sweetheart? It almost felt as if he was trying to get close to her in some way, almost like a friend.
"There's no easy way to say this so I'll just get to the point. Jake sadly passed away earlier today. It appears he had a heart attack just as he entered Bank Station at around about ten this morning. Staff called emergency services but there was nothing anyone could do and he was pronounced dead at the scene."
Anna nervously laughed, what on earth was he on about?
"Don't be ridiculous, we had breakfast together only a short while ago and we're out to dinner tonight, it's business but at least we're going out. Jake wants me to wear my purple dress as it's his favourite. It's at the Shard and I'm so excited, so

you see he can't have died."
Suddenly and without warning she began to sob uncontrollably, loud howling sounds emitted from the Chief's office and everyone in the communal space outside naturally stopped what they were doing and stared towards the closed door. Lifting her to her feet, Lou Garnet pulled her to him and gently cradled the back of her head as the wracking tears of pain continued. Carrying the day's mail, Drew Payton approached the office and was about to knock when he was stopped dead in his tracks by at least five raised voices.
"No!!!!!!"
He turned to look at his fellow officers in total bewilderment but was met by completely blank expressions from all in the room. Even Drew, naive and immature Drew, knew not to go any further. It was a long couple of minutes before Anna finally composed herself enough to stand back from the Chief's embrace. Taking a seat she stared achingly into her boss's face.
"What do I do now?"
"Well not a lot at the moment, there will obviously have to be a post-mortem and……."
"I don't mean that, I mean what do I do? Jake is, was, my world. We had so many plans for when I retire, so many places we wanted to visit and explore. So tell me, what the hell do I do now?"
"I don't know sweetheart but the last thing you

need right now is to be here. Steve Johnson is waiting to take you home."

"Do the team know?"

"I had to tell them Anna, I didn't want anyone to approach you once I'd broken the news, and they can be a tactless fucking bunch at best. Take some time and we are all here for you, you know that. Anything you need just call. Sergeant Johnson will drive you and I'll call and check in on you later today."

Nodding her head Anna left the office without another word. Steve was waiting with her coat and bag in his hand as she walked through the door and looking in the direction of her team, noticed her fellow detectives as they suddenly lowered their heads, engrossed in some mysterious paperwork that had miraculously appeared. The drive over to Holland Park was taken in silence and as they pulled up outside the house Steve's caring offer to go inside with his boss was politely declined.

"Thanks Steve but right now I need some time alone. I'm struggling to take any of it in so it's best if I'm on my own."

Closing the door behind her, Anna took off her coat and then slowly walked from room to room. His shoes were beside the bed, his toothbrush laid in the basin with the residue of paste adhering it to the porcelain, something she had always chastised him about. Again the tears came thick and fast and she so wished he was here now so that she could wrap her arms around him and scold him again for causing her so much pain. Walking back down the stairs she wandered into the kitchen and after pouring herself a large scotch, flopped down onto the sofa. The warm alcohol momentarily brought her a warm feeling but as her mind began to drift back over the last eighteen years the tears naturally began again. Dabbing at her eyes she gave a slight smile when she thought back to their first meeting.

Anna Burns had met Jake Draycott at a Christmas party in late December of 1999. Five years her senior he seemed so worldly and intelligent and Anna was smitten from the off. The couple had talked into the early hours and long after the party had ended. They seemed so in tune with each other, the conversation flowed so easily though neither would have been able to tell you what they had actually talked about. After a whirlwind romance lasting all but three months, they had tied the knot in a small intimate ceremony at St George's Church in Campden Hill and quickly settled down to married life. Initially Jake had been a trainee banker in the city and with his future all mapped out he was determined to give them both a lifestyle to be proud of. After several promotions and company changes and by the time the couple had reached their fifteenth wedding anniversary, true to his word, Jake had reached the top of the ladder in his career. As head of investments at the International Bank Dorfman Munich, who were a well-established and prominent company situated in Canary Wharf, the couple's future was well and truly secure. They had both longed for children, well actually it was Jake more than Anna but it just hadn't happened and Anna had accepted her barrenness without too much upset. In truth it was probably for the best, as they were both so dedicated to their careers that there wouldn't really have been any room for an addition to the household.

When a trust fund set up by his late father matured and with an added mortgage which had a very favourable rate set by his employers, Jake was able to at last purchase their dream home. Renting for their entire married life, the two bedroom property on Royal Crescent in Holland Park was like a dream come true. It was only a small mews house, but traditional in every way and it had the added bonus of a garage which allowed Anna to have a car and drive into work each day, which strangely for London, could be achieved quicker than using the Underground. With money no object, Anna had furnished the property with the very best of designer goods and fabrics. Dinner parties for Jake's clients were commonplace and her life outside of the force was so very different to that of her colleagues. Holidays had always been spent in four and five star resorts and they had both been in good health and had recently been excited about their joint early retirement.

Once again making her way upstairs, Anna entered the spare bedroom that they used as a study and the giant map which Jake had recently hung on the wall now seemed to engulf the entire room. Brightly coloured pins denoted all of the countries they would hopefully be visiting and as she studied each and every one, the tears again began to fall. Sighing heavily, she slowly and methodically removed each pin, there was no way she would be travelling to their planned distant locations, at least not for the foreseeable future.

The Chief called a couple of hours later and having fallen asleep on the sofa Anna was woken by the sound of her phone. The pair talked for a few minutes but it was awkward as there was little in the way of comfort that he could offer. Rinsing out her glass in the kitchen Anna scanned the room. His gym bag sat in the corner and his diary rested against the fruit bowl, Jake, her Jake, was definitely messy and it was one of the things she loved about him, it was annoying at times but she wouldn't have changed him for the world. Now she decided to go upstairs, it was where she felt closest to him and his smell still lingered on the towels and sheets.

Climbing into bed, Anna laid in the darkness just staring up at the ceiling and hoping for sleep to come, a sleep she actually prayed she wouldn't wake up from.

Her prayers weren't answered and she woke when the morning sunlight entered through a chink in the curtains. For a moment she wasn't quite sure if it had all been a bad dream but when she glanced over at the plump, unused bed pillow beside her, she knew that it was all too real. Chief Garnet had informed her last night that the post-mortem would be carried out today and that she was free to make all the necessary arrangements but she just couldn't face it. Instead she pulled the covers over her head and didn't get up until she heard someone banging on the front door at just before noon. Peeking through a gap in the curtains in the vain hope of not being seen, she saw that it was Beth Saunders and when the detective again began to knock, only this time with a little more force, Anna knew she wasn't getting rid of the young woman any time soon. With heavily laden footsteps she descended the stairs. Opening the front door there was no greeting, in fact she didn't speak a single word as she turned her back and walked through into the kitchen. Beth followed behind and placed her bag onto the floor as Anna put the kettle on.
"Chief sent you?"

"Something like that."

"Well there was no need I'm fine. Coffee?"

"Yes please. The Guv thought you might welcome a hand when it came to the arrangements Ma'am." Placing two steaming mugs down onto the breakfast bar Anna climbed onto one of the high stools and beckoned Beth to join her.

"I suppose I do actually, that's if you don't mind? And please Beth, call me Anna, we're not on duty now."

The request felt strange and several times the young woman slipped back and had to correct herself but by the end of the day and when everything was at last in place the pair really seemed more like old friends than senior and junior work colleagues. The autopsy report was finally issued later that day and luckily Beth was still with Anna when she went to collect the death certificate. Jake's report listed catastrophic myocardial infarction as the cause of death.

"A heart attack but he was as fit as a fiddle."

"It's often the way Anna, no one really knows what's going on inside of a person's body."

"I know but he went to the gym, followed a healthy diet, in fact he was always having a go at me about all the fatty food I ate. I just want this nightmare to stop Beth, I feel like I'm on a merry-go-round of grief that will never ever stop."

"Time Anna, time is the only healer. May I ask a

question?"
Anna nodded for her detective to continue.
"Don't you have any family, I mean I'm more than happy to be here but at times like these we usually rely on our loved ones to see us through."
"No I don't. My mum raised me alone after my dad died when she was six months pregnant with me and she never had any other kids. Her family were estranged so I never got to know them and she lost contact with my dad's side pretty soon after he died. She's in a care home now with early onset dementia, so apart from Jake I have, had, no one. That makes him sound as if he's still here but I can't get used to talking in the past tense."
St George's, the same church they had been married in was booked for ten days' time. Save for the ones arranged by the Met, the only flowers Anna wanted on the coffin was a single solitary long stemmed red rose.

The service and cremation passed without event and after a few drinks at the up market bar 'Mitre' on Holland Park Road, Anna soon found herself back at the house and feeling more alone than ever. Hours quickly turned into days and the days swiftly passed into weeks. She didn't clean, hardly ate and had little interest in life in general. Beth would pop in whenever she got the chance and she couldn't be off noticing the obvious decline in her boss. Finally

she decided that enough was enough and on her day off, arrived at the Mews armed with a bag of shopping and cleaning supplies. Anna wearily opened the front door and taking a seat at the breakfast bar, watched as the young detective willingly cleaned away dirty plates and numerous empty wine bottles. Next she unloaded the groceries and set about preparing some sort of a meal. When a plate of Spaghetti Bolognese was placed in front of Anna, the aromas wafting up made her realise just how hungry she was. Ten minutes later and with a full stomach she momentarily stared at her guest before speaking.
"I didn't ask you to do any of this."
"I know you didn't Ma'am."
"I told you Beth, it's Anna!"
Beth took a seat beside the grieving widow and gently took hold of her hand.
"It was, but now it's back to protocol. It's time to get back to business because if you don't, you will disappear so far into your own grief, that there won't be any way back. I'll tell the Chief you'll be back at work next week but I'm sure he'll call you before then."
It wasn't so much of a question but more a statement and Anna strangely didn't argue. Beth Saunders grabbed her bag and before Anna had a chance to attempt a discussion, Beth left the house. Anna was stunned but the more she thought about

it, the more she had to accept that her detective was right. This was no way to live and something Jake most definitely wouldn't have wanted for her. From what Beth had revealed they were no nearer wrapping up the case and Anna realised that she missed her work far more than she cared to admit. Sitting alone in the kitchen Anna Draycott made a decision, it was time to get back to work, solve the case and forge some kind of a new life for herself, whatever that entailed.

CHAPTER SIXTEEN

With a population of just under 3 million, Lithuania, according to Credit Suisse Global Wealth Report 2019, was amongst Europe's highest income groups. Sadly that isn't the case for many of the population as four thousand children in Lithuania are still living in large-scale orphanages and their ranks are swelled by at least a thousand new arrivals each and every year. Approximately 90% of these children still have at least one surviving parent. Lack of community-based services and a non-existent support system for parents, these families are not preserved and the children are hidden away behind closed doors. Many Lithuanians have emigrated in search of a higher standard of living. According to national statistics, the population of Lithuania has fallen by about 180,000 since it joined the EU in 2004. The emigration of parents means that children are often placed into care institutions. The violence found in Lithuanian society at large also affects children and alcohol abuse is a real problem, primarily in rural areas. For one family in particular, this fact carried on being and was completely ignored by all but a handful, especially those that had the power to change what was happening to one sweet innocent little girl.

Punžonys, a tiny village in the east of Lithuania and

close to the border with Belarus, was the home of father and daughter Benas and Ioana, Andris. Benas's wife had passed away when Ioana was just six years old and not long after that her father, in an attempt to drown his sorrows, turned to drink. Benas soon became known as the village drunk and even though several of the locals would look out for his small child, they all had their own families to provide for so more often than not she was left to her own devices. Tending house the best she could, Ioana would at times resort to begging in order to put food on the table. She was often dirty but no one at her school questioned why and by the time she reached secondary school her father had begun to regularly beat her for no reason. Benas was frustrated with his life and the loss of his wife and at times he would take that frustration out on his daughter both by beating and sexually abusing her but it was never rape, even Benas wasn't that stupid. He would force her to perform fellatio and when he had reached satisfaction he would lash out at her, as if everything, even his sorry pathetic excuse of a life was her fault. There was no escape and in the end she would just do exactly as she was told in the vain hope of escaping without being thrashed.

Her nightmare of a life was relentless and continued until Ioana's fifteenth birthday when she was able to secure a part time job cleaning for Mrs Janina

Gabrys, the wife of the local doctor, who's profitable practise covered a vast area of the countryside. It was soon pretty obvious to Janina that the girl was a hard worker and so most days she would leave Ioana to complete her tasks without supervision. Her work was more than acceptable and for Ioana the money came in handy. Every day after school Ioana would trudge in all weathers over to the poshest house in the village and scrub and polish for three or four hours. She was continually exhausted and her school work suffered because of it but it was worth it not having to have to perform those disgusting things on her father anymore, as she gave the majority of her wages to him. The payments weren't given out of the kindness of her heart or a feeling of duty that she had to contribute, her ulterior motive was simple, hopefully he would get so drunk he would be incapable of anything and so leave her alone and for the most part her plan worked.

Holding onto just a couple of euros for herself Ioana saved for almost eighteen months and just before her seventeenth birthday she finally had enough for a passport. Forging her father's signature, as she still needed his consent, her plan was to carry on working until she had saved enough to leave this godforsaken village once and for all, it might take her a couple of years but she was prepared for that. After an unexpected turn of events, things really happened far quicker than she'd anticipated but she wasn't about to look a gift horse in the mouth when six months later the Gabrys went away for a long weekend. Janina asked Ioana if she would come in over the weekend to do a little extra cleaning and to feed the cat. It was music to Ioana's ears, the chance to boost her escape fund and also to get away from her father. With the freedom of not getting caught, she poked around the house looking in drawers and cupboards that she didn't usually get the chance to explore. The Gabrys were certainly doing well for themselves, fine clothes hung in the wardrobes and the sideboard groaned with expensive imported alcohol. For some reason and she didn't know why, Ioana lifted the mattress in the master bedroom and gasped out loud when her eyes fell upon a bundle of stashed money. There was no need for it to be here, Lithuania may have been a bit behind the times but they did have banks, unless the money was illegal in some way? Ioana seized her opportunity, she hated stealing but knew this was her only chance of an early escape and she justified her actions by swearing to herself that when she got settled she would repay every Euro. Quickly heading home she packed a case and that afternoon took the only bus of the day to Vilnius. Purchasing a one way ticket, to what she saw as freedom, Ioana travelled to Belarus and the airport.

After landing at Gatwick and feeling totally lost, Ioana asked for advice and was directed by a kindly customs officer towards the express train to St Pancras. Departing the carriage a little under an hour later she was shocked at the amount of people who all seemed to be going in different directions. Slightly panicking and with no particular place to go, Ioana just wandered aimlessly and somehow ended up next door at King's Cross. The extensive restorations might have been completed in 2013 but the same people still used the station on a daily basis and many of them were of a dubious nature. Ioana's head was spinning with the constant sound of muffled announcements coming over the tannoy system, whistles being blown and train doors closing. Suitcases were noisy as their wheels were dragged over joints in the concrete platform and the enormous amount of commuters queuing for tickets, or eating takeout food as they rushed in all directions, did little to calm her nerves.

As usual, Del Manning was loitering around the station looking for easy prey. Earning a living from young, vulnerable girls, he would befriend them, give them a roof over their heads and then swiftly have them working the streets for him. He never kept a girl for long as his clients liked them young and a street Tom's shelf life was short. They soon gained the hardened brassy exterior that set them

apart from decent women and of late even the curb crawlers were getting fussy about where they dipped their cocks. Spying his next victim, Del allowed Ioana to pass by him and then running up behind her bumped heavily against her back.
"Oh, I'm so sorry sweetheart! Are you okay?"
Whether it was the stress of travelling or the unfamiliar surroundings but Ioana instantly burst into tears. Bingo, Del had a live one!
"Don't cry babe, I'm really sorry but I tripped. Let me buy you a coffee as a way of an apology."
Nodding her head Ioana followed the stranger out of the station and across Euston Road. They continued to walk but when he turned down St Judd Street, Ioana started to worry. Del sensed her footsteps slowing and turning gave her a huge smile.
"It's okay babe, I know the place is a little off the beaten track but it's nice and quiet and they do a killer coffee."
Entering the Half Cup café he guided Ioana to a table in the corner. Sharon Player was the waitress for this shift and she eyed Del suspiciously. Not exactly a regular, he came in often enough and always with a different young girl. He was well dodgy, Sharon was in no doubt about that fact but unless she could prove he was up to no good, then it wasn't worth risking her job by making accusations.

"Two cappuccinos please darlin'. So sweetheart, what's your name?"

Ioana told the stranger and even went on to explain, although not in great detail, how and why she had arrived in London. Every word she spoke made him happier and happier. This one was really young looking and would be a good earner but he needed to tread carefully to get her onside.

"You got any digs sorted yet?"

Although her command of English was pretty good, she didn't have a clue what he meant and it was obvious.

"Digs? A roof and a bed? Where are you staying?"

Her face seemed to fill with panic, it wasn't something she'd thought too much about but now having seen how busy London was, she really didn't have a clue what to do next. As her eyes once again filled with tears, Ioana vigorously shook her head.

"Don't look so worried, you can stay with me. It's okay, you can trust me. Actually I've had to help out several youngsters in the past, that's why they call me the Saint of King's Cross."

Ioana didn't trust this Del one bit but what choice did she really have? After buying her plane ticket there wasn't a great deal of money left and what she did have would need to last her. An hour later they arrived in Soho. His tiny one bedroom flat, situated at the rear of 'One Hour Dry Cleaning' on Wardour

Street, was dank, dirty and absolutely stank of stale food and tobacco as soon he opened the door. Nervously entering the front room, Ioana instantly regretted her decision, the ceiling was low and water stained and held only a single light bulb. You couldn't swing a cat in the tiny kitchen and the sink was piled high with dirty crockery and pots, so dirty in fact that they must have been there for days if not weeks judging by the green mould that had begun to form. The tap constantly dripped causing water to bounce off of the pots and pans and splash onto the floor but when Ioana tried to turn it off it only got worse. The bedroom was no better, filthy sheets and bedding which smelled of urine and Ioana could have sworn she saw a small rat scurry away when she walked into the room. At the moment Del seemed okay but he wasn't that much of a gentleman, to offer her his bed. The lumpy old couch was the only place to lay her head and though doubtful that she would get much sleep, she supposed it wouldn't hurt, at least for tonight. Woken just before six the next morning by the constant sound of hissing from the linen steam press in the dry cleaners next door, Ioana tried to bury her head under the cushions but the acrid stench was even worse than the noise, so she gave up and decided to see if Del had anything in for breakfast. Ioana wasn't hopeful nor was she disappointed, the cupboards save for a couple of chipped mugs, were completely bare.

A week later and when she'd finally managed to find a room in a house share, which was only marginally better than Del's place but whose other occupants had generously allowed her to owe the upfront rent until she got work, it was thankfully time to leave. Ioana was packing her case when she suddenly realised that her passport was missing. Frantically unpacking again and after all of her clothing had been meticulously felt and then shaken, she realised that it had gone. Walking into the small front room which was now far cleaner than when she had arrived, she confronted the man, who up until this point had treated her well.
"Del? I can't find my passport, have you seen it?"
Reaching into his pocket he held up the small burgundy booklet with the Lithuanian coat of arms emblazed on the front cover.
"You mean this one?"
Ioana went to grab it but he moved his hand swiftly out of her reach.
"Not so fast darlin'! Now you've had free food and board for a week and you need to pay me back, I ain't a fuckin' charity sweetheart. I don't know what it's like where you come from but in this country, we all have to pay our own way."
"Of course and I'm so sorry I didn't think, how much do I owe you Del?"

"Two grand should cover it."
Ioana gasped, she had just under four hundred pounds to her name. Suddenly, it all fell into place and even at such a young age, she knew the score. "I haven't got that kind of money and you know it! You really are the scum of the earth."
Instantly Del Manning was on his feet, the kind helpful man that had come to her rescue was no more, as he landed a punch so forcefully into Ioana's stomach that she doubled over unable to breath for several seconds.
"Then you will work it off because if you don't, then the passport stays with me! If I contact the authority they will deport you without a passport, they might even lock you up, you silly little bitch!"
Ioana could feel the tears as they began to roll down her cheeks, she was trapped with no means of escape. And so began Ioana Andris' wretched introduction into prostitution. After taking his cut, the paltry figure Del charged for her left just a few pounds and she knew that it would take years to settle the debt. His clientele were mostly construction workers staying in the city while they were contracting on one of the many large building sites that seemed to be continually springing up all across the city. Many were married men with wives and children back home, wives who were unaware of their husband's antics. Some of the men were even sadistic towards Ioana, as they took out their

pent-up frustration at being separated from their families but Del never muttered a word, just so long as they didn't mark his girl's pretty face.

Early one morning Maggie McKay received a call from Dennis Havers. The Judge was desperate to make a film and even though it was at short notice, he required a young fresh faced girl that very night and was prepared to pay over the odds if she could accommodate his request. As ever, Maggie wasn't about to turn down cold hard cash and informed Dennis that everything would be ready and in place by eight. Summoning Asti Marku, the two walked into her office and Ken Voss slowly shook his head. The pair of them were up to no good, that was for sure. He hated Asti with a vengeance but even Ken knew better than to ever voice his opinion when it came down to the evil bastard that did Maggie's bidding. The man was feared by most and whispers had spread long ago that he was a cold blooded killer. Ken couldn't deny that he had done his own fair share during his time with the firm, Brice had made sure of that but the victims were always either from another firm or had caused the McKay's grief in some way. What Ken had heard about Asti was completely different, the man would kill a grandmother for a fee and by all accounts he had on one occasion, when an overly greedy son wanted to get his hands on his inheritance early. As Maggie

went to close the door she saw Ken staring at her.
"Thank you Kenny, that will be all!"
Walking towards her visitor, she was unaware that Asti was just days away from leaving and that her lucrative alternative side line was about to be severely affected.
"Asti I need a girl and I need her tonight. She mustn't be any older than say eighteen or nineteen or at least not look any older and has to be as clean as you can get, don't want to be giving the punters a dose now do we? Any ideas?"
Asti raised his eyebrows and it didn't go unnoticed. She knew this was a tall order at such short notice so making her way over to the safe she removed a manila envelope and placing it onto her desk, waited for him to pick it up.
"There's fifteen grand in there to help you sweeten the deal. If there's any cash left then it's yours, obviously on top of your usual fee of course."
Nodding his head, Asti simply picked up the package, walked from the room and the fate of Ioana Andris was sealed without her even knowing.
Del was snoozing on the old sofa when Asti tapped on the door and he wasn't best pleased at being disturbed before noon.
"Oi! Answer the door you lazy whore!"
Ioana emerged from the bedroom in her dressing gown, her hair was dirty and hung lankly on her shoulders. Now mentally beaten, she had lost all

pride in herself . Trudging barefoot over the dirty sticky carpet that covered the small hallway, she wearily opened up. Ioana didn't speak, she just left the door ajar and went back to the bedroom. As Asti entered the front room, Del was off of the sofa in seconds. He had only dealt with the Albanian a couple of times in the past but he was only too aware of what this man was capable of and the fear was evident on his face.

"Mr Marku! Long time no see, what can I do for you?"

"I need a girl for tonight, the one who let me in will do."

"Of course my friend, what shall we say? Two hundred an hour any good?"

"She won't be returning to you."

"Woah! Hold on there a minute my friend, that one's a good little earner, I can't just be giving her to you."

In reality, Del Manning knew that he really didn't have a choice in the matter, so when Asti held out a bundle of cash it softened the blow somewhat.

"Here's five grand for your trouble."

"Oh I don't know about that, I mean I stand to lose far more than that over the course of the next few weeks. True, she'll wear herself out pretty soon but the dirty little slut loves cock so much, that I'm coining it in at the moment brother."

His words were far from the truth, Ioana hated

every single man that forcibly entered her and Del insisted on as many punters a night as he could find. After receiving a beating so severe that he had cracked one of her ribs just for complaining, she knew to never refuse him again.

"Okay, six but that's my final offer."

Del greedily snatched the cash from Asti's hand as he nodded his head.

"Have her ready by seven. She needs to look innocent so no trashy underwear and not a word to anyone, or you know what the payback will be."

Del really did know and again nodded his head, only this time it was with vigour. It would be a shame to lose his golden egg but there would always be more prey arriving and he also had her passport to sell which would fetch a decent amount, after all, he had a sneaking suspicion that she wouldn't be needing it again.

Ioana was told to wash thoroughly and dress down in jeans and a blouse. Her hair was tied back in a ponytail and she was given instructions to act very coy like she was still a virgin. The knock came on the door at exactly seven that night and following the stranger from earlier, she nervously climbed into the van beside him. Ioana attempted conversation but when Asti only glared at her in a menacing manner, she immediately shut up. Arriving at the arches, she was shown into the special room that had been constructed specifically for filming. Spying the camera Ioana became uneasy, this wasn't what she was used to and there was no way she would ever allow herself to be filmed, she would rather die than risk anyone back home seeing her naked and performing sex acts. A short while later the Judge and his cronies walked in and save for a black velvet cloak, Michael Lemming was completely naked. Immediately he strolled over to inspect the merchandise and grabbing one of Ioana's small pert breasts he squeezed hard making her cry out in pain. Happy with what had been supplied he pulled on his gimp mask and moved his face only inches from hers. "Good evening my dear, shall we get started?" Roughly taking hold of her hand, the Judge then dragged her over to the bed and pushed her down onto the polythene. Dennis Havers casually passed over a cut throat razor and as the brutal slashing began and the camera began to roll, Ioana Andris screamed but only for a few fleeting seconds.

Back at the arches in the early hours of the morning, Asti began the dismemberment and much like before, removed Ioana's teeth and fingertips before setting off to dispose of her remains. It has actually begun to feel like a game to him and in the weeks between kills he was always on the lookout for places to dump human remains and with Ioana he had definitely struck lucky. On the day of the planned murder Asti had been driving through Manor Park and had spotted three grave diggers as they left off for the day. Parking up the van he entered the cemetery and after a couple of minutes looking about he spied the large mound of earth draped in an artificial grass sheet. This would be perfect and returning in the early hours, he removed his spade and holdall from the van. Jumping down he dug a second shallow grave below the one due for a burial. Placing the legs, arms and head into the hole Asti then covered it over with a light topping of soil. For a brief moment he contemplated getting rid of the entire body this way but thought better of it but it had had given him a great idea to dispose of the torso and driving over to Hackney, he hauled his large bag and spade over the wall into the now disused Abney Park cemetery. Overgrown and seemingly unloved Asti dug a hasty shallow grave and deposited what remained of Ioana's body into the ground.

After getting only a couple of hour's sleep he hadn't been able to help himself and was back at the cemetery to see what would happen. He didn't have to wait too long, the ten am committal for ninety years old Reginald Clements began exactly on time. Taking an inconspicuous viewing spot behind a cluster of small trees so he wouldn't be seen, Asti watched the old man's coffin as it was gently lowered into the ground, perfectly covering most of the remains of Ioana Andris.

CHAPTER SEVENTEEN

On Friday morning, at seven on the dot the alarm burst into life with an ear-splitting and uninvited rendition of Bon Jovi's 'Living on a prayer'. Anna groaned loudly, rolled over and slapped the mute button on top of the digital display. The small silver clock clattered to the floor and she sighed heavily. She was due to return to work and even though as late as yesterday she had welcomed the idea, today she'd changed her mind. Anna knew she wouldn't be able to handle the continuous round of 'I'm so sorry' or 'We've been thinking of you'. It was too soon, even after almost six long months it was too damn soon. To ease her back in it had been decided by the Chief that Anna should do her first shift on a Friday, that way if things became too much she would at least have the weekend to get to grips with her emotions. Opening her eyes she stared up at the ceiling for a second before rolling over to his side of the bed, a side where the sheets were neat and crisp but also incredibly cold. For a moment she smiled when her eyes fell on the framed photo on top of the bedside cabinet. It had been taken three years earlier when they'd spent an idyllic week camping up in the Scottish highlands. The little village of Dornie had been beautiful and the thin scattering of locals had provided the couple with fresh eggs and milk, how she wished she could turn the clocks back even for just one day. Whispering under her breath, Anna asked the same question that she'd asked every morning for the past six months 'Why did you leave me'?

Today, even the short trip to the ground floor was mentally agonising and she hastily ate her breakfast with hardly a pause. Not due in the office until ten, she still had ample time left and now Anna knew she was going to end up twiddling her thumbs until it was time to leave. Maybe a lengthy hot shower would help her to relax a bit? God only knew she needed something and for a second she momentarily considered making a joint from the small stash that Jake had kept for their weekend recreational use. What an absurd idea, turn up on her first day back at work stoned! Anyway, it was probably long past its sell by date and wouldn't give her any relief, just cause her to cough in a wracking way that always had him in stitches. Every single thing she did, no matter how small, always ended up with her thinking of Jake and as the tears once again began to fall, Anna stepped into the shower.

Finally setting off at just before nine, the traffic was heavy but she was so used to the stopping and starting being part of her daily routine, that it didn't bother her in the least. Eleven miles and forty four minutes later, she at last pulled into the small rear carpark at Tottenham Police station and breathed a sigh of relief at the sight of the last remaining space that she knew would have definitely disappeared in the next few minutes. Apart from the Chief's designated spot, it was strictly first come, first served and more often than not she would be forced to find a pay and display. In the rear view mirror Anna checked her face for any tell-tale signs of tears and then making her way over to the building, she walked through the automatic electronic doors. As she swiped her security identification card and entered the inner sanctum of the station, it was suddenly business as usual. The place was a hive of activity and for a moment she stopped and surveyed her surroundings, a building she'd spent the last ten years of her life working in and which now felt so strange and alien to her. Climbing the stairs she headed straight for the Chief's office. The door was ajar and as she entered Lou Garnet looked up and smiled.

"Morning Anna and I must say, it's great to see you back. I won't bother asking how you are as we both already know the answer to that one."

"Thank you Sir. It's good to be back, I just need………"

Her voice trailed off and momentarily she was once again lost in her grief. Chief Garnet gave her a few seconds but then decided it was best not to allow her to wallow in self-pity, no matter how much it was warranted.

"I don't mind admitting, we're between a rock and a fucking hard place where this bastard case is concerned Anna. Unfortunately we are no further forward with our inquiries, whatsoever! Nearly eight bloody months and not a sniff of who is to blame. The tabloids are having a field day and since the fourth and fifth bodies surfaced I'm getting daily calls and fucking emails from the Superintendent's second in command, not to mention the Met's press office."

"Two more?!"

"Yeah, we've managed to keep it under wraps for the time being but we've only got hours, a day at best before the news breaks. For now I can cope with all of that and I want you to take a couple of days to familiarise yourself with anything that has arisen since your leave, although I can assure you, that won't be very much. Don't leave any stone unturned Anna and it goes without saying that you have anything you need and as many bodies as you want at your disposal. We have to stop this bastard before he strikes again!"

"Who's been leading since I've been off."

"Eric Barnes temporarily came out of retirement."

Anna smiled, she and Eric went way back and she'd been crestfallen the day he'd retired two years earlier. Eric was only forty three but looked a good

ten years older. He had given his all to the force over the years and sadly the twenty years' service he'd notched up, showed in every line on his face.
"I don't want to step on anyone's toes Sir. I don't want them all to think I've just waltzed back in here to take over, like I'm demeaning all of their efforts."
Chief Garnet walked from around his desk and gently placed his hand on Anna's shoulder. Putting Eric Barnes to one side, she was one of the finest detectives he had ever known or had the pleasure to work with.
"I can assure you that will not be the case. Eric knew from the off that he was just a stand in until you returned, as did the rest of your team come to that. Once you've settled in I want you to pay a visit to the Lab? Seems there was a problem with the post-mortems on the two bodies that turned up last week, well, one last week and the other a couple of days ago. Some technical issue but it's all sorted now, anyway they worked into the night and the results on the first victim are in, so I want you to go and pay Michael Hanks a visit. He should have completed the second autopsy by now, so I'm praying that he can at least give us something. While you were away, Michael requested the bodies from Wisbech and Cambridge be sent up, I'm not sure why but he may have further news for us, you know the old sod, he's a slippery bugger at the best of times and will wait as long as he can to make his

announcement. Oh and Anna, try not to piss him off again!"

Anna nodded knowingly and then leaving the office, headed in the direction of the incident room. It was like deja vu, her team with the added bonus of Eric Barnes, were still seated just the same as they had been on the first day of the investigation. It was like time had stood still, with very little having been added to the wipe boards.

"Morning everyone! Right, let's get down to work and solve this bloody case once and for all. Beth, bring me up to speed please."

Beth Saunders walked up to the boards, smiled warmly in her boss's direction and then began to go over everything they had learned to date but it really wasn't much. When she had finished talking, there was only silence. Anna sighed heavily before joining her detective at the front of the room. A sixth blank board stood beside the others and Anna began to write with the big black marker pen and with her back to the team, spoke as she did.

"Feel free to butt in at any time you lot. We need to brainstorm and a lot of what we're going to discuss will already have been covered several times before but I'm a firm believer in look, look and look again and sometimes something that's been staring you in the face might, just finally catch your eye. Right, order bodies have surfaced in?"

Carl Wilson was the first to speak but once he did, it

opened the floodgates for the others and they all began to talk at once.

"One at a time please you lot, or I won't be able to hear any of you.

"The little girl. Female A. Male B. Female C and lastly female D. So, what do we know about any of them?"

As her team began to add more and more, Anna scribbled furiously on the wipe board.

"All stomach contents were the remains of an Eastern European style diet. It should already have been done but just to be on the safe side, Beth check out any missing persons from the Eastern European community here in London. Before you all pull me up on that, I know two of the victims surfaced outside of the city but that doesn't mean that's where they actually resided."

Beth Saunders put her hand in the air.

"All of the victims including the child, had traces of semen in most of their orifices, several specimens of semen in fact."

"So we know whoever is doing this is not working alone. They are definitely serial killers but why? Are they all purely sexually motivated? If not, what else could be the motive?"

"Organ transplants!"

"Good Carl but that's already been noted. Has anyone been in contact with the city hospitals?"

The room instantly went silent.

"I've not come back to haul you over the coals for what has or hasn't been done okay? Let's all pull our fingers out and become the Ace team that I know we are capable of being. Carl, find out if anyone on the transplant lists has suddenly removed themselves and if so I want names, addresses, dates and the reason why. Steve, me and you need to pay Mike Hanks another visit. Eric, you can come as well, maybe you will pick up on something we are missing. The rest of you, heads down and let's catch the sick bastards before they strike again."

The drive over to St John's Wood was lengthy as the lunchtime traffic was heavy as usual, not to mention it was a Friday, Anna didn't know why but there was something about Fridays, there always seemed to be more vehicles on the road or maybe that's just the way it appeared. Anna hadn't been in contact with Mike since just before Jake's demise and for the first time ever, she hoped he would go easy on her as she really didn't want him reporting her on her first day back. Michael Hanks was at the top of his field not to mention he had a good ten years on the detective but that wasn't where the problem stemmed from. Five years earlier they had been at a weekend forensic conference, which for some strange reason the Chief had thought would be a good idea for Anna to attend. A weary and very drunk Michael Hanks had made a beeline for her and after her gentle rebuff, it had all gotten a little embarrassing. Anna had been willing to let the matter drop and file it as just a silly drunken mistake but Mike's ego simply wouldn't allow him to do the same, even though he had a wife of thirty plus years and if Janice had found out about his attempt at a one night stand, it would have cost him dearly, financially at least. At every given opportunity he would belittle the detective and she always responded, which only added fuel to the flames and caused heated arguments between the two. It was common knowledge at the station that there was no love lost between the forensic pathologist and Anna but no one knew the exact reason. As they exited the lift, Anna walked in front with Eric and Steve following close behind. No one spoke as they waited for the secure door to be opened and Anna was taken aback when Michael Hanks himself opened up.

"Good morning detectives."

"Morning Michael. The Chief says you may have something for us?"

"I do indeed, follow me."

Anna couldn't get over just how polite he was being and naturally her guard instantly went up, she wasn't and never would be, aware of the fact that Lou Garnet had telephoned ahead and had in no uncertain terms, warned Mike to go easy on her.

Anna didn't go in with a barrage of questions which was her normal method, this time she just waited to see what he had to say. The detectives took seats when offered while Mike Hanks retrieved a manila file from the cabinet, he was old school and always preferred to work from a hardcopy.

"Obviously you are aware that the two bodies, well just the torso's, that were recently discovered were found in very different locations. The first in a disused graveyard, hardly original but there was nothing rushed about it and I get the impression as the grave was dug so shallow and I might be wrong, that the culprit really didn't care if it was found or not. The second is far more interesting. Found in a dumped freezer on a small patch of wasteland just off the North Circular. Nothing of interest in the location, other than it's regularly used for fly tipping. I actually believe that the victim wasn't killed and disposed of there as she had been frozen. I carried out further tests and skin samples show that she could have been dead for many, many months. She may have been the last victim to be found but she could also have been the first poor soul to have lost her life. Anna turned and looked at Steve in utter disbelief before looking back in the direction of the pathologist.

"Is there any way of nailing down the order of the murders?"

"Afraid not, as three of them had been in the water

there's no way of knowing, so they could all have been around the same time. My personal gut feeling is that this last one was indeed the first, almost as if the killer simply didn't know what to do with her, or maybe he was just sloppy and hadn't honed his skills yet. Whatever the reason, out of all of them her torso is the best preserved and unlike the others, all of her internal organs are intact!"

Anna nodded her head but unfortunately they were still no further forward. Mike Hanks then slid a photograph across the table.

"I found the remnants of a tattoo at the top of her torso where her left arm would have joined the shoulder. It's a traditional embroidery pattern. These foreign designs differ greatly from those favoured in the United Kingdom and stem mainly from European folk art."

"So what are you actually saying Mike?"

"That it's almost certain the victim was Romanian. Actually I have had some real fun exploring this avenue of thought and I can also now tell you that in all probability, the male victim, recovered several months ago in Wisbech, was Latvian. He had a large tattoo running down the length of his spine. As you can imagine this got me really excited and I felt compelled to carry out further research. It seems the symbols are for each day of the week and specific to that country."

Mike Hanks handed over two enlarged images but they did nothing to excite her and all Anna could do was to again sigh heavily, something she seemed to be doing more and more of just lately. It didn't go unnoticed, in fact it somewhat irritated the pathologist.
"Well I'm sorry if I haven't given you what you want detective, I'm good but I can't miraculously magic up evidence out of thin air! I would have thought that seeing how you have so very little else at the moment, you would be grateful for any bloody morsels that I am able to throw your way!"
She hadn't realised that her feelings had been audible and now she would have to eat a large amount of humble pie, something she really could do without today. Playing on her personal circumstances, Anna felt guilty at using Jake's death but then she suddenly struggled to hold a grin inside that was so desperate to escape. Jake, her beautiful, wonderful Jake, would have found it absolutely hilarious.
"I'm Sorry Mike but it's my first day back after losing….."
Her willingness to show her vulnerability had him eating out of the palm of her hand and instantly he softened. To berate her any further, not to mention in front of witnesses, would have shown him in a very poor light and besides, he had to make allowances, she was after all only a woman and a

grieving one at that.

"Think nothing of it detective and might I just add, that all of us here at the Lab, would like to offer our condolences in your time of grief. It can't be easy for you."

"No, no it's not Michael and thank you for your understanding."

It worked and when they were all once again outside and out of earshot, Anna suddenly started to laugh out loud making Steve and Eric stare at each other in complete bewilderment.

"Something funny Guv, you sure you're alright?"

"Yes I'm fine Steve, I just played that twat for the fool that he is that's all. Hanks is a nasty piece of work at the best of times and he was obviously playing the concerned gentleman to a lowly woman in distress. Let's get back to the station, maybe someone has come up with something, though it'll be a miracle if they have."

CHAPTER EIGHTEEN

How on earth Bobby McKay had been able to keep his relationship with Diane a secret from Maggie, God only knew but keep it he had, well except for Ken Voss knowing but Bobby knew Uncle Kenny would never rat on him. Every day he was feeling more and more in love but every day Diane was taking him more and more for a ride. After he'd paid for her mother's fake funeral, Diane Buckle had upped her game and now she even had control of Bobby's credit card. Unbeknown to her, the freedom he had given her to spend what she liked would be her downfall.

Meanwhile, Ken Voss was growing increasingly disillusioned with Maggie and what she had turned the firm into. True, he wasn't privy to what went on in the secret room but he had a gut feeling that it was bad and could bring some serious trouble for all of them. Of late business had been slow, there were still several of the Tom's working the streets for the firm and the protection racket was as lucrative as ever but very little new business was coming their way and that alone bothered Ken big style. Maggie's mind just wasn't on the job and he had tried to talk to her but he was shouted down at every attempt. Her father would be turning in his grave if he knew how his Princess was running the firm into the ground, or at least that's how he saw things but there was absolutely nothing Ken could do about it. Lately his thoughts had been more and more on his old pal Philip Magarey, he missed the geezer so much. Known to all as Pup, the two men had been close for many years, well right back to when Harry Pimms had started the firm but Maggie had put poor old Pup out to pasture as soon as she'd taken over, so Ken had no one to confide in, well no one he could trust that is. Pup had been as straight as a die, he might not always have agreed with you but whatever you confided to him would never go any further. Old school and the reluctance to take orders from a woman had been his downfall and Ken had on various occasions tried to warn Pup that he was really skating on thin ice but it had all fallen on deaf ears. Now apart from Ken, the only other old timer, as they laughingly referred to themselves, was Albie Mitchell. The two men had now been in the firms employ for almost fifty years, both joining Harry as young innocent seventeen year olds but they were never what you would call bosom buddies. Albie had always tried to suck up to Harry and he did the same with Brice. It was different when Maggie took charge as she really didn't like him and had solely kept him on as he was, even in his advancing years, good with his fists when it mattered. Ken wished he could have shared his concerns over Bobby with Albie and sought out his advice but he just knew the man would run straight to Maggie and spill his guts.

Walking into the arches one Tuesday morning Ken was surprised to see Bobby seated at his desk. The youngster, well that's what he was compared to Ken's sixty four years, strangely had his head in his hands. Normally the kid would be smiling from ear to ear, waiting in excited anticipation for his uncle to arrive, so that he could share all that he'd got up to that past weekend. Ken strolled over and stopped but Bobby didn't raise his head even though Ken was more than aware that Bobby knew he was there.

"What's up Bobby boy?"

When Booby looked upwards, Ken could see that his honorary nephew had been crying and it was recent as the tears were still wet on his cheeks. Bobby didn't answer, all he could do was slowly shake his head and Ken knew that whatever was troubling the boy was serious, at least to Bobby McKay it was serious. This most certainly wasn't the place for a discreet heart to heart so, in a voice far more jovial than he actually felt, Ken made a suggestion.

"My stomach thinks my throat's been cut so I'm goin' round to Joyce's for my breakfast, want to join me son?"

Wiping his nose with the cuff of his jumper, Bobby

nodded and was on his feet in seconds.
"Anyone needs us, we'll be round Joyce's van!"
The two men walked along in silence until they reached Rope Walk Gardens on Christian Street. Situated at the edge of the play area, Joyce O'Leary ran a traditional burger van, in fact she was second generation and had worked alongside her late father for many years. Joyce knew all of the local villains, most of them used her services on a daily basis and when the council had tried to have her moved on a few years back under the ruse that they wanted to improve the overall appearance of the area, a few words in the right ear and her problems had disappeared overnight. Joyce was old school, anything she heard in the close proximity of her van stayed that way and her clientele appreciated her loyalty. A few times the Old Bill had tried to persuade her and not always in a friendly manner, to give them any information that she might be privy to, conversations she might have overheard or anything she might have possibly seen but it had always been met with a blank expression and the words 'I ain't no agony aunt sweetheart, all I do is serve burgers'.
"Mornin' Kenny love, what can I get ya?"
Joyce O'Leary was now in her early sixties but she had no intention of retiring. As far as she was concerned, her business was what kept her alive and she could often be heard telling punters that the

day she retired would be the day she popped her clogs.

"Usual darlin' and get the boy the same will you? I'll be seated at my regular table."

Joyce laughed out loud, the reference to his table sounded as if it would have been better suited to a fancy restaurant up West, instead of one of the green plastic garden tables that sat on either side of the serving hatch. The onions sizzling on the hotplate smelled fantastic, it was a trick Joyce regularly used if trade was slow, shove a bowl of onions on to fry and within minutes she would have a queue of salivating passers-by forming something approaching an orderly line. With two steaming mugs of tea and two double cheese burgers perched on a tray, she delivered the food personally to Ken's table.

"Especially for you! Freshly cooked and brewed to order!"

"Thanks babe."

Ken handed over a twenty and waved his hand in dismissal when Joyce said she would be back in a second with his change. It was the same scenario every day and the eight quid tip was always gratefully received and soon mounted up over the course of a week let alone a month. Never wanting to take the man for granted, Joyce had actually began to save Kenny's tips in a jar that sat beside the fridge and she almost had enough stashed up to buy a ticket to Benidorm, to visit her daughter and grandkids.

"So Bobby, are you goin' to tell me why the fuck you have a face like a smacked arse?"

Bobby swallowed the mouthful of burger which tasted really good and laid the rest of the overfilled bun down onto the table before sighing heavily.

"I gave my credit card to Di. She told me she needed some bits and bobs, lady stuff I think. Anyway, when I got home yesterday my credit card bill was waiting for me Uncle Kenny and Di's run me up a big debt. I ain't got access to my dad's money and I ain't got the cash to pay it off and I daren't ask Mags, she'll go ballistic. My dad left me money but she keeps a tight rein on it. Did you know I had a lot of money Uncle Kenny? I'm a rich man I am, that's what my Di says. Di wants to move into the house but I daren't tell her that Mags will never allow that, she treats Buxton Street as some kind of shrine and she's always on at me about cleaning and stuff. I'm in a right pickle Uncle Kenny really I am."

"Ain't this Di woman got any money of her own?"

"Nah, she only works a couple of hours in the afternoon so not much left over for any niceties or so she keeps tellin' me."

"So, how much are we talkin' about?"

"Fifteen."

"Fifteen fuckin' grand!?!"

Ken silently thought for a moment, he could tell Maggie but undoubtedly that would start world war III or, he could go and have a word with the gold digging bitch himself. He decided on the later but didn't share his decision with Bobby. Reaching into his trouser pocket he pulled out a wad of cash and handed it to his nephew.

"Here's a monkey, use that to make a payment and I'll sort you out some more next month. Have you got your credit card back?"

Bobby took another bite of his burger and at the same time anxiously shook his head.

"Fuckin' well do it then! I'll help you out this time Bobs but I ain't a bank and I sure as hell ain't fuckin' paying for your bit of stuff's luxuries. Understood?"

"I'll do my best Uncle Kenny but my Di is a force to be reckoned with and if she don't want to do somethin', nothin' will make her."

Bobby's last sentence cemented Ken's decision and later that day he would be paying the Buckle bitch a visit.

A little after four that afternoon Ken Voss left the arches, telling the others at the unit that he had a bit of business to deal with and wouldn't be back until tomorrow. Making his way to Madur Singh's corner shop, it didn't take Ken too long to find out that the slag had a flat on White's Row over in

Spitalfields. Madur knew exactly who Ken was and he offered up the information without question. Diane had been getting out of hand lately, the woman had no morals and was blatantly open regarding what was going on with the McKay kid. Madur hated what she was doing to young Bobby, maybe she was about to be taught a lesson, whatever the reason, he had no intention of forewarning her regarding her impending visitor.

The large block of well over forty flats was run down to say the least even though it was owned by the borough and Ken wondered what on earth Bobby must have thought the first time he came here because he certainly wasn't used to this type of abode. The family home on Buxton Street may have been Victorian in construction but that was where it ended. Everything was high tech and high gloss, Brice had been so particular and Bobby had been brought up in the lap of luxury. The outside of the building was in dire need of a repaint and the bullet holes in the concrete, obviously from a past drive by shooting told him all he needed to know. Pushing on the main entrance door he walked straight inside as the video entry system had long since given up the ghost. The main stairwell smelled of stale urine and was liberally littered with bottles and food wrappers. A couple of the ground floor front doors had been boarded up to deter squatters and one

door even had a metal grill, so that the door could be opened but access denied if the occupant didn't like the look of someone, or to delay a raid, Ken guessed it was a crack house. Climbing the concrete staircase to the upper landing was no better, the whole place reeked and the open balcony was full of clothes hanging out to dry and screaming kids running up and down the concrete walkways.
'Come dine with me' was almost over and Diane Buckle was engrossed. It was one of her favourites and she hated being disturbed when it was on so when she suddenly heard a knock at the door she spoke out to an empty room 'Who the fuck is that, can't a person have five fuckin' minutes to themselves?' Reluctantly she hauled herself from the sofa, now she was going to miss finding out who had won and she wasn't best pleased at being interrupted. Strangely, when she opened the front door and came face to face with Ken Voss she wasn't the least bit fazed.
"Yeah?"
"Diane Buckle?"
"Yeah, who wants to know?"
"I'm Bobby's uncle and I need to have a chat about him."
Shrugging her shoulders, Diane turned and walked back in the direction of the front room, just in time to see the closing credits of the show she was almost addicted to.

"Fuck it! I've missed the end now."
Ken walked over the threshold and as he made his way through the small hallway he wrinkled his nose at the stench of the place. Outside had been bad enough but this was disgusting. There wasn't any one distinct aroma that he could put his finger on, it was more of a complete combination of cooking oil, unwashed or damp linen, mixed in with stale cigarettes, sweat and God only knew what else. What on earth was Bobby thinking? He wasn't used to this, he'd been brought up in almost sterile conditions as Brice had also been somewhat OCD about cleanliness. Entering the room he saw the woman perched on the sofa wearing the broad grin of a Cheshire cat that made him want to smack her face from one side of the room to the other. Diane was a big girl, who dressed in leggings at least two sizes smaller than she actually was, her breasts were massive and hung down almost to her waist and Ken couldn't for the life of him understand what Bobby was attracted to.
"So, what's up with Robert? He ain't hurt or anythin' is he?"
Her show of concern was insincere and it showed. Without waiting for an invitation of any kind, Ken sat down on the newly acquired sofa and wondered if McKay money had paid for it. Glancing around the room he could see through the piles of linen, that most of the other furnishing were little more

than a few months old and it was obvious that a large chunk of the debt had been spent on the front room but you can't make a silk purse out of a sow's ear, which was exactly what the woman before him had attempted to do.
"Bobby's fine, well except for the shed load of debt that he's in, debt accrued by you I might add."
In seconds Diane was on her feet and now standing less than a foot away from Ken. Her arms were folded indignantly across her ample chest and her face was set in stone as she peered down at him.
"Who the fuck do you think you are?! Bargin' into my gaff and castin' fuckin' aspersions? You can get the fuck out, right now!"
Now Ken was on his feet and he towered head and shoulders above his host. Grabbing her by the front of her top as he roughly pulled her towards him.
"The spendin' stops now you slag! Do you understand me?"
Instead of a fearful reaction, Diane Buckle started to laugh.
"Get your fuckin' hands off me you muppet! When my Bobby finds out about this you're a dead man."
"Sweetheart, your Bobby couldn't fight his way out of a fuckin' paper bag, why do you think I'm here."
Diane pulled away sharply and they both heard the ripping sound as her top split its seams.
"Fuck! This was brand new and now you've ruined it. Right, I'm goin' to tell my Bobby you tried it on

with me, ripped my top when you tried to feel my tits! Then we'll see how mad he can get. The best thing you can do mister, is to fuck off right now!" Ken had to admit that he was onto a hiding to nothing, the bitch was crazy and there was no way she was about to toe the line. It would have been a different story if Brice was still alive, he would have been round here himself and the slag would have disappeared without trace but that wasn't possible now so he had no other option, he would have to tell Maggie and let her take over the problem. It wasn't going to bode well for his relationship with Bobby but the kid's welfare was all that really mattered and Ken had promised when Brice was on his death bed that he would look out for the boy when Brice had gone. Whatever the outcome, Bobby would be fine in the end, though he couldn't say the same for the leery, greedy bitch he'd just had the sad misfortune to meet.

"Look sweetheart! Just hand the credit card back and we'll say no more about it."

"Fuck off!"

"I've tried to warn you to stay clear darlin' but you won't listen will you? Pretty soon it will be out of my hands and you will have to deal with the consequences."

"Oh just fuck off out of it old man, you don't scare me!"

Ken left the flat but he was in no mood to take

things further tonight. Tomorrow would be soon enough but for now, he needed a stiff drink, in fact he needed several. Inside Diane mulled over what had just happened. She could do as she'd threatened but that would just create a mess and the last thing she wanted was for Maggie McKay to get involved. For now it would be best to just keep her trap shut in the hope that it would all hopefully blow over. Whatever the outcome, there was no way she was going to walk away from her cash cow without a fight.

CHAPTER NINETEEN

The following day Ken Voss was at the arches long before anyone else. A couple of months earlier Maggie had relented and given him back his keys to the front roller shutter but he was under strict instructions never to attempt entry into the newly adapted room. He would have had to have been Houdini reincarnated to do that as the door was not only steel plated but secured like Fort Knox. Ken wasn't here to pry but simply because he hadn't been able to sleep the previous night and as Joyce didn't open her burger van until eight thirty, there wasn't really anywhere else to go. Pacing up and down, he was at least grateful when Albie Mitchell strolled in.
"Shit the bed Kenny?"
Albi had been a part of the McKay firm for years and had thankfully survived the thinning out when Maggie had taken over fully. He was always good for a laugh, was reliable and loyal to the boss but Ken didn't trust him as far as he could throw him, especially when it came down to telling Maggie anything she wanted to know.
"Somethin' like that, how come you're about so early?"
"I always like to get here before her fuckin' ladyship, you know what she can be like and I for

one don't want to be in the firing line if she's in one of her bleedin' moods."

Just as the word 'moods' left his lips the door opened and the woman in question strode in and it looked like she'd had a bad night as well. Maggie's peroxide bob was dishevelled and the blouse she wore was fighting to contain the ample bosom that was desperately trying to escape. Ken thought back to the first time he had met her when she was just a little girl. A pretty, timid, little thing who clung to her father's legs for reassurance. He'd watched her grow into a stroppy teenager and then into a beautiful young woman, her looks were stunning and she had the figure of a model but years of overindulgence were now at the fore and there was nothing whatsoever appealing about this bully of a woman.

"Albie. You're early Kenny, shit the bed?"

"That joke has already been cracked Mags. Actually I'm here before time as I really need to have a word with you and I don't feel it can wait."

"Sounds a bit ominous, come through. Albie put the kettle on, I'm gasping."

Just like the lapdog that he'd sadly become, Albi Mitchell almost sprinted over to the small kitchen area and Ken couldn't help but slowly shake his head in despair as he followed his boss through into the office.

"Take a seat but I hope it's not goin' to take too

long, I have a lot on today."
Doing as he was told, Ken waited a few seconds for her to hang up her jacket and handbag and then join him.
"So?"
"I don't know if you're aware of the fact that Bobby has a girlfriend?"
Maggie laughed out loud but not in a comical way, the sound was mocking and cruel.
"A fuckin' bit of stuff?! You're havin' a laugh ain't you? What female in her right bleedin' mind would look at that fuckin' retard?"
"Well he has and it's been goin' on for close on a year now. I've been monitoring things and until yesterday there didn't appear to be any harm in it."
"Firstly, why am I only fuckin' findin' out about it a year later? I think you need to remind yourself where your bloody loyalties lay Ken and it ain't with that bleedin' halfwit."
"Don't call him that Maggie, he's your flesh and…………"
For a fleeting moment they just stared at each other but Ken didn't go any further, there was no need and besides, if he brought up Bobby's parentage he knew she would only kick off.
"So you were saying, yesterday? Why what happened?"
"I came in and found the poor little sod in tears. Seems he gave her his credit card and now she's run

him up a shit load of debt. I paid her a visit but the greedy bitch ain't budgin', said she'd tell Bobby I tried it on with her."

"And did you?"

"Of course not, you know me better than that."

"So, how much are we talkin' about?"

Maggie wasn't the least bit worried about Bobby's pain and suffering, all she cared about was the fact that her soppy twat of a brother, well that's what everyone thought he was, except Ken knew the real truth, was wasting her hard earned cash. She didn't recognise Bobby's inheritance, as far as Maggie was concerned every penny belonged to her even if her father hadn't seen it that way.

"This is exactly why I keep him on a short reign where money is concerned. Honestly though, never in a million fuckin' years would I have thought that the thick twat would have the brains to apply for a credit card. So, are you gonna tell me how much or not?!"

"Fifteen grand."

Ken waited for the shit to hit the fan and he didn't have to wait long.

"The money grabbing fuckin' bitch, I'll kill her! I'll fuckin' kill that soppy little cunt as well, where is he?"

Ken sighed heavily, he knew this would happen but what choice did he have? He had tried to sort it himself but when that didn't work, he had to tell her or that conniving cow would continue to take poor Bobby further and further into debt.

"He ain't here yet Maggie but go easy on him when he gets in will you? He doesn't know that I've been to see her, at least I don't think he does. You go in all guns blazin' and he'll dig his bleedin' heels in. Whether you like it or not, the boy is old enough and hopefully has enough sense between his ears to sort out his own finances now and you don't want that to happen, now do you? If you piss him off, he'll take control of the money Brice left him and probably end up pot less within a short space of time."

For the first time in her life Maggie McKay actually took notice of someone else's advice. Her dad had left most of his estate to her, well for her to administer appropriately as and when needed but he had also left her bastard almost a million in trust and there was no way she was about to let him waste her father's hard earned cash on some old slag.

"I want to know all there is."

"I asked about but there ain't much to know as far as I'm aware. She's a single mother, with several previous kids who were all given up for adoption. She had a stint as a Tom, works part time in the shop on the corner of Buxton Street and deals a little wacky baccy from behind the counter, unbeknown to the owner, or at least I think it is. That's about it really. Oh and she's a right dirty cow as well, her flat smelled like a fuckin' toilet and looked no better than the council tip."

"Get me her address and the hours that she works."

"I know where she lives but I'll have to pay the shop owner a visit to find out her hours. How soon do you want to know?"

Maggie stared into Ken's face and her expression was totally blank, a look he'd seen many times over the years and he was now beginning to wonder if he should have kept his mouth shut after all. This was going to end badly and at the end of the day, the woman who was going to be on the end of Maggie's wrath, hadn't personally done him any harm.

That afternoon as Diane Buckle, accompanied by her little girl, entered the inner stairwell of the flats on White's Row, Albi Mitchell was following close behind. Maggie was already inside waiting, after her man had expertly picked the lock ten minutes earlier. She'd wandered around and her face had grimaced in each and every room. It was a fact of life that a lot of people are poor but there was no excuse to live in squalor, soap and water cost next to nothing but this place needed condemning and it wasn't the building itself. Maggie imagined what her dad would have thought about it all and what a dressing down he would have given Bobby for even entertaining such a filthy bitch. As soon as Diane stepped into her home Albie shoved her with force, grabbed the child and slammed the front door shut. As Diane was roughly pushed in the direction of the front room, it felt as if everything was happening in slow motion and she hardly had a second to draw breath let alone scream out. Albie then disappeared into the kitchen with a crying Tasha held close to his chest, he wasn't much good with kids but the sight of the giant bar of chocolate that he pulled from his pocket soon silenced the little girl. Albie just hoped that the sweet treat would last until Maggie had sorted out whatever business she had come here for. Spying the unwanted guest seated on her new three piece, Diane was suddenly shaken back to reality and was no longer scared. A fighter from a young age, she was more than capable of taking care of herself and that talent had come in handy on more than one occasion in the past when she'd been on the game and a punter had cut up rough or had refused to settle his bill.

"Who the fuck are you and what are you doin' in my gaff?"

Seated in one of the new armchairs, Maggie looked the bitch up and down. What the fuck was Bobby thinking, she looked exactly what she was, an ex-Tom.

"Seems my late father's money has recently furnished this tip you call a home?"

Instantly Diane could feel her knees begin to wobble

at the realisation of just who was sitting in front of her and now she was really frightened. It was one thing to take care of yourself and have a bit of confidence but quite another to take on a menacing gangster who would never allow a person to get one over on them. Any repercussions should she lash out, would go on for a long time and Diane really didn't want any more aggro in her life.
"Whaa, whaa, what do you want?"
Maggie silently studied the woman's face, this could go one of two ways, the bitch would either roll over and do whatever she was told to, or end up, well Maggie didn't want to go down that route just yet.
"My brother is vulnerable Diane, I can call you Diane?"
Diane Buckle vigorously nodded her head, the woman could call her anything she wanted just so long as she didn't hurt her. There was no thought for her child, Diane only feared for her own safety because as far as she was concerned, everyone else was replaceable.
"As I said, Bobby's not quite the ticket but you already know that don't you? It's the reason you sought him out and have screwed every penny you could out of him. Well it fuckin' stops now!!!"
Maggie was out of her seat in seconds and was now standing so close to the woman that Diane could feel Maggie's breathe on her face.
"You've got two weeks, then, I want you to just

disappear."

"But where will I go, what about my job?"

Maggie gently ran a long highly polished fingernail down the woman's cheek as she gently spoke.

"Quite frankly darlin' I don't give a flyin' fuck but if you should ever show your face in London again or have any and I mean any, contact with Bobby, then you will disappear permanently. Do you get my drift?"

Not waiting for a reply, Maggie promptly headed in the direction of the front door while Diane remained rooted to the spot in complete shock and disbelief.

"Albi! We're goin'!"

With a face smeared in chocolate and on hearing the shouting coming from the front room, Tasha ran to her mother crying when she saw the strangers leave.

"Mummy! Mummy!!!"

"And you can stop fuckin' whining you little bitch! I have enough fuckin' problems to deal with now, without a snotty nosed brat clingin' onto my new gear!"

The stench of the place had been overpowering and Maggie couldn't wait to get outside into the clean fresh air, well as fresh as it could be for London. The incident hadn't fazed her in the least, she was quite prepared to return if necessary but the past and her own infamous reputation in London had taught her that the odds against that needing to happen were low.

A day before schedule, Diane Buckle was packed and ready to leave and by lunchtime all of the stuff she had managed to sell would be picked up. The council had organised an anonymous swap with some bloke in Wales so she had new accommodation already lined up. Diane didn't much like the Welsh but at least her and Tasha would have a home and she desperately hoped that it was far enough away that Maggie couldn't find her if she had a change of heart. The furniture hadn't brought in much over fifteen hundred but it was more than enough for their travel and to be quite honest, Diane couldn't wait to leave. There was one last task to see to and sitting down on the floor she put pen to paper.
My dear sweet Bobby
I know this will break your heart but me and Tash have gone away and we won't be coming back. Your sister came to see me and told me that if I didn't leave and cut all contact with you then she would kill us. I'm sorry baby but I just can't stay so we're off to Spain for a new life.
Love you always
Your Di Di xx

The letter was a foolish attempt at some kind of payback to Maggie McKay and the mention of

Spain would be enough to put her dozy now ex-boyfriend off the scent. If she was being forced to start a new life then she didn't want some retard trying to track her down and causing aggro. Sealing up the envelope she taped it to the back of the front door knowing that once he'd been inside, he couldn't be off missing it on his way out.

Bobby had innocently planned on a romantic evening after deciding that he was going to ask Diane to marry him. Rather than turn up to find out she'd already made plans, he called ahead to tell her would pick her up around seven as he had a surprise. Not wanting to reveal what was happening, Diane had played along and now he was as happy as a sand boy. Approaching her front door he was surprised to see it was slightly ajar, a definite no, no, in this area at least. Walking inside he closed the door behind him as he called out her name but there was no reply. It took Bobby only a moment to realise that the entire place had been stripped bare. There wasn't even a picture left hanging on the wall and now he was starting to panic. Walking swiftly through to the bedrooms he stopped when he reached Tasha's room. Without her new cute white furniture, the Cinderella wallpaper looked tatty and unloved. It wasn't until he turned to leave that he saw the envelope and snatching it from the filthy gloss paint work, he tore

it open with a feeling of foreboding. Bobby slowly began to read the note and as he took in each heartbreaking word, he slid down the wall into a crumpled mess on the floor. He must have stayed that way for quite some time because when he eventually stood up he could see that it was dark outside. A few minutes later he heard a key in the lock and momentarily hoped that Diane's plans had changed but as the door opened he was greeted by a smiling middle aged man who introduced himself as Evan Thomas. Evan began to explain that he was the new tenant but Bobby didn't hang around to listen to anymore and barging past the man, ran down the stairs two at a time. Deciding he had to find her no matter what, Bobby taped into his list of contacts as he walked back towards Buxton Street.
"Hello Bob's, unlike you to call this late kid?"
"She's gone, she's left Uncle Kenny and I don't know why. Did you see her, did you say something nasty and that's why she left? She said Mag's paid her a visit, what did she say to her?"
The pain was evident as his voice began to rise in a crescendo of fear and Ken thought he then heard the gentle sound of sobbing. This was so wrong and he wished with all of his heart that he hadn't opened his big fat gob in the first place.
"Look Bob, I had to tell Maggie. You know, the debt and everything and it wouldn't have stopped sunshine, she would have bled you bleedin' dry."

"What did she do? Oh no Uncle Kenny, what did she do?"

"You have to calm down boy. Now I don't know what Maggie did, maybe she just had a word with her and told her to get out of your life but there ain't anythin' you can do about it tonight. Go home, sleep on it and we can have a chat in the mornin'. We'll find out what happened with Maggie then. What do you say?"

The line went dead and now Ken was worried. Bobby could be highly strung at the best of times and with low intelligence, there was no knowing just what he would do next.

Reaching home Bobby McKay placed his key in the door and then flicked on the lights. As usual, the house was deathly quiet as he made his way into the kitchen. Opening one of the cupboards, he did something he'd never done in his life before, he pulled out a bottle of his father's scotch. Thirty minutes later and now more than a little tipsy, Bobby had come up with a plan, he was going to fly out to Spain and bring his Di Di home! The safe, located in the back bedroom and where Brice had set up a study/office, had been sunk into the wall. It used to contain large bundles of cash, stocks and of course the family passports but Bobby hadn't looked inside for a long, long time. Removing the picture that concealed the metal box he opened it up but there weren't any passports inside. All it contained were papers with dates, times, locations and names he'd never heard of written on them. There were also five DVD cases and now intrigued, he took one out and staggered downstairs to the front room. As the disc began to play and the bloodcurdling screams started, he couldn't believe what he was seeing. Turning down the volume, he just stared hard at the images trying to see where it was but nothing came to mind. He did however recognise Alina from when she'd visited the arches and as the scene played out Bobby began to feel his stomach heave and then the retching started. Running through to the kitchen he vomited every ounce of the food he'd consumed that day, not to mention the vast amount of scotch, into the sink. Finally composing himself he went back into the front room and ejected the disc. It looked new, as did the other four when he went back upstairs to check. They certainly hadn't been there when his dad was alive, that left just one person, his sister! Placing the viewed disk into his jacket pocket he then put the others back into the safe, locked it and rehung the picture. As he tried to think of what to do, Bobby continued to drink the whisky before finally passing out on the front room floor. He'd had all intention of going to see Maggie, find out what she had said to his Diane and also to ask where his passport was but that would now have to wait until the morning.

CHAPTER TWENTY

For the second day running Ken Voss was at the arches long before anyone else. He wanted to be the first to see Maggie and break the news that Bobby knew she had gotten rid of Diane. That's if her brother hadn't contacted her already? Ken accepted that he would have to bear the brunt of her wrath, it was how she worked, always lashing out at the messenger, not caring who she hurt or offended. It was one of the nasty traits she had inherited from her mother and something Brice had tried again and again to stop his daughter from doing but his endeavours had always fallen on deaf ears. Now that he wasn't around to at least try and correct his princess, everyone was afraid to be the bearer of bad news. It wasn't anything Ken hadn't experienced before but maybe this time he would stand up to her, maybe now it was time for a few home truths.

Maggie was on cloud nine when she entered as a few minutes earlier Dennis Havers had been on the phone and was requesting yet another evening of fun for the Judge. Quite frankly she didn't like the bloke, he was shifty and smarmy but she did like the vast amounts of cash that had been coming her way via the requests. Sam Wenner was more or less out of the picture nowadays, they still met for the odd meal or a drink but he had been honest and said the whole thing now sickened him to the stomach. Maggie had just shrugged her shoulders, at least she didn't have to pay him any money and it was one less person to deal with or hear complaints from.

"Morning Kenny, you really are gettin' a right old early bird ain't ya?"

"I need to speak to you."

"Again? Really?!"

This was all she needed, she had an event to plan and he wanted to discuss some menial problem that for some reason he couldn't handle himself.

"Can't it wait only I'm a bit busy this morning?"

"No not really Maggie, I think this could be urgent."

Sighing heavily she searched in her bag for her office key. Even before her new line of business had begun the door was always kept firmly locked, she trusted absolutely no one and that went for her entire workforce as well.

"Sometimes Kenny I wonder what I fuckin' pay you for, my old man might have liked havin' you around but I'm startin' to wonder if it's about time you retired like your old pal Pup."

Waving her hand in the general direction of the office, she followed behind and then waited for him to step aside so that she could open up. There wasn't anything too incriminating inside but all the same, this was her own private space that she loved

and she had, after her father's death, decorated it so tastefully. No one dared to venture inside without an invitation and apart from her Chelsea home, it was the only place she could think properly.
Hanging up her jacket, Maggie scanned through the post as she spoke.
"So, spill your guts, what's goin' on?"
"Bobby knows you went to see his girlfriend."
"And?"
"He phoned me late last night and he was in a hell of a state. I didn't realise he was that keen on the woman. Maggie, it sounded like he was raging when he spoke, well apart from when he was crying that is. The poor little sod sounded heart broken."
Ken instantly wished he hadn't let slip that last piece of information but before he had a chance to even try and rectify what he'd said, Maggie went in for the kill.
"What a twat! That's exactly what I mean, no true McKay would ever fuckin' blubber like a baby but then he ain't a McKay is he? He's just like his father. I bet Ciaran could have turned on the water works if he didn't get his own way."
Maggie again laughed out loud with a mocking, almost sadistic tone.
"We'll never know about that though will we Ken? Anyway, I can handle that little bastard, you worry too much Kenny. Now if you don't mind I really have to get on with business."

Ken nodded his head and then turned to leave. He'd done his best but she wouldn't listen and once again he'd bottled out of having a go and saying what he really felt. She gave the boy no credit whatsoever and Ken knew if she wasn't careful, little Bobby McKay could be his mother's downfall, possibly all of their downfalls. Maggie never referred to him as her son and Ken wondered if she'd actually begun to believe that he really wasn't. There was something slightly unhinged about the woman, he'd always thought that even back when Brice was alive but it was a belief he'd had the nous to keep to himself.

As soon as the door closed, Maggie sat back in her chair and removed her diary. Usually it was locked away in a hidden place at home but not today, today she was definitely going to need it. At the thought of her next big payday she wore a wide grin as she searched through her list of contacts. Finding Asti's details, she tapped in his number and waited for her call to be answered but it just kept on ringing which oddly, was very unlike him. Deciding to give it ten minutes in the hope that he would call her back, she busied herself with overdue paperwork regarding the legitimate properties the firm owned, properties that were rented out in an attempt to deflect any interest that the Old Bill might show if they ever had reason to look into the McKay Empire. Maggie couldn't concentrate and five minutes later she was just staring at blurred lines. She had a gut feeling that there was something wrong! Having no address for the Albanian meant she couldn't pay him a visit and after four further attempts at contacting him by phone went unanswered, she slammed her mobile down onto the desk in frustration. Without him she was fucked! Wracking her brains she tried to think of someone else that could help but she trusted absolutely no one and now it looked as if she was going to miss out on a shed load of cash and upset the Judge who in this niche market, was her only real client as his minions wouldn't dare act without his say so.

Bobby woke with the mother of all headaches. Even though he was heading towards thirty it had been his first real experience with alcohol and now as he swallowed two paracetamol, he realised that scotch probably hadn't been the best choice. Glancing at the clock he saw that it was almost noon and he should have been in work a good two hours ago. Usually he would be rushing around desperate not to upset his big sister by being late but something inside him had changed. He was angry, normally a placid soul, it was an emotion he rarely felt but now because of what she had done, as far as he was concerned she could just go and fuck herself! He would get to the arches when he was good and ready and not before. Taking a shower, he put on his big fluffy dressing gown and after drinking two pints of water, slumped down into Brice's old armchair and drifted off to sleep. Half an hour later he woke again and though not gone entirely, he could feel that the headache was slowly starting to lift. Bobby decided that now would be as good a time as any to face his sister and let her know just what he thought of her so with tentative steps, he gently made his way upstairs to get dressed.

Outside the sun was shining and Bobby took his time as he walked to work but the good weather didn't make him feel any better. He realised that he was about to go head to head with the woman he had feared for his entire life and that notion alone, made a chill run down his spine. As he stepped into the arches everything was continuing as usual, Albie Mitchell was making a brew and the newest recruit, Si Boswell, was glaring at one of the computer screens in utter confusion. Uncle Kenny was studying the Racing Post and looking up, stood up from his desk as soon as he saw Bobby come in. It was a somewhat feeble attempt at barring his way but the expression Bobby wore, told Ken that trying to stop him was going to be far easier said than done.
"Now Bob, don't do anythin' stupid!"
"Get out of my way Uncle Kenny, I've kept my trap

shut for far too long and that fuckin' bitch has treated me like dirt, well no more! I want to know where my Diane has gone and what that cow has said to her!"

Strangely Ken didn't continue to argue and instantly stepped aside. Maybe it really was time for a few home truths, even if he hadn't had the balls to do it himself. In reality Bobby McKay was the only one in a position to do it anyway. Bobby didn't knock or wait to be invited inside and with one turn of the handle the office door flew open and crashed against the adjoining wall.

"What the fuck!"

"Shut your trap Maggie! You evil, vindictive cow! Why did you interfere in my business, it had nothin' to do with you. Where is Diane?!!!"

"When the old man's money is being wasted on some trashy piece of skirt like it's goin' out of fuckin' fashion then it does have somethin' to do with me you little prick! That gold digger has gone for good, so just get over it!"

Every word being said could be clearly heard by all out in the reception area and as Maggie tried to make her way to the door in an attempt to close it and keep private business, private, Bobby roughly grabbed her chubby, gold encrusted wrist.

"Get your fuckin' hands off of me you retard!"

Bobby instantly let go but not because he was scared, this was the first time she had ever called him that, well in earshot at least. He knew he was different to others, knew he had been far slower than his peers at school but a retard?! Was that what he was? Maggie saw the pain on his face but it only fuelled her fire and what came next was to change both of their lives forever.

"I should have gotten rid of you when I had the chance instead of listening to my fuckin' father! You have only ever been an embarrassment to me. Who in God's holy name would ever want a son like you, I would have been better off keeping the fuckin' afterbirth!"

"Are you tellin' me I'm your son?"

"Hallelujah, the penny has finally dropped! You didn't think the mighty Brice McKay would spawn something like you did you? You're no different from your cunt of a father and you should have been put down like a rabid dog just as he fuckin' was!"

"You're lying, I don't believe you Mags!"

Bobby ran blindly from the room, he couldn't bear to hear any more of her lies and when he was once again out in the reception area he made a beeline for Ken Voss.

"Tell me it ain't true Uncle Kenny, tell me that evil bitch ain't me mother?"

The revelation left everyone in the arches standing open mouthed in shock. Ken could only hang his head in shame and when he looked up again he momentarily saw the tears in Bobby's eyes before he ran at speed from the building. Enraged, Ken simply couldn't let this go unchallenged, couldn't hold his tongue any longer and marched into Maggie's inner sanctum

"You nasty, spiteful fuckin' bitch! Why the fuck did you tell him? What on earth did you think it would achieve?"

"Maybe the thick twat will keep on runnin' and if I'm really lucky he'll throw himself off Tower Bridge and do us all a fuckin' favour!"

Maggie's eyes were bulging and she was red in the face. A few strands of her heavily processed hair had stuck to her sweaty forehead and in that fleeting moment Ken was sure he had never seen anyone so ugly, or evil looking.

"Well I just hope it was worth it 'cause he could end up bringing you down!"

"What the fuck do you mean?"

"He might be slow Mags but he ain't that fuckin' daft. How much do you think he really knows about this firm?"

Maggie McKay flopped down into her leather chair with a thud. True he had seen a lot of what went on, even overheard a lot of conversations but surely he wasn't bright enough to know what most of it meant, at least she hoped he wasn't. Thankfully he hadn't been privy to anything regarding her recent side line, she'd at least had the brains to limit that information to only a select few and even then it was strictly on a need to know basis.

Bobby ran until he couldn't run anymore and then he slowed to a walk, only stopping at one of the numerous convenience stores to purchase a bottle of scotch. After waking up feeling like shit earlier this morning, he'd made a promise to himself to never touch the stuff again but things had changed and all he now wanted was to get so out of his skull that he couldn't think about anything. Stepney Green Park came into view and entering Bobby sat down under a black poplar tree that overlooked the Astroturf court. Opening the bottle he placed it between his lips and immediately downed almost half of the contents as easily as he would have done with a can of Coke. His surroundings soon began to swim and blur and shortly after he laid back onto the grass and slept. Every couple of hours or so he would occasionally rouse and drink a little more but eventually he was out for the count entirely. When he finally came to, the court was lit up by floodlights and a group of men were playing an evening game of five-a-side. When they began to continually watch him, thinking that he might be some kind of pervert or kiddie-fiddler, Bobby realised it was time to move on. Staggering drunkenly to his feet he once again started to walk with no real destination in mind. By now he was out of drink so stopping to buy more whisky, he then sat down on the steps of Hackney Town Hall. As the crow flies he'd covered little more than three miles but his legs felt as if he'd done a marathon. Being midweek the place wasn't exactly buzzing and after opening up the bottle and swigging far more than was good for him, Bobby was approached by one of the local winos.

"Give us a swig mate!"

"No, go away!"

Bobby clutched the only thing able to make him forget close to his chest and when the tramp all of a sudden reached out to snatch the bottle of Bells, a tussle ensued. There was far more verbal assault than anything physical as both were too far gone to have any real fight in them but they were still able to cause enough of a commotion to draw the attention of two beat bobbies who were about to come to the end of their shift.

"What's going on you two?"

"Greedy bastard won't share oooffissicer!"

Old Tom Nugent was known to everyone in the area. He'd been an alcoholic for years and was generally a good sort and not out for trouble. Looking this newcomer up and down, PC Fielding could tell by Bobby's clothes that he wasn't a run-of-the-mill drunk in the usual term of the word. Making a kindly gesture, Officer Fielding attempted to help Bobby to his feet but everything rapidly changed when Bobby viciously lashed out in frustration.

"Fuck off copper! Get your fuckin' hands off me! Do you hear?!"

Twenty minutes later and Bobby McKay found himself in the custody suit of Lower Clapton Road. Booked in as a drunk and disorderly, he was swiftly shown to a cell to sleep it off and Bobby didn't resist. Quickly taking a seat on the concrete bench, he was snoring loudly after just a few minutes.

For the rest of humanity at least, it would turn out to be a lucky night, Keith Forbes had drawn the short straw for the late rota as custody sergeant. As it goes, Keith was a nice bloke but he was also incredibly nosey and as he bagged up the few possessions of Robert James McKay, he came across the DVD which had been removed when Bobby was patted down before being taken to the cell. The case was blank and flipping it over Keith couldn't see any writing but it did have the smudges of finger prints so he knew it had been used which intrigued him. It was now just after three in the morning and being a quiet night, Keith simply couldn't help himself and before he knew it had slipped the disc into the drive of the custody computer. Making himself a coffee he returned, took a seat behind the counter, loosened his trousers and was all ready to tune into what he imagined was porn and if he was

really lucky, it would turn out to be a homemade one. Keith had been able to watch several of those in the past before they were sent down to evidence and they always made for good viewing. As he took a sip of his drink, the hot liquid was instantly spat out in shock when he saw what appeared on the screen. This was serious, deadly serious and with the bodies that had been turning up recently he knew he had to tell someone. Using the internal phone he called up to the small CID unit. Detective Bhavesh Chowdhury, known to all as Vesh, was none too pleased at being disturbed. Vesh loved the graveyard shift, unless of course it was a weekend, as he was able to catch up on reading or his other favourite pastime, gaming. He treated his personal Xbox like a shrine and tonight he was about to reach his highest level to date on 'Man of Medan'. Momentarily distracted when the phone rang, his opponent from somewhere in America he assumed, took the final points.
"What!!?!"
"I think you need to come down to custody Vesh, there's something you have to see."
Vesh slammed down the handset and angrily closed the screen of his PC. This had better be good or fucking Keith was going to get the mother of all bollocking!

Within the hour all hell had broken loose. Keith

and Vesh had tried to wake Bobby up to start an interview but he was completely out for the count. Vesh knew that to hold onto potential evidence and quite possibly impede an investigation was a sackable offence, so as much as it went against the grain, the evidence had to be passed over to Tottenham nick as they were the ones dealing with the torso cases and this could possibly be connected. Protocol had to be maintained at all times, it was something Vesh was a stickler for but deep down he would have loved to have gotten his teeth into this one.

CHAPTER TWENTY ONE

Anna Draycott was enjoying possibly the most restful night's sleep she'd had since Jake's death so she wasn't best pleased when he mobile burst into life at a little after four am. Reaching over to the bedside table and with bleary eyes, she grabbed her mobile but struggled to make out who was calling. It was Eric Barnes and aware that he would never call at such an ungodly hour she knew it was serious. Sitting bolt upright in the bed, as Anna pressed connect, she willed it not to be news of yet another torso being found.

"Guv?"

"This had better be good Eric?"

"We've had a development and new evidence has just come in. I would have waited but I really think you need to see this ASAP."

"Give me an hour and I'll be with you. Have you called in the rest of the team?"

"They're on their way as I speak. I think we might have a real chance of cracking it this time."

His last words went unheard as Anna had ended the call and was already in the bathroom turning on the shower.

Both Eric and Steve Johnson were waiting outside on the rear steps of Tottenham Station as Anna pulled into the carpark. Seeing their faces suddenly

made a shiver run down her spine, she hadn't been called in like this for years and it could only mean one thing, they had something big. Almost running over to the building, Anna was taking her coat off before they were even inside and as she walked at an exceptionally fast pace, the two other officers were struggling to keep up with her.
"Right! Eric bring me up to speed?"
Eric Barnes had retired holding the rank of Detective Inspector and with time served, he outranked Steve by a country mile. He hadn't been brought back for the glory, just to cover Anna in her time of need so he wasn't about to try and steal anyone's thunder.
"Actually it was Sergeant Johnson that received the info, so better it comes from him. Steve?"
"A couple of Hackney plods picked up a drunk and disorderly a couple of hours ago and he had a DVD in his possession. I'm just warning you, it was viewed, don't ask me why but what came to light will shock you to the core."
"Don't over egg the pudding Steve, just tell me what's what."
"That's something I'm definitely not doing Ma'am. It's pretty horrific stuff, seems someone has been making snuff movies and this could very well be connected to our inquiries."
"Do we have the evidence here?"
"Yes guv, I drove over to Hackney and collected it

myself."

"And the bloke? Any info on him?"

"At the moment he's drunk as a skunk and asleep but who he is? Well, that's where it gets a little more interesting, he's the younger brother of Maggie McKay. The McKay's run………"

Anna abruptly cut her sergeant off midsentence. She had only ever dealt with Ms McKay once and that was back when she'd first just joined the department but it had been a meeting she would never forget. It had been Anna's initial interview as a detective and involved the brutal torture of an unfortunate street Tom named Florence Devereux. David Granger, a solicitor of dubious nature had been in attendance but he wasn't needed as Maggie McKay tore Anna to shreds. Within a week Florence had mysteriously left town and the case had instantly fallen apart, leaving the young detective constable with a considerable amount of egg on her face.

"I'm well aware of who the McKay firm are. Those lowlifes have been up to no good for years but they are on the ball and as yet we've never been able to pin anything on them, though it's not through the want of trying I can tell you! Are we all set up for a viewing? I want the whole team to see this."

"It's pretty bad Guv."

"I don't give a rat's arse Steve, we're trying to catch serial killers here and those poor victims have suffered more than we could ever imagine. I want everyone to see what's on that disc! Has anyone made coffee?"

"Bubbling away as we speak Ma'am."

"Be a love and grab me a cup would you? I'm still not awake properly and I want to be firing on all cylinders when I speak to the team."

The incident room was a hive of activity as they entered but silence fell on the room as soon as Anna and Eric walked in.

"Sorry for hauling you all from your beds but we might finally have a lead. I've only just got here myself so I don't know what the footage you're about to see will contain but I have been informed that its gruesome. Anyone who doesn't wish to see it should leave the room now."

Anna had to give them the option but everyone in attendance knew that should they have opted out, then their career in the Met would have been all but over. Steve entered the room with Anna's coffee and after a couple of sips she was rearing to go.

"Right then! Let's get started shall we?"

When the recorder stopped you could have heard a pin drop.

"Steve, get the McKay bloke over here now and I don't give a fuck if he's still sleeping off the excess."

Two hours later and Bobby had been woken, forcibly given copious amounts of coffee and was hastily on his way to Anna's station. He wasn't taken to a holding cell but directly to interview room number two. There was a slight delay while they all waited for a duty solicitor to be duly brought in but once Mark Hallowell arrived it was all systems go. Mark was given a quick rundown regarding what had been found and after a brief conversation with his client, by eight forty five that morning they were finally ready to begin. Before the interview got underway, Mark asked to speak privately with Anna.

"I hope whatever you have to say will be quick as I need to get going on this, so how can I help Mr Hallowell?"

"After briefly speaking with my client, I am under the impression that he is of low intelligence."

"Aren't all of these villains a bit thick? After all, if they weren't we would never be able to do our job now would we?"

"I wouldn't exactly class Mr McKay as thick but I would place him within the special needs spectrum. Now even though this won't stop the interview from proceeding, I would ask that you take this information on board Detective Inspector and tread very carefully, because if I feel at any time you are using or abusing his mental health in any way whatsoever, then I will cease the interview without hesitation."

"Understood and thank you for giving me the heads

up. Shall we?"

Guiding the solicitor back into the room, Anna took her seat and Mark Hallowell sat down beside Bobby. Chief Inspector Garnet and Steve Johnson were now in attendance but were discreetly observing from behind a two way mirror as Anna was to lead the interview with Eric as her second. They had worked together on several arrests in the past and they seemed to flow effortlessly when it came down to grilling a suspect. Switching on the recorder and after introducing everyone in the room, Anna got down to business.

"Mr McKay, when you were arrested earlier this morning, you had in your possession a DVD. What can you tell me about its contents?"

Bobby stared at her wide-eyed, he'd completely forgotten about the disc until now and suddenly he recalled its contents and knew he was in big trouble. His head was pounding and all he wanted was to be at home, tucked up in his bed. Anna knew exactly how he was feeling and for a moment felt pity for the man, she'd had the same experience numerous times in the past, especially since Jakes death and it wasn't pleasant coming down from a bender.

"The sooner you explain things Bobby, I can call you Bobby? The sooner you will be out of here."

"It isn't mine lady honest, I found it."

"Where?"

"In the safe at home."

Anna nodded cautiously in the direction of the mirror and it was a signal for Steve to apply for a search warrant.

"So who do you think it belongs to then Bobby?"

"Only me and my sister have keys, well dad had one but he died."

"So it's Maggie we need to speak to?"

Bobby was beginning to relax, he hadn't even thought to ask how they knew his sister's name and he puffed out his cheeks, exhaled deeply and rolled his eyes upwards as he spoke.

"I wouldn't if I was you. Mag's is mean and nasty and she could hurt you. She made my girlfriend go away you know?"

They were somewhat deviating from the original conversation and Anna had to get back to what was important but she also now agreed with the solicitor's earlier statement regarding the suspect's IQ and realised she had to tread extremely carefully with her questioning.

"Don't you worry about that Bobby. Now, who else might know about what's on that disc?"

"It's horrible, made me sick and I mean really sick."

"Yes it is and we have to stop whoever has done this to that poor girl, from ever doing it again. So come on Bobby, who else knows about it?"

Bobby thought for a moment. He didn't want to get anyone into trouble but his dad had told him that liars only dig a big hole for themselves and he didn't want to do that.

"Uncle Kenny works for us but I'm sure he wouldn't be involved. Uncle Kenny is nice and takes care of me, like when Diane ran up the credit card it was Uncle Kenny who sorted it all out well kind of but….."

"Bobby, where is your key to the safe?"

"Oh I don't carry it with me, far too many muggers about or that's what Mag's says. It's safe under my batman figure in my bedroom. My dad bought it for me a long while ago you know and it's one of my prized possessions and……"

"I think we can take a little rest now Bobby. Are you hungry?"

Bobby slowly moved his head up and down, his headache was still bad but his stomach was rumbling noisily.

"Oh yes please lady, my dad used to say men march on their stomachs. He was funny you know, a real……"

"That's fine Bobby, you go with the officer and I'm sure he will fix you up with something really tasty from the canteen. Okay?"

Bobby stood up and joyfully walked from the interview room without a care in the world. If the truth be told, he was actually enjoying all of the attention and for someone to talk to him as an equal for a change, felt really good. Again Anna nodded in the direction of the mirror signalling Steve to arrange an arrest warrant for Kenneth Adam Voss and Margaret Amelia McKay. Bobby was taken back to his cell and as promised, some hot food was brought to him just as Anna re-joined her team in the incident room.

"Steve, did you get the warrant?"

"Yes Guv, I also applied to search the business premises, thought we could hit there and the house at the same time, so no warnings can go out?"

"Good thinking. Beth, you're with me. Eric, you partner Steve and the rest of you just get into two groups, one with me and Beth and the other, well I don't need to say do I? Call SCO 19 and get them to attend."

"Do you really think that's needed Ma'am, I mean do you really think there will be firearms?"

Normally Anna would come down hard on any of her team if they challenged her but she knew Beth was asking out of fear rather than judging Anna's leadership.

"I don't know Beth but I'm not about to take any chances with the team. You know as well as I do that these crimes are about as serious as it gets and the culprits are looking at long stretches if convicted, so there's no telling what they might do if cornered. We leave when we have confirmation and an ETA from SCO 19. Does anyone have any questions?"

No one spoke and within seconds everyone had

gotten into groups and made their way to the rear carpark, which had long since been the designated meeting point when a job was about to go down.

Things moved fast and within the hour both of the properties were on the verge of being searched and Anna had told her officers to be thorough and leave no stone unturned. As there was no one home, the door of Buxton Street was forced open with the big red key' or as her team referred to it, 'Big Bertha'. It wasn't necessary to use force at the arches as Ken Voss had politely opened the door in the roller shutter as soon as they'd knocked. He'd seen them approach via the CC monitors and spying the armed response team, knew it was a no brainer not to open up. Past experience had taught him you could play deaf but they would just break their way in and cause untold damage and when you added highly charged officers carrying Glock 17s into the mix, it was a whole other ball game. Maggie was in her office and Ken had been alone in the reception area and was just about to go to Joyce's for a late breakfast bap.
"Good morning officers what can I do for you?" Anna stepped forward, she wasn't fazed by his size and not because she had her team behind her. These people were bullies and earned their reputation by instilling fear into those who were too scared to stand up for themselves.

"Where is Margaret McKay?"
It had been years since Ken had heard Maggie referred to as Margaret, she hated the name and would have been even angrier that it was being used by the Old Bill. Pointing in the direction of the office he smiled in Anna's direction. Anna marched through the open reception area accompanied by Detective Carl Shaw while Beth, in the company of two uniformed officers, took Ken's details before arresting him for murder and the accusation rocked him to the core! He couldn't deny the fact, though he would never admit it to anyone, that he had ended several people's lives over the years but there had been no one since long before Brice had died. Ken didn't resist as he was placed in handcuffs but his voice sounded agitated as he spoke.
"And who exactly am I supposed to have murdered?"
Beth couldn't tell him and only replied 'persons unknown' as she continued to read him his rights.
"No! I ain't fuckin' having that copper! Who exactly am I supposed to have fuckin' murdered?!!! You come in here like a mini fuckin' army, what's with all the fuckin' hardware!!?!"
"Mr Voss, I would advise you to calm down, I am also reminding you that you're under caution so just be careful. Take him to the van please."
Before Beth had time to take a breath she was approached by Detective Dave Wilson. Dave had

been Beth's mentor when she'd first joined the unit and she had nothing but the utmost respect for the man.

"Come and have a butcher's at this Beth, you're never gonna fuckin' believe it!"

Walking over to a door that had also been broken down by Big Bertha and the one that separated the two units, the detectives stepped inside and then entered the soundproofed room.

"Oh my God! This is where it all happened. Those poor, poor souls, whatever did they go through?"

"Doesn't bear thinking about Beth but I think one of us should go and interrupt the Guv, don't you?"

When Beth entered the office she saw her boss standing in front of Maggie's desk and in the middle of reading the woman her rights. Maggie McKay just smirked for the entire time as Beth waited for Anna to finish.

"Guv, you need to come and see this."

"Be with you in a minute Beth, cuff the sick bitch Carl and put her in the fuckin' van."

Over on Buxton Street, the search was carried out with relative ease and knowing where and what they were looking for made things simple for Eric and Steve. Opening the safe and finding five other discs was exhilarating and neither of them could wait to get back to the station and tell Anna. The rest of the house was searched simply as a matter of course but nothing else came to light, so after the door was secured, it was back to base.

Once again the DVD's were played to the team in the incident room and hushed discussions took place while the moving images were showing but when they came to the final one and the tiny, innocent face of Kahla Hussein appeared, the room was deathly silent. Even though she was already dead on the film and a large scar ran the length of her torso, as the masked assailant moved closer to the innocent little girl, there wasn't a dry eye in the room. Several voices were heard as they called out 'Evil bastard' and 'You sick cunt!' but Anna didn't tell any of them to be quiet. She figured they had to let out their emotions as cases like these could have serious enough effects on the mind, without the added stress of actually having to see the atrocity played out in front of them. Finally, Beth Saunders ran from the room sobbing uncontrollably and Steve was duly dispatched to try and calm her down. Switching off the monitor, Anna scanned the room looking for any reactions before she at last spoke. "I'm going to interview that bitch we picked up. Eric, I want you to take the bloke. The rest of you, go through the evidence and find me more, anything that ties these sick bastards to at least one of the murders."

Just as she'd been several years earlier, Maggie McKay was as cool as a cucumber. She hadn't recognised Anna which was a blessing but when her solicitor arrived, Maggie was advised to answer 'no comment' to anything she was asked, at least until they knew what the Old Bill had up their sleeve. Eric had a little more luck with Ken Voss. Having arrested the suspect several years earlier, pleasantries were exchanged before the interview took place, when it did, Ken ignored all advice from his brief. After being asked what he knew about the firm making snuff movies, the look on his face told Eric that there was no way on earth Ken was involved.

"Look here detective, I may have my fuckin' fingers in a few dodgy pies and plenty more besides but you know about me, have done for some time no doubt and I'm old school. Those sick bastards have no place in the world I live and work in."

"What about Maggie?"

Ken was struck dumb for a few seconds as he thought about the locked room at the arches, about having his keys taken away and Maggie not really bothering anymore about what business was being generated by her men.

"Straight up! I ain't got a fuckin' clue what she gets up to these days. Her poor old dad would turn in his bleedin' grave if he saw the state of his business now but what can I do? She's the one that gives the fuckin' orders. What went on in that room is as much as a surprise to me as it was to you, the door was always locked and none of us were allowed inside. When Brice was alive it was used to dish out a bit of punishment if someone stepped outta line but then she had it converted to somethin' that none of us were privy to. I know she has some fuckin' Albanian called Asti something or other. He does a spot of work as and when, a right hard bastard by all accounts but that's as much as I know. You ask any of the boys, Albie, even old Pup, not that he's been around for a while. They'll all tell you the same, Maggie McKay is a law unto herself."

Eric concluded the interview and for the time being Ken was taken back to his cell. He had some real thinking to do, he wasn't a grass but it was now time for self-survival because if Maggie got the chance she would serve his head on a platter and it didn't matter that he wasn't involved so long as she saved her own skin.

When Anna broke for a coffee Eric took a seat to discuss how things were progressing.

"Has she said anything?"

"Not a dickie bird but then I knew she wouldn't. What about Voss?"

"No, but not because he didn't want to, just couldn't tell us anything because it seems he's been kept in the dark regarding firm business of late. Seems the McKay woman either works alone regarding the

films or with outsiders that Ken Voss knows nothing about. He did mention an Albanian but the name didn't check out so it was probably an alias."
"You believe him?"
"Actually I do Anna. I've had a thought and it's a bit irregular but we need more than those movies."
"What's on your mind Eric?"
"Let me show Voss the footage, see if he recognises anyone. It's a long shot but it's got to be worth a try ain't it?"
For a moment she was silent as she mulled over the request. Showing a potential suspect crucial evidence, even if that suspect would probably walk away without being charged, was highly irregular.
"I see where you're coming from Eric but I would need to run that by the Chief. He's been called to a meeting with the top brass and he's not fully up to speed with all of the developments yet. Leave it with me and I'll run it past him as soon as he gets back but in all likelihood, even if he agrees it won't happen until tomorrow and that means holding Voss overnight."
"I somehow think, in the grand scheme of things, that's not too much to bear on his part and I have a feeling that Mr Voss, though reluctant in the past, would be only too happy to help us out this time."

CHAPTER TWENTY TWO

The next day, Anna was in her office at just before seven. Going over and over the evidence again and again, still didn't result in enough to charge Maggie with anything significant. They could use the Pornography Law, 63 sub section 7 'Life threatening act' (possession of extreme pornographic images) but at best it would be a short stretch at Her Majesty's pleasure and at worst, a heavy fine and a suspended sentence. The case still wouldn't be solved as the killers would remain unknown, so never brought to justice and the victims would also remain unidentified. Plus there was absolutely no proof that Maggie was involved in the manufacture or even that she was distributing the material. No, Anna needed more, a whole lot more! The case was a ticking time bomb and they all knew it was just a matter of time before the arrests were leaked. The media were now involved and because the Met could offer little in the way of advancement, the daily tabloids had begun to have a field day and she was more than aware that no knowledge would just enhance their imaginations and they would report their suspicions, true or false. Reporters were camped outside of the station and any moment Anna knew she could, probably would, be taken off of the case, or at least be made to answer to the bods on high as to why she and the CPS hadn't as yet brought a prosecution but apart from making her feel like a failure, it wouldn't change anything as they just didn't have enough evidence. If they took Maggie McKay's involvement out of the equation, which presently wasn't anything on a large scale in any case, they had no other names regarding who was carrying out these horrendous atrocities. Rapping her fingers frustratingly on the top of her desk as she tried to think, she was suddenly stopped when Drew Payton tapped on the door and meekly walked in.

"The chief would like to see you Ma'am."

"Thanks Drew, I'll be there in a minute."

Well this was it, this was probably when her career was going to go down the proverbial pan but she had one last pitch to make, one last desperate chance at finding the killer or killers. The central office was strangely quiet as she entered but not because it was empty. In fact the place was full to capacity and her team were all beavering away at their work stations but after last night's high, everyone was now feeling deflated not to mention dead tired. Knocking on the door Anna waited to hear the word that was probably going to seal her fate.

"Enter!"

Taking a deep breath, she corrected her posture and now standing tall, she walked inside.

"Good morning Sir, you wanted to see me?"

Chief Inspector Garnet stood at his window and looked exhausted as he motioned for her to take a seat.

"I'm not going to beat about the bush Anna, yesterday was appalling and before you try to defend yourself, I'm not talking about you, your team or the sterling work you have all been doing. I'm talking about the verbal beating I received from Superintendent Miles Crow, not to mention the other five or so minions in the room, who felt it necessary to tear strips off of this department. I have the arrest files here but bring me up to speed with what's really been happening.

"Yes Sir, of course. Well, we know Maggie McKay is involved but as yet we only have her on possession. The cases holding the discs have been sent for finger print analysis but I'm not hopeful. The brother isn't involved, he has a very low IQ and I think it was just a case of being in the wrong place at the wrong time re his arrest. He's angry with his sister, or mother as it goes according to Kenneth Voss, over some personal issues but that's another story. Voss? Well Eric's convinced he isn't involved either but Eric did come up with something, though it's highly irregular Sir."

By now Lou Garnet was seated behind his desk and after the dressing down he'd received the previous day, was open to any suggestions no matter how small or off the wall they might be.

"I'm at the end of my tether with this case Anna. It's like we've hit a brick wall so fire away!"
"Eric wants Voss to view the DVD footage. It's a long shot but he feels that Voss might just be able to recognise someone and we will at least have a name or names. I know it's highly irregular Sir but at the moment possession is all we have and we won't get a better chance at this, in fact this could be our only chance!"
"Do it!"
Anna smiled and was on her feet in seconds. Now out of the Chief's office she fired orders left right and centre. Drew was to set up the viewing equipment, Eric was to join her in the interview room and Steve was to escort Ken Voss. Ken was then taken back to Interview Room Two where a monitor and player had been installed. When he was brought in Anna and Eric were already seated and Ken nodded to the man who he'd thought was in charge and then looked at Anna with utter disdain, as much as to say 'Who the hell is she?'
"Take a seat Kenny. This is my superior Detective Inspector Anna Draycott."
Anna didn't smile and kept her expression deadly serious but she softened her tone as she spoke.
"You're aware of the reason we arrested you Mr Voss and……"
"I already told him! There's no fuckin' way I'm mixed up in any of that sick shit so if you…………"

"It's okay, it's okay! We accept that you haven't been involved but we are certain that your boss Maggie McKay somehow has been."

Ken was tired, tired of being held here and tired of Maggie's shit, shit that had obviously culminated in both of them being arrested and him having no idea what was going on. She was a disgrace to her father's name and Brice would have a fit if he was here but he wasn't and Ken owed her no loyalty whatsoever.

"I wouldn't put anythin' past that bitch!"

"We have five recorded discs Ken, showing the horrific murders in great detail, the only problem is the fact that we have no names."

"So you want me to have a gander and see if I can recognise anyone? I ain't no fuckin' grass copper!"

"I am not asking you to inform on anyone but this is a whole different ball game Mr Voss. All I'm asking is for you to take a look at the images and if you can, identify any of the poor souls that were subjected to this abuse and ultimately lost their lives because of it."

Ken took a moment to think about what was being said to him. If it ever got out that he'd assisted the Old Bill, especially if that help had resulted in someone doing time, then he was finished but could he live with himself if he didn't at least try and help?

"On one condition? If I recognise anyone then I will

give you a name but that's it, I ain't ever testifyin'. You know only too well, that in the circles I mix in it would be like writing my own death warrant."

Anna smiled for the first time since Ken had walked into the room, it was actually the first time she'd had anything even remotely to smile about in God knew how long.

"That's fair enough Mr Voss, that's all we're asking. Drew, Steve, you can both leave the room now. Eric do the honours please."

The discs were shown in no particular order and with each one Anna studied Kens face for any kind of reaction. Peteris' death was first and he showed no emotion, nor did he with Khristina's or Ioana but when it came too little Kahla he suddenly asked to take a break. Anna saw him wipe a tear from his eye but still he offered nothing.

"Who could do that to a poor little kid for fuck's sake?!"

"I know, it's sickening but did you manage to get anything from the footage?"

"No, like I said I never stepped foot in that room and I only know it's the arches because you told me it was. Look, you've got the discs and the place and the only person with keys is Maggie, so isn't that enough?"

"Sadly no. Oh we can charge her with being in receipt of obscene material but I want a murder charge Mr Voss!"

They were down to just one remaining disc and after the last four, Anna wasn't pinning her hopes on it.

"Shall we get this over with?"

Ken nodded his head and once again Eric pressed the play button on the remote. Suddenly and without any warning Ken sat bolt upright in his chair and then suddenly leaned forward so that he could get a better look at the image.

"Stop it!"

Eric instantly hit pause and he and Anna were immediately on tenter hooks waiting to find out who or what Ken had recognised. The footage from this disc hadn't been shot at the arches, it was the very first kill which had happened in some derelict barn, and somewhere Ken didn't have a clue about.

"That's Alina Balan, she worked for Maggie first in the clubs and then as the hostess at some sordid weekend sex parties that I was also not involved in. Can you play it just a bit more?"

Finally they were getting somewhere and Anna nodded for Eric to resume the film until Ken again uttered the two words that she was longing to hear.

"Stop it!"

Strangely he didn't speak for several seconds as his eyes darted from Anna to Eric and then back to Anna again. He was weighing something up in his mind, almost as if he didn't know whether to say what he'd seen. Anna could have been mistaken of course but to her it felt as if the big man was now frightened.

"Ken? What's wrong, what have you seen?"

Ken Voss just stared open mouthed at Anna for what felt to her like an eternity but was in fact only a matter of seconds. She was desperate to hear what more he had to say and willing it to be something substantial.

"What you agreed to earlier, that I would give you names if I could but from then on in I would be left out of it? Swear that it still stands!"

"Mr Voss, I am a woman of my word and Eric here will testify to that. Anything you tell me in this room will remain strictly confidential, of that I can assure you."

Again Ken nervously glanced from one detective to the other but finally he exhaled deeply and then slowly bowed his head in agreement.

"On the last film, if you look closely, a man comes in and for a fleeting moment before he puts on that fuckin' gimp mask, well you can see his face."

Anna told Eric to rerun the film and after several attempts he was able to pause on the exact moment.

"It's only a fleeting glimpse I know but that is Lemmings, the Honourable Judge Michael Lemmings no less!"

"The High Court Judge!?!"

Ken nodded and at the same time he had a wry smile on his lips. Anna stared at the screen for a second and then looked at Eric. Both of their mouths were open in total shock and Eric slowly shook his head in utter disbelief.

"We need to look into this further Mr Voss."

"Can I go now?"

"Sorry but not for the moment I'm afraid."

"This is gonna be a white wash ain't it? That perverted old cunt won't see a days' time in the clink will he?"

Anna was already out of her chair and after having removed the disc was now standing at the door. Turning, she faced Ken Voss with the same deadly serious expression of earlier.

"That view of the Met might well be held by the criminal fraternity but I can assure you, the man in the film will be charged and will receive the same punishment as any other member of society. In my opinion Mr Voss, when a person partakes in criminal activities, especially activities as abhorrent as these, then all privileges must go out of the window.

"Heard it all before sweetheart but we'll just have to wait and see won't we?"

The question was rhetorical and Anna hurriedly left the room without responding.

Swiftly returning to her office, she made a phone call and within minutes had left the station and accompanied by Beth Saunders, was on her way to

New Scotland Yard. Opened by the Queen in 2017, the building is vast but Anna knew exactly where she was heading and it wouldn't be entering through the main entrance. At the very rear of the building on the ground floor was a small unassuming door that led directly to the offices and laboratory of the Central Forensic Image Team. There was still stringent security to go through but it was more streamlined than the main reception area, as the office was only visited by employees of the police force. Anna hadn't been here for quite some time but she hadn't forgotten her way around and with Beth following in hot pursuit, they were soon standing outside the door of Detective Chief Inspector Richard Walker. Richard was time served and had taken on the role of head trainer after a lifelong interest in photography and of course having successfully undertaken and passed intensive training himself. He now headed up the Lab team and trained new recruits who were destined to work in one particular field of police work. With the advent of CCTV imaging several years earlier, the department was now inundated with work but Anna didn't want a minion for the task she was asking for, she wanted the best, now all she had to do was convince Richard of that. Their paths hadn't crossed for a long time, so she hoped he would still be as approachable as he'd been in the past. Seeing her and Beth coming along

the corridor through the blinds that dressed his interior window, Richard was out of his seat and opening the door just as Anna was about to knock.
"Well bless my soul, if it isn't Anna Draycott! You're a sight for sore eyes not to mention a blast from the past."
Richard then leaned forward and gave her a friendly kiss on the cheek.
"Sorry to hear your sad news Anna."
"I didn't think you would know?"
"News travels fast in our game, you should know that. Please, come in."
After introducing Beth and getting the formalities over with, Anna explained what she required and that at the moment it was imperative to not share the results with anyone as it was presently a very sensitive issue. All the time Richard nodded his head sagely.
"As you know, we have a crack team of experts here Anna. We follow a systematic forensic process, and use human skills when assessing a person's suitability to join us and as it goes, I have a great guy….."
"It has to be you Richard, you're the only one I feel comfortable trusting this with."
Again he nodded.
"Well it must be your lucky day as I've just had an appointment cancelled so I can have a look now if you like. Would you like to observe? Most people

are fascinated by the process?"

"Thanks, we'd like that very much."

The three made their way down what felt like numerous long corridors and then into a large laboratory where several men were seated in front of high tech computers but none of them bothered to look up from their work as the detectives passed by.

"These guys work under immense pressure but that said, they all love their work. We've been able to play a key part in bringing down some notoriously hardened criminals and at times it's been purely on the evidence we've been able to supply directly from this Lab."

Richard suddenly stopped and took a seat in front of a vacant monitor and Anna and Beth each stood to one side. They were mesmerised at the speed in which the man worked. The first thing Richard did was to install the disc and make a copy from which he would actually work and then handed the original back to Anna.

"Can't be too careful, plus this way we can never be blamed for ballsing up the evidence!"

Next, using various software programs Ricard enlarged and adjusted the pixels and then lifted an image of the Judge from the disc. Clapping his hands with almost childlike glee he pressed print and within a few seconds a high quality, almost photographic picture spewed out of the printer.

"You're lucky, whoever shot this footage used a very high end camera, which makes my job a whole lot easier. You wouldn't believe some of the crap we're handed with the expectations of receiving back a crystal clear image. Contrary to what you see on CSI and other TV shows, that just isn't possible with the technology we have available, well at least not at the moment."

Anna couldn't thank her colleague enough, though she hadn't mentioned who the image was of and Richard Walker hadn't asked. Had she or Beth been able to see Richard's face while he was working, it might have been a different story. This wasn't the first time he'd been asked to enhance the face of Michael Lemmings but Richard knew that this could possibly turn out to be the last. Before Anna had even driven out of the carpark, Richard was on the phone to the office of the Chief Superintendent some six floors above his own. He hated going behind Anna's back but his career was far too important to him and if it ever got out that he had turned a blind eye, that career would most definitely have been in jeopardy.

CHAPTER TWENTY THREE

Bobby had been released from custody just a few minutes before Ken Voss and when Ken stepped out into the bright sunshine, he saw his adopted nephew sitting on a low wall that in the distant past, had at some time been made into a flower bed but was now overgrown and unloved, a bit like Bobby he thought.
"Hello Kid! Whatever are you doin' here?"
"Oh Uncle Kenny I'm in so much trouble, Maggie will kill me when she finds out what I've done!"
Bobby didn't seem to have the intelligence to ask why his uncle was here and Ken ruffled the young man's head just as he'd always done and at the same time laughed in an attempt to put Bobby at ease.
"Calm down kiddo and don't go worryin' about things you don't even know will happen. What say we make our way over to Joyce's and I treat you to a slap up breakfast? We can have a long chat about everythin' and put the whole bleedin' world to rights if you like?"
Bobby was on his feet in an instant, Uncle Kenny always had a way of making things alright and suddenly Bobby was hungry, even though he'd been given food only a short while ago.
"Actually I'm starvin' Uncle Kenny, I could eat the jokey and chase the horse."

"Is there somethin' you ain't tellin' me boy?"
"Like what?"
"You ain't queer are you?"
Bobby looked at Ken with a puzzled expression, as if he didn't have the faintest idea what Kenny was on about.
"It's eat the horse and chase the jockey you muppet."
Bobby now looked more confused than ever.
"Never mind, come on walk up a bit."

When Anna got back to the station she didn't let on about her findings to anyone, there was further research needed before she was prepared to share anything. Switching on her computer she logged onto Google and typed in the Judge's name. Sitting back for a moment while the images loaded, it felt like forever and she impatiently drummed her fingertips on the desk. It was one thing Kenneth Voss telling her who the person in the footage was but it was quite a different matter when it came down to her taking that information to her boss. She needn't have worried, the first face profile to appear was proof enough and with the enhanced photograph that Richard Walker had provided gripped firmly in her hand, she headed to the Chief's office. His door was wide open and seeing his empty chair Anna turned to Drew Payton with a quizzical and somewhat disappointed look on her face.

"Where is he?"

"Got summoned to New Scotland Yard Ma'am and he wasn't best pleased I can tell you."

Anna's brown furrowed with confusion, what on earth was going on?

"Let me know the moment he gets back!"

On arrival at the Yard, Lou Garnet was immediately escorted up to the office of Chief Superintendent George Madden. It was a step up from yesterday when his dressing down had come from the second in command, Superintendent Miles Crow. Now Lou was about to attend a meeting he hadn't requested and with the highest of the high to boot. He had absolutely no idea what this was all about and that fact alone had him slightly nervous and on his guard. Unlike yesterday, there were no minions or secretaries, this meeting was private and that alone unnerved Lou even further.

"Good afternoon Chief Inspector, please take a seat."

"Sir."

Waiting for his superior to begin, Lou looked around the high rise office. The furnishings were expensive and would easily have been in keeping in a five star hotel. Glancing out of the window, he was in awe at the view and momentarily compared it to his own box of an office, that up until now he'd been quite happy with.

"Nice isn't it? I never tire of looking at it."

"I can imagine Sir."

Lou wanted to add 'you lucky bastard' but knew better.

"Now it has been brought to my attention that you are investigating one of her Majesty's High Court Judges."

Lou stared at the Chief with a totally blank expression, what on earth was going on? Raising his hand he asked for permission to speak, which was duly granted.

"I'm sorry Sir but unless you're privy to information that I have yet to receive, then I don't have the first idea what you are talking about."

"I can appreciate that as the news was passed down to me less than an hour ago, so I quite understand if you've yet to be brought up to speed. The Judge in question is the Honourable Michael Lemmings no less. I understand the importance of the high profile case you are currently working on and the need for it to be brought to closure, especially for the general public but a high court Judge cannot be seen to be involved. Not only would it leave the Government with egg on its face but potentially bring the entire judicial system into disrepute."

Again Lou Garnet raised his hand and once again he was given permission to speak.

"Can I at least find out what my team have

unearthed before we go down that road?"
Suddenly the Superintendent's tone changed from one of friendliness to one of authority and Lou could instantly tell that he wasn't being asked, this was a direct order.
"No you cannot! You will do as you are told or suffer the consequences. I'm aware that this case needs putting to bed ASAP and that is why the Judge will assist you in any way possible to bring the culprits to justice, he has no choice in the matter. When this is all over he will be dealt with in house and that is an end to the matter. Good day Chief Inspector!"
Knowing better than to try and argue, Lou thanked the Chief Superintendent for his time and then drove at speed back to the station. Anna didn't need to be told of his return as he barged straight into her office some twenty minutes later and she nearly jumped out of her skin as the door smashed against the wall.
"What the fuck is going on Anna?!!"
She was shocked that he already knew she had something, you couldn't keep a secret in this place for love nor money and she should have known that. Strangely, this time she didn't mind too much, although by the look on his face, her boss didn't appear too pleased?
"We not only have a name for one of the victims but we have a positive ID on the murderer Sir."

"Show me."

Anna removed the disc from her bag and placed it into the drive of her computer but she was still confused. The Chief wasn't happy and why had he come to her office? She couldn't remember him setting foot in here before now, or if he had then it had been a long, long time ago. As the DVD played Lou leaned over her shoulder and Anna talked him through their findings. Halfway through the viewing Chief Garnet stood up, walked around to the other side of Anna's desk and purposefully took a seat.

"You can switch it off now Anna and I'm sorry but you're definitely not going to like what I'm about to say. Fuck, I don't like it myself but my hands are tied and there's absolutely nothing I can do about it."

Anna suddenly had a sinking feeling, he'd been to the Yard so Richard Walker must have spoken to someone.

"The Judge is strictly off limits to this inquiry."

"What?!!!! I can't believe what I'm hearing Sir, he's not just simply involved, he's the actual bloody killer!"

"I realise that and it sickens me to the core but you know as well as I do the rules dictate that we must follow protocol. There's no damn choice in the matter, we have to go along with what the top honchos tell us to do. He will be coming in and he's

well aware that he has to assist us, so that at least might help us nail Maggie McKay in all of this."
"This stinks Sir!"
Lou Garnet violently slammed the palm his hand down onto the table in sheer frustration and Anna now thought she might just have pushed things too far.
"Do you think I don't fucking know that?!!!"
Quickly getting up from her seat, she stormed past her boss and out of her office. Almost marching through the communal space she didn't look at any of her team. The hours and hours that they had all invested, lost time away from their families and loved ones, time they could never get back and for what? In the ladies toilets and after making sure that the cubicles were empty, Anna Draycott broke down and sobbed uncontrollably.

That afternoon and accompanied by legal representation, the Right Honourable Judge Michael Lemmings attended an interview at the station. He wasn't under caution and to begin with took a holier than thou attitude. Eric Barnes was once again Anna's trusted ally and because this was such a sensitive matter, Chief Garnet was also sitting in.
"Tell me Mr Lemmings, what involvement did Maggie McKay have in the making of these atrocities?"
"I wouldn't call them atrocities my dear, I rather

like to think of them as art films."
"You sick bastard!"
"Maggie!!!"
Lou Garnet had to stop his detective before she stepped too far over the line for him to pull her back.
"Mr Lemmings, I will politely ask you once again, what involvement did Maggie McKay have in the making of these atrocities? You can evade the questions all you like you piece of shit but if you don't play ball and tell us what we need to know, your protection from prosecution could easily disappear."
"That would simply never happen, Detective!"
"Don't be so sure. These murders are high profile, the public are scared and saving your livelihood and high social standing isn't worth the hassle this case will bring if we don't get some answers!"
"Look, I only ever met the female in question once and for a very short amount of time at that. I have a man that arranges things and he dealt directly with this gangster woman. By all accounts she's a very unsavoury human being, so please simply speak to Dennis Havers. As for making the films, initially she did that without my permission, the sneaky little bitch!"
"Really? You really expect us to believe that?"
"It's the truth, well initially at least."
The Judge giggled in a childlike way and it was

almost too much for Anna to bear. She tried desperately to hold her composure as she didn't want the Chief to step in and take over if she lost her rag.

"One last question, why remove the organs and cut off the heads and limbs?"

The question made Michael Lemmings laugh out loud and Anna was repulsed by the arrogant, monster sitting before her. She now understood how a person could so easily kill another because right now if she'd had a gun in her hand she didn't think it would have been too much of a struggle to pull the trigger.

"Doctor Dewala, Mr Dewala to you, is a member of our select little group and a damn fine surgeon I might add. He came up with the idea of organ transplantation, a kind of by-product if you like. Making these films doesn't come cheap so it was a way of recuperating some of our costs. Actually it turned out far more lucrative than we could ever have imagined. I didn't realise that a kidney could command so much, did you Detective?"

Again the Judge began to laugh and Anna knew that she really couldn't deal with anymore of him today, not without ending up on a charge herself for doing him some serious injury. The Chief, as always, could read her like a book and noting the frustration in her voice, nodded his head in her direction. Anna knew what that meant and swiftly

brought the interview to an immediate close.
"That will be all for now but be available should we wish to speak to you further."
"Please would have been nice!"
Anna barged past the brutal and sadistic excuse for a human being and marched off down the hall. Michael Lemmings then turned towards Lou Garnet, his face was red with anger and he wanted an apology.
"I think you need to teach that bitch a lesson in manners Chief Inspector and I will expect her to apologise for her behaviour and tone towards me forthwith."
Lou, still silently raging over his meeting with the Superintendent, also couldn't take much more and turned on the arrogant, self-opinionated and poor excuse for a human being, with a vengeance.
"You're not on the bench now you old twat so I would keep my fucking trap shut if I were you! All it takes is for someone to let something out and the shit will really hit the fan. You are hanging on by a very fine thread and I've just about reached the end of my tether with the fucking judicial restrictions that are placed upon the force when someone, in this instance you!, is as guilty as fucking sin but is allowed to walk away scot free."
Michael Lemmings began to cough and splutter but was still able to utter a few more words even though his representative had placed his hand onto

the Judge's arm in an attempt to silence him. "You wouldn't dare and besides, the institution would leave no stone unturned to find out where the leak came from and the book would be thrown at that person from a very tall height. Whether you like it or not detective, at the top of the tree we all look after our own!"
Lou didn't reply but gave a look that told the Judge it would be a very bad idea to test him any further. The Chief was well aware that he would now probably be summoned to the Superintendent's office for another dressing down but to be honest he really didn't give a shit and this time he would, come hell or high water, have his say no matter what George Madden tried to threaten him with!

Dennis Havers was arrested that afternoon though charges were yet to be brought. When faced with the evidence and informed what Michael Lemmings had said, Dennis instantly spilled his guts regarding exactly what had happened, times and dates, not to mention naming Sam Wenner. There might be honour amongst thieves but when it came down to these lowlifes, they would sell out anyone to save their own pathetic skins. When Sam was brought in he was a little cagier and would only admit to his connection going as far as introducing the relevant parties to each other. He didn't give Maggie up, that wasn't his style and he just hoped that she would return the favour even though his involvement had thankfully been minimal. The custody suit was rapidly filling up and they now held three suspects connected to the same case. The doctor had yet to be located and it would take the team several hours longer to learn that Adesh Dewala had boarded flight DEL562 to India almost twenty four hours earlier. After being invited to an urgent meeting with the Superintendent, Michael Lemmings had then forewarned his old friend and Adesh, knowing that this situation would almost certainly arise one day, had already moved vast amounts of money and bonds back to his homeland. The UK signed an extradition treaty with India back in 1992 but proceedings were incredibly slow and very expensive, not to mention the fact that this case would probably never see the inside of the Old Bailey, so money and resources wouldn't be wasted on an extradition order. All in all it was turning into a farce and Anna was pinning all her hopes onto charging Maggie. The second interview was to begin in the morning but for now Anna called it a day, she was dead tired and feeling incredibly deflated and let down.

Ken and Bobby's breakfast chat had gone well, at least as far as Ken was concerned. Bobby had explained about getting arrested and that the Old Bill had taken the disc out of his pocket. In almost a childlike way Bobby explained what it contained and asked his uncle if he'd had anything to do with it.

"Sunshine, I might be a lot of things but murdering women and kids ain't among them."

For a moment Bobby looked confused as he tilted his head slightly to one side with a quizzical expression on his face. He stared intently at his uncle but didn't say anything.

"What?"

"You said kids?"

"No I didn't you must have misheard me."

Ken could have kicked himself, this was exactly the thing he had feared would happen. Sometimes you let things slip without thinking about it and that could easily get you in a whole heap of trouble.

"You did Uncle Kenny! You said 'I may be a lot of things but murdering women and kids ain't among them'. What did you mean?"

"It must have been a slip of the tongue. Eat your burger before it gets cold! We have to make some plans 'cause it looks like Maggie is goin' to be charged and we will have to keep the firm afloat. It's time for you to step up to the plate kid, think you're ready?"

Bobby grinned from ear to ear and Ken hoped that his last sentence had been enough to put his breakfast companion off of the scent and stop him asking anymore questions.

That night as Anna lay in bed unable to sleep her mind raced as she tried to come up with an idea that might help them in some way. If they couldn't charge that monster maybe the powers that be could somehow make sure he never did it again. It wouldn't be just or fair but life wasn't fair, something Anna knew only too well. Closing her eyes she again tried to get some rest but her mind just couldn't shut off. What about the victims? If anything was to come out of this horrific crime spree it was to at least give all of those poor lost souls a name, she, the entire Metropolitan Police Force come to that, surely owed them that much?

CHAPTER TWENTY FOUR

Yet again after another fitful and broken night's sleep, Anna was seated behind her desk at Tottenham Station by six am. With all of the thoughts still racing through her mind, thoughts which had kept her awake for most of the night, she was now dog tired but she was also a woman on a mission. The team had strangely all turned up for work early but that may have been helped along by the call she'd made to Steve Johnson in the early hours of the morning. Anna now gave them strict instructions to once again go through the database, with a fine-tooth comb if necessary. They were all told to double check for any missing persons of Eastern European descent in the last two years and note any distinguishing marks. Drew, in his naivety spoke out of turn and Beth cringed when she looked at the Guv's face.

"Ma'am we've already done that and more than once! If you want my opinion, it's just a complete waste of time and resources."

Anna slowly nibbled on her bottom lip. It was a peculiar trait she had when angry and all that had worked closely with her over the years recognised it and knew to keep a wide berth.

"Detective!!! I did not ask for your opinion and I'm fast becoming pissed off with the way you continually feel you have the right to challenge me!

You may well have done it all before, as you so eloquently put it but this time you will include the information on the very unique tattoos that have recently come to light courtesy of Michael Hanks. If you still insist on querying my orders, get the fuck out of this room and off of this case right now!" Drew instantly hung his head in embarrassment and the rest of the team sloped back to their desks. Anna may have been a small woman in stature, just five feet tall in heels but you really didn't want to come up against her if her cage had been rattled and the recent developments in this particular case had done precisely that.

Before the shift was over they had miraculously discovered the names of three of the victims. Obviously Alina Balan through information supplied by Ken Voss and they were now just waiting for a family member to arrive from Romania to provide a DNA sample. It was so infuriating that the other two bodies had been in the system all along. Anna was aware that Cambridge and Wisbech had previously fucked up in the most glorious fashion but this latest correspondence really took the biscuit. In just a few hours, both stations had contacted her team and revealed that they had unknowingly, which was a total joke, somehow misplaced files on two of the victims being reported missing by relatives months earlier.

In particular a young Russian woman in Cambridge, who to date has never surfaced. Anna immediately telephoned Larry Hanwell at Parkside station and the Cambridge Inspector had been expecting her call.

"Anna, so good to hear from you and before you continue, I must apologise profusely regarding the late information you have recieved. I have since had my officers trawl the city's close circuit monitors on the date in question and there was footage of a woman being forced into a white van on the night that the young Russian woman went missing. The registration plates were false so sadly we are no further forward."

"The driver?"

"The street was poorly lit and added to the fact that the cameras are now old and need replacing, I...."

Chief Hanwell momentarily stopped speaking when he heard Anna noisily sigh.

"As I was about to say, the image was too grainy to get a clear profile I'm afraid. I will send over a copy of the missing person's report and......"

Not waiting for him to finish Anna slammed down the handset in sheer frustration. There had been the mother of all cockups but she was damned if any of her team would be held accountable when it was all over, that's if it would ever be all over. Quickly making her way to the Chiefs office she relayed all that had now come to light.

That evening both Sofija Kalnins and Dimitri Chenyshevsky had been informed of the possibility that their loved ones were unfortunately deceased. Having to fly over from Russia, Dimitri wouldn't arrive for a couple of days but Sofija had agreed for DNA samples from her baby to be taken at a local hospital the following day. It was a step, albeit a small one, in the right direction but Anna wanted all of them named, the other female and the little girl!

For most of the day everything had been in place for Maggie's second interview but various unexpected delays had meant that they only got around to starting at just before four that afternoon. Anna knew she had the woman bang to rights but she needed irrefutable proof and really didn't want to have to apply for an extension but the clock was ticking. Maggie almost strutted into the interview room, she was tired and riled with how long everything was taking. Sitting next to her solicitor, she sighed and tapped her fingers on the table as she waited impatiently for Anna to switch on the recorder and introduce everyone. Her heavy sighs didn't go unnoticed and that alone gave Anna a brief moment's pleasure.

"Ms McKay, we have reason to believe that you were involved in the production of pornographic material, though I do use that term loosely. What I probably should have said is 'snuff movies' and a total of five bodies have surfaced in connection to those so called movies."

"No comment."

Anna didn't let the reply rile her, she had yet to get to the best bit and couldn't wait for Maggie's response.

"We will shortly have confirmation on the identities of Alina Balan, Peteris Jonsons and Khristina Chernyshevsky and we are still working to find out who the other two victims are. Can you assist us in anyway?"

"Fuck off copper, I ain't got a clue what you're talkin' about."

"For God's sake woman, you have been named! The recordings were found at the home of your late father and forensics found several different blood groups in a secure room inside your business premises, all of which match at least four of the victims. You or others may have tried your best to sanitise the area but fortunately for us, your housekeeping skills were not up to par."

Inwardly Maggie was starting to panic, though you would never have guessed by the front she was showing. She was tired and not thinking straight as images and conversations rapidly ran through her mind and she could only come to one conclusion, Asti was to blame in all of this. He obviously hadn't disposed of the victims properly or sanitised the room adequately enough. She had the option to grass him up but that would have only been by giving his name, if in fact that was his real name and besides, it would be a cardinal sin in her world to assist the police in any way whatsoever. Without any further discussion with her solicitor she suddenly fired a question that shocked not only David Granger to the absolute core but also everyone else in the room.

"You spoke to that old cunt the Judge yet?"

"We have spoken to several people in connection with this Ms McKay but presently you are the only person of interest to us."

Maggie ran her open fingers through the peroxide bob that was now greasy and in dire need of a wash. As she slowly spoke she stared directly into the eyes of Detective Inspector Draycott and Anna felt a chill run down her spine. The woman was evil, pure and simple. She showed no remorse or pity for the victims and fleetingly, for some reason Anna thought of Myra Hindley's arrest photograph. The likeness was frighteningly identical, a hard faced human being, totally void of any compassion or regret.

"I get it, you lot are closing ranks as usual but you ain't making me the fuckin' scapegoat I can tell you! I need a bloody break, I have to speak to my brief and its fuckin' urgent so don't try and refuse me."

Reluctantly Anna agreed to a ten minute recess and switched off the recorder. She didn't like the fact that Maggie seemed to be taking charge but she couldn't really deny the request and in all honesty she needed a break herself. Leaving the suspect and her legal representation she headed out along with Eric and the Chief, to grab a quick coffee.

"What do you think she's up to Sir?"

"Haven't got a clue but I expect we'll find out soon enough."

"You got any thoughts Eric?"

Eric Barnes took a moment before he answered. He'd been witness to this kind of scenario many times over the years and it certainly wasn't looking good. The crafty bitch had something up her sleeve, that was for sure but Anna was so obviously stressed that he didn't want to add to her burden until it was absolutely necessary.

"Not really Anna and it's best not to speculate."

Fifteen minutes later Eric and the Chief were the first to re-enter the room but Anna was stopped by David Granger, just as she was about to go inside.

"Excuse me Detective Inspector but before we begin again, might I have a quick word?"

Anna eyed him suspiciously, she didn't trust legal reps as they always had an ulterior motive and it rarely came down in favour of the law. Nodding once, she put out her hand and guided him into a small side room that had previously been used for interviewing but was now little more than a storeroom.

"How can I help you Mr Granger?"

"This is a delicate matter and I would just like to add that in no way do I condone the criminal acts that have been mentioned here today. Now, what I am about to say is strictly off the record?"

"Fire away, I'm not exactly in a position to record what you're saying now am I?"

"My client wishes me to inform you that should she be charged with any of the offences previously discussed, she has copies of all of the movies which are stored in a secure secret location. Furthermore, Ms McKay has instructed a member of her staff to release the discs to the media should Judge Michael Jennings walk away from prosecution and she ends up being the only one charged."

Of course none of the statement was true but Maggie was shrewd. She knew they wouldn't charge a High Court Judge, so the bluff was her get out of jail card because there was no way on God's earth that the government or the big boys in the Met, would ever allow any of this to hit the headlines.

"Thank you Mr Granger and in light of what you have just told me I feel we need to delay proceedings for a while longer. I shall be applying for an extension to hold your client, so could you please inform her that she will be here for quite a while yet."

Opening the door to the interview room Anna

poked her head inside and as she beckoned Eric and the Chief to come out, she noticed that Maggie McKay was now wearing a broad grin on her face. The extension was granted without challenge and Anna had asked for the maximum ninety six hours. Now seated in the Chief's office, she revealed all that the brief had said to her.

"So what now Sir?"

"This is way above my paygrade and for now I will need to seek further advice. First thing in the morning I'll pay the Superintendent another visit but my gut feeling, is that this is all going to go tits up!"

Initially after being told that the Judge was not to be involved it had felt like a very hollow victory for Anna but now she wasn't convinced there would be any kind of victory at all. Visiting the custody suite on another matter entirely, brought Anna a moment's pleasure but it wouldn't last long. Maggie had only just been told of the extension and she could be heard going ballistic in her cell. Anna just couldn't help herself and making her way along the corridor she opened the inspection hatch and smiled. Instantly Maggie was kicking and punching the door and as much as it was going to bring satisfaction for what she was about to say, Anna was really grateful that she was on the opposite side of the door. Maggie was most definitely a force to

be reckoned with and on a physical one to one, Anna knew she would never have stood a chance.
"Kick off all you like McKay but you're here for the duration, actually I was the one who just secured the extension of time."
"You cunt, you fuckin' bitch, I'll kill you......."
Anna left the custody suite with a smile on her face but deep down she knew it might well be short lived.

The following day at nine am sharp, Chief Inspector Garnet was again seated outside of the Superintendent's office. He already knew how this was all going to pan out but it had to be made official before he broke the news to his team and Anna in particular.
"Come!"
"Good morning Sir."
"Inspector. I really hope you have some good news for me and we can now close this case and finally release a statement to the media? The lack of any real information being available has caused the general public to go into a state of panic and the phones are ringing off the hook. No one feels safe and that isn't ever a good situation for anyone."
"Not exactly Sir. It seems Ms McKay has an ace up her sleeve and I wanted to bring the matter to your attention before any decisions were made."
The Superintendent sighed heavily, why couldn't

things just simply go to plan?

"Maggie McKay has copies of all the discs and has informed us that if she is charged and not Judge Lemmings, then she has given instruction that the footage be released to the red tops. Now whether this is true I'm not certain but I'm not prepared to take the chance without your approval."

George Madden didn't speak for a moment, things were now really getting out of hand and he too needed to seek advice and recommendation from a higher level. In the wrong hands these discs could do irreparable damage to the Met, not to mention the government but the press were out for blood, so this case needed to be brought to some kind of closure as soon as possible.

"You'll have to leave this with me Lou, it's a big decision."

The Chief nodded, stood up and left the office. It always amazed him how the bigwigs were full of authority and calling you by your title one minute but as soon as their back was against the wall they wanted to be all pally, pally.

As Lou pulled out of the car park, the Superintendent was asking for an urgent meeting with the Commissioner. There were several ranks above him including the Commander and Assistant Commissioner but time was of the essence and even though he knew his actions wouldn't be looked upon favourably by his superiors, George had broken protocol and gone straight to the top. An hour after a deflated Chief Garnet had got into his car, the Commissioner was on her way over to King Charles Street, just off of Whitehall, accompanied by the Chief Superintendent. George really hated coming to the Home Office and thankfully it wasn't a regular occurrence but all the same he was nervous and edgy. He felt that the suits looked down upon anyone in a uniform, well, all except the Commissioner. She was a law unto herself and could quite easily have made the decision regarding the case. For some strange reason she wanted reassurances and George wondered if the Judge had more than the clout of his father's peerage.

As the massive glass building came into sight, Chief Superintendent Madden could feel his palms begin to sweat and he felt immense relief when the Commissioner instructed him to wait in the foyer until and only if, he was called to give any details. There was little love lost between the Home Secretary and the Commissioner, two women in one kitchen never worked and the Home Secretary took any opportunity to make the Commissioner look small. It was unprofessional and something the Commissioner didn't want to be seen or heard by anyone who ranked below her. In all the meeting lasted for a little over thirty minutes and in that time the Commissioner learned just how high the connections held by the Honourable Judge Lemmings went. He was a very close friend of a senior royal, to the degree that he was often a house guest at Sandringham over the Christmas period. If anything regarding this case was ever to be associated with the occupants of Buck House it most certainly wouldn't be good for the Royals nor for the equilibrium of the government as Lemmings had initially been introduced to the family by a former prime minister. George Madden wasn't called into the meeting and was simply given the outcome in the car on the way back to New Scotland Yard.

Back in his office Chief Superintendent Madden made the call but the news wasn't given over the telephone, instead he invited Lou out for a late lunch that day. As soon as he heard the invitation Chief Garnet knew what he was going to hear wouldn't be good but still, there must be more to it for him to have received an invite, so just as protocol dictated, he graciously accepted. At just before noon he was shown to a table in a select, roped off area on board The Yacht. He'd been told to attend in uniform and now he could see why. Permanently moored at Temple Pier, The Yacht is a high end eatery and favoured by the hierarchy of the Yard. It was far above Lou's normal level of dining and while he didn't exactly feel uncomfortable in the surroundings, he knew this wasn't normal practice for the likes of him.

"Thank you for coming, please take a seat Lou." George ordered drinks and idle chitchat followed but it was uncomfortable for Lou. When the food had been chosen and the starters brought to the table, George at last began to explain what was going on, or at least as much as he had been told, regarding what they were expected to do.

"So basically they all walk away scot free? Hardly law abiding Sir, if you don't mind me saying that is?"

"For the record Lou, this all galls me as much as it does you but we are talking about the involvement, even if it is indirectly, of some of the most influential, powerful and high-ranking people in this country. If news of this ever got out, by association alone it would be devastating. You know as well as I do what the backlash was from the Profumo affair and that was almost sixty years ago, so imagine what could happen now? The freedom of press has moved on significantly since then and as much as it saddens me to say this, this scandal could actually bring the country to its knees."

"And just how do you expect me to deal with this? What exactly do I say to my team?"

Lou listened and while George talked, Lou sighed

several times.

"So you see, although no charges will be brought, the culprits will be made to pay. Unconventional I know but at the end of the day, the most important fact is that they will be dealt with and no other parties will get dragged into it and the crimes will cease once and for all."

"I need clarity Sir, exactly how will they be dealt with? I'm going to have to face a barrage of questions when I get back and in all honesty, the men and women on my team have worked tirelessly on this case so they deserve the truth."

"I'm sorry Lou but I'm not at liberty to disclose any details other than they will be dealt with, my hands are tied I'm afraid."

Getting into his car, George didn't drive directly back to the station, he needed time to think, time to work out exactly what to tell the team. Luckily he always kept a raincoat in the boot of his car and after parking up he put it on to conceal his uniform. The greasy spoon on Bruce Castle was three roads away from the station and far enough that the chance of being spotted by one of his men was minimal. Lou spent over two hours in the place, observing customers from all walks of life come and go but by four thirty that afternoon he couldn't put off facing his detectives any longer. After settling his bill for the numerous mugs of tea he had consumed, Lou Garnet made his way back to the station with a more than heavy heart.

CHAPTER TWENTY FIVE

To alleviate the chance of any potential eavesdropping, the central office was completely cleared on the orders of the Chief and Anna, along with Eric Barnes, was called to Lou's office. While the Chief had sat mulling over things in the cafe, he realised that this was far too much to place on one person's shoulders. Anna would need someone to confide in because Lou was under no illusion that at times in the future, she would have serious doubts about the decisions that they had been forced to make. Eric was time served and would soon go back into retirement but he was also a very trusted colleague and Lou knew he would make a good confidant should his detective inspector need to ease her burden at any time.
"Please take a seat."
Lou looked at them both for a few seconds before he eventually spoke, what he was about to reveal so went against the grain and this now felt like the lowest point in an otherwise unblemished career. Instructions had been handed down that only the bare minimum should be revealed but Lou trusted both people sitting before him and besides, they knew they were bound by the Official Secrets Act.
"It's a no go I'm afraid. McKay has to be released and there will be no charges brought against either her or the Judge."

"What?!!!!"

Anna shot up and began to pace around the office, finally she stopped but when she did, she violently punched the door in sheer frustration and her voice was raised as she raged.

"For fuck's sake Guv, they are guilty!!! Doesn't anyone give a shit about that! Or is it me being thick, am I missing something here?"

"Don't be so absurd of course you're not and I'm more than aware of their guilt Anna, now if you will just calm down for a moment and listen to me, you may begin to understand."

Doing as she was asked she reluctantly took her seat and as she did so, rubbed at her throbbing knuckles. Chief Inspector Garnet spent the next five minutes or so explaining in great detail why the charges wouldn't be brought and what would happen next, although even he wasn't privy to the exact details. They were between MI5 and the Home Secretary alone and unbeknown to anyone else, a plan was already being put into force by the security services. By the time Lou had finished speaking Anna had tears of frustration and sadness in her eyes. Frustration that their hands were tied and there wasn't a thing she could do about it and sadness for the victims, who would never receive the justice they so deserved.

Calling all of her team back into the incident room, Anna stood at the front shoulder to shoulder with

the Chief and Eric. When everyone had congregated and all murmuring had finally stopped, Lou would be the one to address the team. It had been agreed that they needed to show a united front, if only for appearances sake but right at this moment in time Anna felt as if she'd been stabbed in the back and all she could think of was walking out of the place and never coming back.
"Thank you everyone. Now I have to break some devastating news and after I have finished, there will be absolutely no questions, do I make myself clear?"
The murmuring began again and only stopped when Chief Garnet slammed his hand down onto the table.
"I said, do I make myself clear!!!"
Everyone nodded their heads and Anna scanned the room and in particular, focused her attention on Drew Payton but he had his head hung so low that she couldn't look into his eyes.
"There will be no charges brought and McKay will be released. This comes under the heading of national security, so the file is now closed. From now on, you will all revert back to the cases you were previously working on. The bods at the Yard have been so gracious and kind in offering to fund a memorial for the victims and I expect you all to attend, not just out of duty but because we weren't able to give the victims what they so rightfully

deserved. As far as this outcome goes, I'm sorry but it's out of my hands and this is how it has to be. Those on high have made the decision and after all, they know best!"

His sarcasm was noted by all and with that Anna marched briskly from the room before anyone was able to see the tears in her eyes. Making her way to the custody suite she slammed down the inspection hatch to Maggie's cell.

"You might have gotten away with this one you murdering bitch but I swear as God is my witness that I will make it my duty to bring you down. From now on you won't take a fucking shit without my knowing about it, I'm going to haul your vicious arse in here every chance I get!"

"Fuck off copper and open this bastard door!"

Now Anna laughed and in this moment of absolute devastation, the look on Maggie's face brought a wry smile to the Inspector.

"The extension was for the maximum time allowed, so on my reckoning we have you for almost another three days. Enjoy your stay!"

Maggie again began to kick off but just like before, it fell on deaf ears. It didn't take long for the news that there would be no charges to filter down through the ranks and Maggie McKay's temporary incarceration would be made as unpleasant as possible.

Ken Voss arrived at the arches early and within the hour had contacted Eryk Kowalska. Eryk was instructed to demolish the room he'd constructed and it needed to be done that day, of course he would be handsomely compensated and that phrase alone saw the torture chamber dismantled in record time.

As yet Bobby hadn't shown his face which somewhat concerned Ken but after calling him, Bobby assured his uncle that he just needed a bit of time on his own and would be back at work within a couple of days. It was strange how quickly things got back to normal and none of the lads seemed to have a problem taking orders from Ken, he just hoped he wasn't jumping the gun by taking over the reins so soon. The street Tom's were brought back into line and Albie was given the task of engaging a few more girls. A long firm was being planned where a company would be set up and legitimately purchase goods paying the suppliers promptly, earning respect and a good credit score. The goods would then be sold on to the general public for a little above cost and then after a lengthy time of trading, a large order would be placed but the Long Firm would then disappear overnight without paying a single supplier. In the past Brice had regularly done business this way and if handled correctly, the rewards could be vast. Ken also scaled up the extortion game by several notches. All in all, in just a few days Ken Voss had put the firm back on track.

Bobby had spent the time since his release alone in the house mulling over everything. He knew he wasn't the brightest spark in the box but something was being kept from him and he didn't like it. When Maggie got back she would make him suffer and he was scared, so scared that he'd taken the handgun from the safe, cleaned it and filled the chambers in readiness. It was strangely something his dad had taught him when he was little and Bobby had learned fast. Whatever Maggie had planned for him, he didn't intend to take it lying down, for once in his life he was going to prove them all wrong and be the man his dad had always wanted him to be.

Maggie hurriedly exited the station first thing on Wednesday morning and she smelled like a garbage bin. She hadn't washed in days and her stomach was rumbling through lack of food. Apart from a couple of slices of dried bread, she had only been given water but she hadn't once complained. If the bastards had thought they would grind her down, they'd been sorely mistaken! She was a McKay and that name stood for more than those muppet's could ever know. There was no one outside to collect her, so hailing a cab she told the driver to take her over to Roland Way. She was in desperate need of a shower but told the cabbie to wait all the same. Abe Goldman, like his father before him, had been a black cab driver for well over thirty years and even though he lived out of the area and travelled in each day from Enfield, he still knew exactly who Maggie McKay was. When she'd told him to wait, there was no question Abe would refuse her and twenty minutes later she was back outside and ordered him to take her over to the arches.

On the same day Maggie was released from the station, Bobby McKay arrive at Pinchin Street and he was in a good mood. He now had a grip on his emotions but he wanted answers to questions that everyone always seemed to evade answering. The lads all patted him on the back when he entered and striding forward he made a beeline for his sister's office.
Ken looked up from some loan shark papers he was in the middle of issuing and smiled warmly when he saw who'd just come in.
"Hello Bob, good to see you kid."
Bobby flopped down into the armchair on the opposite side of the desk.
"You too Uncle Kenny. Kenny?"
"Yeah?"
"I need to ask some questions and I want you to be

honest with me, now that I'm the head of this firm and before you say anythin', I know you'll be runnin' things but I don't want to look like a fuckin' twat anymore. I want them all to take me seriously, even if I am a bit slow at times and I can't do that if they think they know secrets about me that I ain't been told about."

Ken had known that sooner or later this would happen, it had been coming for a long time and maybe now was the time to reveal the truth.

"I understand what you're sayin' kid but I don't think I'm the one you really need to speak to."

"I know but the person I need to get answers from is a complete bitch! You know that when I came in here and had a go at Mags she got angry with me. Kicked off big style and said she wasn't my sister but my mum? Said she hated me and wished I'd never been born. I know my sister can be a right spiteful cow Uncle Kenny but was that all it was, or was she tellin' me the truth? I really need to know once and for all."

Now Ken felt backed into a corner with no way out.

"What say we go and grab some breakfast?"

"No! I want the truth and I want it now Uncle Kenny."

Ken Voss rubbed at his brow with the tips of his fingers, why, oh why hadn't she kept her big mouth shut? This was all going to cause so much unnecessary hurt and would accomplish absolutely nothing.

"Okay, okay! I'm not happy about it and I shouldn't be the one to tell you this Bob but as no one else is prepared to, I suppose it falls to me. I know you've asked me before and I didn't confirm it either way so in answer to your question, yes, sadly it is true, Maggie is your mum but Brice brought you up as his own and…."

Within a few minutes of Bobby's arrival the door again suddenly opened and Maggie strode in. Surprised, the men glanced up from what they were doing and as soon as they saw her, were on their guard. Albie looked sheepish, Maggie had seen that look many times over the years and when his eyes darted in the direction of the office, she could feel the anger begin to build up inside.

"Who's in there Albie?"

Albie Mitchell remained silent and Maggie stomped towards him.

"I said! Who is in my fuckin' office?"

"Voss and Bobby but Maggie I don't think they knew you'd been released."

"Obviously fuckin' not!"

Maggie marched towards her office and pushed open the door just in time to hear the tail end of the conversation.

"He's right!"

Instantly both Ken and Bobby looked towards the now open doorway only to be greeted with a seething Maggie, who then slowly walked across the carpet in her high heeled stiletto shoes. As she spoke she directed her words towards Bobby alone and Ken closed his eyes for a split second as he knew only too well what was about to be said. "Some fuckin' lowlife raped me, that's how you were conceived. I didn't love you then and I don't love you now. Actually, if the truth be told I fuckin' hate you for ruinin' my life! I never wanted to keep you either but the old man felt differently and persuaded me out of getting an abortion but by God, I wished I hadn't listened to him! Then you came out a fuckin' retard and I would have put a pillow over your sickening little face but dad made sure I was never alone with you. I think he knew what I would do, so removed the temptation but do you know somethin'? You sicken me to the pit of my stomach, you're no good to anyone and I doubt whether you ever got it up with that fuckin' old whore you were in with. What a fuckin' state she was, but then I……….."

Maggie's sentence was halted when Bobby pulled out the handgun. Instantly Ken was out of his seat but Bobby didn't waver nor wait for Ken to try and stop him and taking aim he shot his mother squarely in the forehead. The look of sheer surprise on her face as she fell to the floor brought a smile to Bobby and he ginned as he tilted his head slowly to one side. It was the first time in his entire life that she had been surprised about anything he'd done. Ken ran from his side of the desk and stood over the body, stunned and unable to believe what the hell had just happened.

"Bobby!!!!!! Fuckin' hell, why!?! What the fuck did you do that for!!?!"

"She was rude about my Di, you can't go about slaggin' people off Uncle Kenny, it's not right."

"Bob! You can't just fuckin' shoot people willy-nilly because you don't like what they are sayin'. What a fuckin' mess!!!!"

Ken raced out into the main area and told Albie and Chris Freeman to disappear pronto and to make sure they kept their mouths well and truly shut. It was obvious that they had heard the gun but not one solitary question was asked. As they hastily excited through the door in the roller shutter, neither however noticed the white transit parked up across the road. The van was fully loaded with the most up to date satellite equipment that any government could wish for and seated inside were two MI5 agents and three cleaners.

Returning to the office Ken found Bobby pacing up and down.

"What do we do now Uncle Kenny? I've done a bad thing haven't I?"

"Well it ain't exactly good son, now is it?"

Bobby dropped to his knees and placing his hands over his head, began to rock back and forth like a

child. Kens heart went out to the young man. Poor Bobby McKay, for his entire life he'd been either used as a verbal punch bag by his own mother or was the butt of everyone else's jokes. This all had to stop now and Ken was going to make damn sure that it did but he also now realised that Bobby was a liability, not to mention a bit of a loose cannon, something he never could have imagined.
"Nothin' we can't clear up sunshine. I want you to go home and stay there until I call you. I'll take care of all this and then I'll pop round to Buxton Street and make sure you're alright. How's that sound?"
Without warning Bobby was suddenly back on his feet and had lovingly flung his arms around his uncle. As he clung on for dear life he made small steps from one foot to the other.
"I love you Uncle Kenny."
"I love you too kid. Now on your way, I have stuff to take care of."
As soon as he heard the door in the roller shutter slam shut, Ken pulled out his mobile and tapped in the number of a contact, who on the rare occasions when they had been forced to meet, had actually made Ken feel physically sick. After several rings it was finally answered and Ken informed the person on the other end, that a consignment of meat was ready for collection.

Over the past thirty years Harry Cunningham had

been employed at some time or another, by most of the London firms. In fact Brice had been a client on several occasions but Ken couldn't recall Maggie ever using the service. A pig farmer by trade, Harry was the perfect disposal man for anyone who had been rendered surplus to requirements. A portly man who resided in a remote hamlet in Norfolk, he was the soul of discretion. His dress was eccentric to say the least and invariably brought sniggers from all who came into contact with him. A checked shirt was always open to the waist, no matter what the weather. Long shorts were held up with garish red braces and a piece of blue rope acted as a makeshift belt. Wellington boots and a deerstalker hat completed the outfit, an outfit more regularly seen donned by hillbillies living somewhere south of the Mississippi rather than in a small English hamlet. Harry was always accompanied by his son Henry and daughter in-law Martha or Mar as she was referred to. Henry and Mar eerily bore more than a striking resemblance to each other and it was locally accepted that the pair were actually brother and sister. The idea sickened most of the bosses but it never stopped them calling on Harry when in need. Now it was Ken's turn and by darkness that day, the odd looking trio pulled their wagon up outside the arches. Ken had made himself scarce as soon as he'd ended the call but had given Harry instructions of where to find the key

and what to expect inside. Payment for the job would be hidden in an envelope under the kitchenette sink unit. Expecting to return the following morning and all would be well, Ken was shocked when his mobile rang at just before five to midnight.
"Yeah?"
"I dunno what you be aplayin' at me ole booty but there ain't na meat ta be collected here. Bloody place is empty and as clean as our Mar's quim on a church Sunday."
Ken grimaced, he didn't have a clue what the inbred was talking about and told them to stay where they were and he would be there as soon as he could.

With little traffic he covered the journey from his flat on the Clichy Estate in Stepney to Pinchin Street in just over five minutes. More than a little pissed off, Ken marched into the arches to find the Cunningham's seated in the office and swigging from a bottle of rather expensive malt whisky that Maggie only kept for visitors. The room, apart from its occupants, sparkled and there wasn't a single trace of blood to be found on the carpet or walls.
"See what I said ole boy, place is bootiful, clean as a whistle."
Ken just sighed, what the hell was going on?
"I'll just get you a bit of cash for your trouble then."
"Ain't na need for that me ole booty, our Henry's

already had the cash away. It's been a reet long trek down here and it only be fair we get what we was supposed to."

Ken looked towards Henry who was now on his feet. The man even towered above Ken who wasn't much short of six feet himself. It was no time to argue or he could possibly end up with the same fate he'd planned for Maggie.

"Fair enough, I can't expect you to work for nothing. Well if you'd like to be on your way I'll get locked up and call it a night, it's been a strange bleedin' day I can tell you."

Harry tapped the peak of his hat and the three trudged out of the office without another word. More than a little relieved when he heard the door close and the billowing old wagon splutter into life, Ken took a seat behind the desk and rubbed his forehead with the back of his hand. For the life of him he couldn't even begin to work out what had happened. Had someone stumbled upon the body and was now setting them up for blackmail? If they were, then it wouldn't be too long before they made contact. There really was nothing for it, he would just have to sit tight, wait and see if anything occurred and then just deal with it as and when.

CHAPTER TWENTY SIX

Three days passed and there had been no blackmail demand or anonymous contact. Ken knew it was too soon to be overly confident but he reasoned that if there was going to be an attempt at blackmail, then surely they would have heard something by now. Making his way to the arches, he picked up a copy of the Standard. Tossing it onto the passenger seat of his car as he cautiously watched an approaching parking warden, he was about to turn the key in the ignition but was instantly stopped when he casually glanced down and caught the front page headline out of the corner of his eye. In that second everything stopped and frantically grabbing the tabloid all thoughts of the traffic warden went straight out of the window.

'Notorious Whitechapel gangster found dead after apparent suicide'.

'For over thirty years, Margaret McKay terrorised the vicinity of Whitechapel and beyond. Yesterday her body was discovered in the garage of her mews home in Chelsea. A police statement issued late yesterday afternoon stated that Ms McKay was about to be arrested in connection with the torso murders.' The article went on to further add that there were no other persons of interest at this time. At the bottom of the story in small font so as not to stand out, there was another small section.

'The Met also announced that there is to be a private memorial service for the murder victim's families in due course, which will be held at a secret location.' Ken couldn't stop grinning, those crafty bastards couldn't charge her for whatever reason but they'd made good use of her corpse. Sitting bolt upright he suddenly had a thought, they must have been watching the arches the whole time and knew it was either Bobby or him who was responsible. Would they now get their collars felt? Then again, what would be the point of that, the Old Bill had what they wanted so surely it would be best to let sleeping dogs lie. Grinning from ear to ear Ken decided that as soon as he got to work, he would take Bobby round to Joyce's for a slap up breakfast to celebrate. His glee was suddenly brought to an abrupt halt when the warden tapped on the passenger side window. Ken smiled and put his hand up as he started up the engine and pulled away, today nothing could dampen his good mood.

At the station it felt like a hollow victory, not just because the team hadn't actually solved the killings or the fact that if Bobby McKay hadn't innocently spilled his guts, then Maggie would still be in business without anyone being the wiser. What really bothered all of those who had worked on the case, was the fact that only three of the victims had been identified and the one that gave them, Anna in particular, the most heartache, was the little girl. With the incident room closed down until the next big crime occurred, the mood in the communal office was naturally sombre. Eric was packing up the last of his things when Lou walked in. The Chief was whistling and oddly seemed in a happy mood, which certainly couldn't be said for the rest of them.

"In my office when you've got a minute please Eric and bring Anna with you. Oh, and by the way, we need to plan her leaving do, let's have it here this Friday shall we? I suggest plenty of piss and a takeaway. I have a yearning for an Indian but I'll leave it up to a general vote."

Lou didn't wait for a reply and Eric knew it was more of a statement than a request but then he had to admit that none of them were in the right frame of mind for a knees-up at the boozer, least of all Anna, so holding it here was definitely preferable to their local pub. Eric made his way to Anna's office to relay Lou's message about wanting to see them both and found her sitting at her desk just staring blankly into space.

"Anna? You okay darlin'?"

"Yeah I'm good thanks Eric, just totally gutted that we couldn't solve it in-house and bring those bastards to justice."

"You can't win 'em all sweetheart and you just have to let it go, or you'll never have a moments peace."

"I know Eric but it wouldn't feel quite so bad if they had been lesser crimes but in all of my time in the Met this one has to be the sickest and cruellest. Anyway, what can I do for you?"
"Chief wants to see us, you okay to go now?"
Nodding she got up from her seat and the two made the short distance through the central shared area in silence.
"Come on in the pair of you. Close the door and take a seat. Now I expect you've both seen today's Standard?"
Eric and Anna just looked at each other with blank expressions. Lou then opened up the folded copy that was lying on his desk and pushed it forwards. Anna's face was a picture as she read the wording and about to ask what the hell was going on, she was stopped when Chief Garnet held up his open palm.
"Let me continue. Last night I received an anonymous text informing me to buy today's issue of the Standard and also the Daily Mail.
Again he pushed a newspaper towards them.
"Page four, top right hand corner."
Anna was flabbergasted as she slowly read aloud the small inch by three inch column.
'The body of High Court Judge the Honourable Michael Jennings was found at his Knightsbridge residence at the weekend. A family spokesman revealed in a statement that the death has been

listed as natural causes. The funeral will be held at the private chapel on the family's Wiltshire estate and members of the Royal Household are expected to be in attendance but as yet no names have been released.'

Eric had been listening intently and now staring at the Chief in disbelief, he could only shake his head.

"Karma always finds a way Eric and while this may not have panned out how we all wished it to, I think the outcome couldn't have been much better under the circumstances. The government have saved hundreds of thousands, which would have been wasted on trial costs and those poor lost souls and their families have at least received some kind of retribution, even if they will never be aware of that fact."

Still stunned, Anna and Eric got up to leave but the Chief had one last piece of information that would finally give them all closure.

"Before you shoot off, as you're both aware, the Met had provided the funds for a memorial as a goodwill gesture and to try and show them in a good light no doubt. The families of those identified have made their own arrangements but the joint funerals of the two unidentified victims will be held first with the memorial following directly afterwards. It will be held next month but the location hasn't been announced to the general public. Only officers who worked on the case and of course the relatives of those identified, are expected to attend. Trinity Church has been chosen, I think the powers that be thought that holding it over the water would reduce the chance of the tabloids getting wind. Highly emotional events can lead to loose lips and that's the last thing the force needs right now. Please discreetly inform the team that they should all make themselves available."

The next two days dragged by, no big cases had come to light and the team were filling their time with small scale burglaries and street robberies. On Friday afternoon, at a little after five, Anna put on her coat and picked up her bag. Glancing around the room she then wearily locked her office door for one last time. The station was eerily quiet as she slowly made her way along the corridor but as soon as she pushed open the doors to the communal space, cheers suddenly erupted. Someone sparked up a portable cd player and the sound of Tom Jones belting out 'She's a Lady' suddenly filled the room. It was blatantly obvious that the Scotch had already been flowing freely, everyone was in such high spirits but at least it was good to see them all in a happier frame of mind. The aroma of curry filled the air and her nose was drawn to a table in the corner piled high with takeaway containers in readiness for a veritable feast. Anna's good health was toasted several times and then everyone made a beeline for the food but as the Chief walked past her, she gently touched his arm.

"Can I have a quick word Guv?"

Lou Garnet worryingly glanced at the rapidly disappearing food that he'd been thinking about all day. It was bound to be gone if he delayed any further but he couldn't deny Anna's request on her last day.

"Sure! Eric, make sure you save me some or you bastards will be picking up the tab. Come into my office Anna it's a bit quieter there."

Slowly she closed the door behind them and when she heard his next sentence she couldn't stop a tear escaping but she didn't turn around.

"What can I do for you Detective Inspector? Feels a bit strange that this will probably be the last time I call you that."

"That's what I want to speak to you about Guv. I don't want to retire, I need to work, need to have something else in my life other than mourning Jake and I know I will just sit at home twiddling my thumbs."

"I never wanted to lose you in the first place! You're one of the best officers I have ever known and of course you can stay sweetheart, that goes without question. You're young and will be here long after me, probably be the one to replace me no doubt."

Now she turned and the tears were flowing freely

but she was also smiling at the same time.
"Come on, let's get back to the party and those reprobates hadn't better have bloody stuffed all that food or demotions will be on the cards!"
Chief Inspector Garnet tenderly placed his arm around his Detective's shoulder as they walked back to the others. He wouldn't announce the news yet, Monday morning would be soon enough and besides, he was starving and desperate for a Biryani if the greedy bastards had left him any.

A month later, on the day of the memorial and about to head off for the service, the internal phone rang, in fact every phone in the central office was connected and designed to only stop when someone picked up. Being the last to leave, Anna grabbed one of the receivers just in case it was an emergency, in all honesty she would have done anything to get out of attending today. It was less than a year since Jake's death and ever the professional, she still didn't know if she could handle setting foot inside a church or dealing with grieving relatives yet.
"DCI Draycott?"
The station receptionist sounded nervous when she realised who had answered, Anna's notoriety as a hard-nosed copper was legendary but also undeserved.
"I have a Mr Kenneth Voss on the line for you Ma'am, shall I put him through?"

Anna sighed deeply as she reluctantly replied 'I suppose so'.

"Detective, it's Ken Voss. I heard about the service over at Trinity's and......."

"How could you possibly be privy to that information Mr Voss, the location has been kept a closely guarded secret?"

Ken laughed out loud, he wasn't mocking her so much as her naivety.

"Please call me Kenny and us criminals know about most things in advance Detective, that's the reason we ain't all banged up and you're not out of a job yet. The reason I'm calling, I was wondering if you would mind me attending? I know I work on the opposite side of the law so to speak but something about all of this has really played on my mind, guilt I suppose."

"But you weren't involved?"

"I know but its left a bad taste in my mouth. I should have known, should have been more on the ball and been able to stop that evil bitch!"

"Mr Voss, Kenny, this is a free country and you can do as you please, though I would ask, that if you do decide to attend, you do not make yourself known to the relatives. That would be adding salt into their already open and weeping wounds. Goodbye."

Anna hung up and then flopped down onto one of the numerous chairs that were scattered around the room. Would she ever stop being shocked and stunned at the actions of other human beings?

The two funerals were basic and so desperately sad. There were no relatives to speak words of love for Ioana Andris and as the small coffin containing the remains of Kahla Hussein came down the aisle, Anna reached over and placed a single pink rose onto the tiny lid. There wasn't a dry eye in the church and all of the officers involved bowed their heads low in respect and also in an attempt to conceal the tears that none of them could stop from flowing. The bodies were going straight for cremation, so the team stayed seated in readiness for the memorial. A few minutes later the relatives of those identified looked lost and totally forlorn as they began to enter and seeing them only brought back Anna's own loss. Khristina's father was the first to stand and speak and his eulogy was utterly heart breaking, in fact the depth of pain seemed to deepen with the words of each family member. Elena Balan was next and she spoke of how proud she was of her daughter, of the struggles they had endured after the disappearance of her husband and how Alina had been determined to make all of their lives easier but there was no interpreter, so most of her words were not understood but her wracking sobs spoke volumes to all who were there. Finally it was the turn of Sofija Kalnins. Walking slowly to the front of the church with her baby in her arms,

Sofija scanned the rows of pews filled with people she didn't know.

"We came to your country so full of hopes and dreams. We made a new life for ourselves, put a home together and were truly happy for a while but someone ruined all of that when they took the life of my beloved Peteris. He was a good man, a hard worker, a man of morals and loyalty but he didn't get to meet his son, he never even learned that I was pregnant because of what some monster did to him in this, your country! This memorial is kind and you all seem very nice and we thank you, my baby and me but it won't bring Peteris back."

Sofija hung her head as she returned sobbing to her seat and for a brief moment the church was silent. The only sound to be heard was the gentle cooing from a solitary pigeon high up in the rafters. Chief Inspector Garnet then gave a reading from Psalm 33:18 beginning 'The Lord is close to the broken hearted'. Anna was supposed to have read it but on seeing Kahla's coffin had gone into an emotional breakdown and it had taken quite a while for her to compose herself, so much so that the Chief didn't want to risk a repeat performance. When the service finally ended and the attendees at last began to filter out, the haunting chords of 'Abide with Me' could be heard playing low in the background. Outside, as normal everyone just stood around in the churchyard not really knowing what to do next and Anna was one of them until she was unexpectedly approached by Ken Voss who tapped her on the shoulder.

"Can I have a word?"

They walked away from the crowd so as not to be overheard, though Anna really didn't have a clue what he was about to say.

"I thought that went well Detective Inspector under the circumstances."

"Yes Mr Voss I suppose it did but I still don't fully understand why you are even here?"

"Like I said, I feel guilty. Before Maggie's father passed away he asked me to watch over the two most precious people in his life, Maggie and Bobby. I failed him and because of that a lot of people got hurt, innocent people. I should have known what was going on, I was aware of what she was capable of but I didn't see it coming."

"Hindsight is a wonderful thing Mr Voss, how different the world would be if we were all able to go back and change things."

"Please, it's Kenny and yes it would be. I wish you all the best in your retirement Inspector."

"Oh I'm not retiring Kenny, in fact I'm only just getting started! Seems the London criminal network doesn't actually know everything after all. I need to get off now but I'm sure our paths will cross again in the not too distant future, Mr Voss!"

Anna nodded her head and then slowly walked

towards her waiting car. It was now time to get back to their chosen careers, even if those careers were at opposite ends of the law. Kenny had a sinking feeling that the Old Bill would be gunning for his and every other firm in London from now on. In fact he was sure of it but the thought still made him smile, it would soon be business as usual for all of them.

THE END